Medieval and Renaissance Texts

The Friar's, Summoner's and Pardoner's Tales from The Canterbury Tales

General Editor A. V. C. Schmidt

Geoffrey Chaucer

The Friar's, Summoner's and Pardoner's Tales from The Canterbury Tales

Edited by N. R. Havely

 Holmes & Meier Publishers · New York

Published in the United States of America 1976
by Holmes & Meier Publishers, Inc.
101 Fifth Avenue, New York, N.Y. 10003

Library of Congress Cataloging in Publication Data
Chaucer, Geoffrey, d. 1400.
    The Friar's, Summoner's, and Pardoner's tales from
the Canterbury tales.

    (Medieval and Renaissance texts)
    I. Havely, N. R. II. Title.
PR1867.H38   1975   821'.1   75-19090

ISBN 0-8419-0220-8
ISBN 0-8419-0224-0 pbk.

Printed in Great Britain

Contents

Abbreviations

The following abbreviations are used in the Introduction, the Textual Notes and the Commentary:

'Manly and Rickert' – *The Text of the Canterbury Tales, studied on the basis of all known manuscripts*, by J. M. Manly and E. Rickert (Chicago, 1940)

'Owst' – *Literature and Pulpit in Medieval England*, by G. R. Owst (2nd edition, Blackwell, Oxford, 1961)

'Robinson' – *The Complete Works of Geoffrey Chaucer*, edited by F. N. Robinson (2nd edition, Oxford University Press, London, 1957)

'Skeat' – *The Oxford Chaucer* (6 volumes and Supplement), edited by W. W. Skeat (Clarendon Press, Oxford, 1894–7)

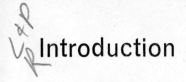

Introduction

The Three Pilgrims

Chaucer's Friar, Summoner and Pardoner are all parasites upon the medieval Church. They live off this huge and powerful body by converting its spiritual authority in society into material profit for themselves. This is one basic similarity between the three characters. Their basic difference is one of rank. About a third of Chaucer's pilgrims hold some kind of office in the Church, and among these the Friar (from the evidence of his portrait and the way that the Host addresses him) seems to be of higher standing than the Pardoner and Summoner. The Summoner is probably the lowest-ranking of the three. Unlike the Friar and Pardoner he would not even have been ordained, and so would not have been able to live off the Church by preaching and giving absolution as they do.

But in the degree of their corruptness there is very little to choose between these three. If all the Church pilgrims were placed in order of moral merit, the Parson would be at the top of the list, characters like the Prioress somewhere near the middle, and the Friar, Summoner and Pardoner all together at the very bottom. Later on in this Introduction we shall look at the way Chaucer exposes particular faults and vices in each of these three characters. But first of all it may be useful to look briefly at the basic relationships that exist between them.

All three characters are said to be very much at home in the place that the medieval preachers denounced as 'the devil's church' – i.e. the tavern or alehouse. We are told that the Friar 'knew the taverns well in every town' (ll. 33–4 of his portrait, in this volume). The Summoner is so addicted to 'strong wine, red as blood' that it seems to be the best thing to bribe him with (ll. 13–15 and 27–9 of his portrait). The Pardoner is also very attached to the 'liquor of the vine', and he insists on stopping at a tavern for a 'draught of moist and corny ale' before beginning his *Tale* (ll. 33–40, 164 and 168 of the *Pardoner's Tale*). This fondness for wine, ale and taverns seems fairly harmless at first sight – but for Chaucer's audience, brought up on the metaphors of the preachers, it would probably have helped to emphasize the extent to which the three characters have betrayed their trust.

There is a friendship between the Summoner and Pardoner which itself has something of the appearance of a drinking-companionship. This is suggested by the way they ride along together, singing – the

1

Summoner with a garland like that from an inn-sign on his head – the Pardoner with his yellow hair straggling free (ll. 44–6 of the Summoner's portrait, and ll. 1–15 of the Pardoner's, both in this volume). The title of their song (*Come hither, love, to me*) and the style of their performance also point to their common interest in attracting, controlling and fleecing the innocent and ignorant, and perhaps suggest that there is a sexual element in the relationship between the singers – the effeminate treble Pardoner and the lusty bass Summoner.

But besides being the Pardoner's friend the Summoner is also the Friar's enemy. This enmity is more productive for the *Canterbury Tales* than the Summoner's and Pardoner's friendship, since it results in the Friar and Summoner both telling their *Tales* against each other. These *Tales* themselves give birth to another friar (Friar John in the *Summoner's Tale*) and another summoner (in the *Friar's Tale*), who are their central characters and the focal points for their satire. This 'reproduction' of the characters of Friar and Summoner in each other's stories can cause confusion when the *Tales* are being talked about.

But the developing relationship between the two types of character has quite a clear basic purpose. The rough, violent summoners and the smooth, subtle friars counterbalance one another; they throw into relief one another's vicious and ridiculous features. This is also true in a more limited way of the relationship between the pilgrim-Summoner and the Pardoner in the *General Prologue* – especially when they are shown singing together the bass and treble lines of their song. As we shall see, contrasts between 'rough' and 'smooth' are essential to Chaucer's presentation of such characters later on, in the three *Tales* and their dramatic framework.

The Friar

The portrait of the 'merry' and prosperous Friar comes early on in Chaucer's *General Prologue*. It follows those of two other well-to-do clerical characters – the fastidious Prioress and the sleek Monk. The Friar may not be of such high rank as they are within the Church, but his status within his Order (l. 7), his impressive appearance (l. 54) and his fine manners and accomplishments all suggest that he is not much further down the social scale. Apart from the Prioress and the Monk, the other Church pilgrims are in different ways socially inferior to the Friar. The more dedicated clerics – the

Clerk and the Parson – are less prosperous than he is (ll. 52–4). The other thoroughly corrupt ones – the Summoner and Pardoner – lack his veneer of gentility.

The Friar in his professional capacity represents a comparatively late development within the medieval Church. The Orders of Friars had been established less than two centuries when the *Canterbury Tales* were written. There were several reasons for the founding of these Orders. It was felt that there had been a decline in the quality of parish priests, who were certainly not all as competent or conscientious as Chaucer's Parson. Many of the better recruits to the Church had been attracted to the cloistered life of the monasteries. Not all of these became so luxuriously corrupt as Chaucer's Monk, and many of them did important work for the Church and society. But there was still a need for the kind of cleric who would work in much closer contact with the common people.

This need was met first of all by the founding of Orders of 'mendicant' (begging) friars by St Francis of Assisi in Italy (in 1209), and by St Dominic in France (in 1215). The Dominican friars were the first to arrive in England, in 1220, followed by the Franciscans in 1224. There were four Orders of friars by Chaucer's time (see l. 3 of the Friar's portrait – the other two were the Carmelites and the Augustinians). But, for the purposes of Chaucer's satire, the pilgrim-Friar is not associated with any one of them in particular.

The original friars tried to live in imitation of the first Christians – the Apostles. They took vows of poverty, chastity and obedience, like monks, and both St Francis and St Dominic laid special emphasis on the first of these. Their followers were not supposed to own property, even in common, and were meant to support themselves by begging. Chaucer's pilgrim-Friar isn't exactly dedicated to poverty. He keeps to the letter of this rule rather than the spirit. He is said to be 'the best beggar in his convent' (l. 45).

The friars also set out to meet a very pressing and immediate need, by giving religious instruction to all people – especially the poorer classes. It was mainly in this way that they made their mark on the Church and the society of their time. They became the leading teachers, preachers and missionaries of the later Middle Ages. Chaucer's Friar, however, doesn't seem to have much time for any of these important activities. He is very active as a 'limitour' (a friar licensed to beg on behalf of his convent within certain limits) and as a confessor – but we are told nothing about any contribution towards scholarship or spreading the Gospel. His flippant remarks about learning and preaching in the *Prologue* to his *Tale* (ll. 7–13) and his hypocritical little homily at the end of it (ll. 378–400) suggest that he is interested in this kind of work only when he can get something out of it for himself.

Much the same is true of the Friar's attitude towards the profitable business of hearing confessions. We are told that he did this 'sweetly', that his absolution was 'pleasant', and that he was also very persuasive about the advantages of giving 'silver to the poor friars' in lieu of penance (ll. 14–25 of his portrait). He prepares his 'clients' for this kind of argument by claiming to have more 'power of confession' than a parish priest. The friar in the *Summoner's Tale* (ll. 152–3) goes even further than this, and suggests that confessions should be made to friars because parish priests are not very good at 'probing delicately into a conscience'. The parish priests themselves naturally resented the expansion of the friars' activities, both in this area and in the others (e.g. baptisms, marriages and burials) that provided them with so much of their income. Although the original friars had not set out to compete for custom in this way, by the middle of the thirteenth century (over a hundred years before Chaucer was writing) complaints were being made against them for doing so.

The friars also made enemies because of their dependence on begging. Their opponents in the Church and the universities were already condemning them for this by the end of the thirteenth century, and by Chaucer's time the tricks of the begging friar, wheedling his way from door to door, seem to have become a standing joke. Chaucer makes this joke turn a bit sour by showing how his Friar could expertly charm money out of a widow who herself 'had not so much as a shoe' (ll. 46–8 of his portrait).

Was this kind of attack justified? It would certainly not be a fair judgment on the original ideals expressed in the *Rule* of St Francis (see Vol. I of the Pelican *Documentary History of England* for a translation of this). But between their foundation and Chaucer's time the friars had found it increasingly difficult to stick closely to these ideals in the face of pressures from the secular world, with which their work brought them into such close contact. The most important of the rules to yield to this pressure was that of poverty. The friars needed from the first to build convents, as regional bases from which to work, and churches to accommodate the growing number of those who wanted to hear them preach. The monks had long been getting money and land for this kind of purpose from the wealthier classes in society, and the friars were soon able to do the same. Financial success tempted them both to provide for themselves in a more elaborate way than their founders had intended – and to concentrate their attention on the rich and powerful rather than the poor and needy.

Resentment of the friars' activities was expressed not only by their rivals for wealth and power (the parish priests, the monks and the university teachers), but also by reformers and satirists, who pointed to the gap between the worldly success of the Orders and their original aims and ideals. William Langland (a contemporary of Chaucer), speaking about Charity, says wryly that 'Once he was seen in a Friar's frock, but that was a long time ago, in St Francis's time, and since then he has been seldom known in that Order' (*Piers Plowman* – Penguin translation, p. 224). The satirists, how-ever, concentrated mainly on describing the friars' underhand methods of begging and infiltration into positions of influence. They* saw them as a plague of busy insect-like creatures, spreading over the face of the land and getting everywhere. As the Summoner says at the beginning of his quarrel with the Friar, 'A fly and also a friar will fall into every dish and every business' (ll. 7–8 of the *Words between the Summoner and the Friar*, in this volume). (Examples of similar points of view can be found in pp. 373–8 of *Chaucer's World*, edited by E. Rickert – a very useful collection of translated material about the lives of Chaucer's contemporaries.)

Chaucer himself, though, is more imaginative in his satire than most of his contemporaries, and he shows vividly how in his Friar a smooth professional manner goes together with a sleek and pros-perous appearance. Near the beginning of the portrait he mimics the slick patter of the confessor's 'sales-talk' (ll. 18–25). And at the end he tells us how, after the Friar had been singing and harping, 'his eyes twinkled brightly in his head, as the stars do in the frosty night' (ll. 59–61). Through details like these he conveys very powerfully the hypnotic charm that such successful swindlers must have had.

The Summoner

The fiery-faced Summoner is one of the last and most grotesque of the pilgrims described in the *General Prologue*. With his scabby

---

* Like Chaucer's Wife of Bath at the beginning of her Tale (D 864–81).

cheeks, loud voice and the garland on his head, he stands out in sharp contrast to the smooth-faced, anaemic Pardoner who accompanies him, and to the sleek and prosperous Friar with whom he later quarrels.

His job, as well as his appearance, also contrasts with the Pardoner's and Friar's. Although all three were closely associated with the Church, the Summoner's work was more secular and more clearly defined; he was a minor official of the ecclesiastical courts. In Chaucer's time there were two main ecclesiastical courts in each diocese. They were presided over by, respectively, the bishop and the archdeacon, who was (and still is) the assistant to the bishop in the administration of a diocese. Chaucer's Summoner seems, from what he says in lines 32–6 of his portrait, to be attached to an archdeacon's court. His job would have been to summon people to the court, and make sure that they appeared – sometimes even acting as a kind of detective. He would also have acted as usher while the court was in session.

The summoner in the *Friar's Tale* also works for an archdeacon, and the Friar, before describing his activities, gives a long list of the kinds of case dealt with by such courts (ll. 39–56). This includes disputes, like those over wills and marriage contracts (ll. 43–4), which would now be handled by civil courts; crimes against the Church, like simony (l. 45) and failure to pay tithes in full (l. 48); and moral offences, like fornication, prostitution and adultery (ll. 40–2).

The archdeacon had power to impose penances upon offenders, but by Chaucer's time he was usually prepared to accept money-payments instead. This is what the pilgrim-Summoner is talking about when he tells a lecher that he will be 'punished in his purse' (l. 35 of his portrait). Summoners in general may well have been tempted to imitate their masters' profiteering by accepting bribes instead of reporting offences or making arrests. Chaucer gives an example from the Summoner's 'scale of charges' in lines 27–9 of his portrait: a quart of wine secures a year's freedom to fornicate.

The pilgrim-Summoner not only lives off lechery in this way, but is also himself 'as lecherous as a sparrow' (see ll. 4 and 30 of his portrait). The summoner in the *Friar's Tale* is not actually said to be a lecher himself, but he does exploit lechery and is actively involved in a prostitution racket. He not only takes bribes (like the pilgrim-Summoner), but also forges summonses in order to be able to extort them at will.

It is not certain, however, that all, or even most, of the summoners in Chaucer's time were actually as corrupt and unscrupulous as the two described in the *Canterbury Tales*. But the fact that they made a living (whether honestly or dishonestly) out of following up rumour and scandal was probably enough to make them generally unpopular. Those who were not (like the children and young people in lines 6 and 41-3 of his portrait) afraid of the Summoner might well have been actively hostile to him. The Friar says that summoners were often beaten up (l. 21 of his *Tale*) – and the records of at least one of the church courts (at Canterbury) seem to support his claim.

Attacks of a different kind were also made on summoners by reformers and satirists – although these did not become so much a part of literary tradition as those on friars did. Langland mentions summoners briefly and contemptuously, together with other disreputable characters, in *Piers Plowman* (Penguin translation, pp. 78, 80 and 86). Earlier on in the fourteenth century an anonymous poet, satirizing the Church courts, describes summoners in this way: 'Six or seven summoners sit there, misjudging all men alike, and stretching out their roll [of names]. Men of the household and every man's servant hate them, because they put every parish in pain and enslave it.' (translated from *Political Songs of England*, edited by Thomas Wright, p. 157).

Chaucer also shows how a summoner can 'enslave' people. In the portrait of the pilgrim-Summoner we are told that 'he had the young people of the diocese under his control as he pleased, and knew their secrets and was their only adviser' (ll. 41-3). Later on, in the *Friar's Tale*, he describes a summoner who keeps an eye on the vices that can be exploited in his neighbourhood, by means of a network of spies. In this way Chaucer creates a more sinister impression of the summoners' activities than the previous satirists had done.

In his portrait of the pilgrim-Summoner, though, Chaucer concentrates mainly on what is sinister, disgusting and contemptible in the character's physical appearance and private behaviour. The Summoner's eyes, for example, don't 'twinkle in his head' attractively, as the Friar's do. They are set 'narrow' in his fiery-red, pimply face, beneath scabby brows (ll. 2-3) – and so help to express the calculating greed, corruptness, and perhaps even ignorance (ll. 17-24) that Chaucer associates with him. His disease (probably a form of leprosy) is not only symbolic of his generally corrupt way of life. It might also, according to the medical authorities of Chaucer's time, have been caused by his lecherousness and been made worse by his diet of garlic, onions and leeks, accompanied by 'strong wine, red as blood' (ll. 12–13).

There is a strong note of contempt, as well as disgust, in the description of the Summoner's behaviour – especially after he has been drinking such strong wine. His drunkenness unleashes his rowdiness and reveals his ignorance (ll. 14–24) – and his playfulness in riding along on the pilgrimage with a garland on his head and a cake as a shield simply increases the grotesqueness of his appearance (ll. 44–6). Such details of appearance and behaviour make a very sharp impression in the Summoner's portrait. They underline what we are told about his sinister and corrupt activities, and make the genial phrase, 'good fellow', which Chaucer uses to describe him and his friends, ring very hollow indeed.

The Quarrel between the Friar and Summoner

The Friar and Summoner start attacking each other some time before they start telling their *Tales*. Their enmity first breaks out early on in this group (Group D) of the *Canterbury Tales*, in a stormy interlude between the Wife of Bath's *Prologue* and her *Tale*. The Wife's *Prologue* is itself aggressive and challenging in tone, and has already called forth one respectful tribute (from the Pardoner – D 163–87) by the time the Wife reaches the end and promises to move on to her *Tale*. At this point the Friar breaks in and laughingly points out to her that she has been a long time in getting round to it.

From Chaucer's point of view there are probably some sound technical advantages in having an interruption here. The Friar's remarks forestall criticism about the huge length (over 800 lines) of the Wife's *Prologue*, and might have prevented 'smart' people like him from making similar witticisms when the poet was reading the *Tales* to an audience. They also lead to a quarrel which in turn helps to link the whole of Group D more firmly, by ensuring that the Friar and Summoner will be ready to start telling their *Tales* against each other just as soon as the Wife has finished hers.

The Friar himself may also have some personal or even professional reasons for making the interruption. The tone of his remarks to the Wife is teasing rather than critical, and suggests that he is trying to get on closer terms with a woman who, in spite of having buried five husbands, is still physically attractive – and financially well off, too. His portrait in the *General Prologue* (ll. 10,

27 and 46–50) makes it clear that he has a 'way' with 'worthy women', and he may well be trying it on here.

But the Friar isn't given the chance to betray his motives more clearly. Before he can get any further with the Wife, the Summoner breaks in with his satirical complaint about friars being as much of a nuisance as flies (ll. 5–8). The violence of the Summoner's attack suggests that he also has some personal or professional motives for getting involved. He seems to be taking offence at the very tone of voice in which the Friar has been speaking to the Wife, and to be defending her with a kind of crude chivalry against this smooth sort of approach.

The differences of tone and manner between the Friar and Summoner are strongly marked in the rest of this passage (ll. 9–21). The Summoner's language continues to be vivid and violent. He twists the Friar's witticism about the Wife's 'long preamble' into a gibe at his prosperous 'ambling' appearance, and freely peppers his other remarks with oaths, curses and exclamations. The Friar, on the other hand, seems to keep fairly cool in the face of this aggressiveness. He speaks to his enemy with mock-respect as 'sire Somnour', and tries to head off his attack by promising to 'tell a tale or two about summoners'. His language at this stage is much more restrained; his strongest oath in reply to the Summoner is 'by my faith', and he continues to be polite to the Wife when she sarcastically asks him for permission to go on with her *Tale*. From this point of view, the Summoner's claim that the Friar's patience is gone (l. 21) seems to be just wishful thinking. At the end of this preliminary round of the contest the Friar's character still preserves the smooth and polished appearance that has been presented to us in the *General Prologue* – whilst the Summoner's behaviour strengthens the impression of grotesqueness and violence that he has already made.

These are the main personal differences that emerge at the beginning of the Friar's and Summoner's quarrel. But is there also a professional rivalry between them? As we can see from the *General Prologue*, their methods of working are very different, but they are both engaged in roughly the same line of business – the exploitation of the common people in the name of religion. But this very broad similarity of purpose is almost the only evidence of professional rivalry that is given to us. It's possible that the prosperous, highly-sexed Wife of Bath is the kind of character that both Friar and Summoner would want to get their hooks into. But in their quarrel over her, and in the Tales that result, neither of them shows in detail how their interests might come into conflict. The *Tales* each give an account of the tricks of friars or summoners, but neither shows them *together* as rivals. This may be because each of the two characters is trying to expose and discredit the other as fully as possible, without showing himself to be guilty as well. But another reason could be simply that Chaucer wasn't interested in going into the details of any special, long-standing rivalry that might have existed between the professions. Differences of temperament and a *general* sense of rivalry seem to be good enough motives for a quarrel between two such villains. And the device of staging such a quarrel, in which the pot and kettle both call each other black, may have seemed especially interesting to Chaucer, as a satirical idea that was worth experimenting with.

This experimental interest in the Friar's and Summoner's quarrel might also help to explain why it is not linked in any way to the next group of *Tales*, or rounded off neatly. From this point of view it contrasts with both the other main quarrels in the *Canterbury Tales* – between the Miller and Reeve (in Group A), and the Pardoner and Host (in this volume). The Miller's and Reeve's quarrel is linked to the beginning of the *Cook's Tale* by a few humorous remarks (A 4325–38), and the Pardoner and Host are reconciled by the Knight (*Pardoner's Tale*, ll. 672–80). But there is no such link between the Friar's and Summoner's quarrel and the *Clerk's Tale* (which follows it) – nor is there the slightest hint of a reconciliation. Perhaps Chaucer wanted to leave room for the other pilgrims to take up some of the issues – as well as to keep these two characters ready to tell tales against each other on the return journey from Canterbury.

The Friar's Prologue

The quarrel between the Friar and Summoner has remained quietly simmering during the *Wife of Bath's Tale*. We are told at the opening of the Friar's *Prologue* that he has been casting dirty looks at the Summoner throughout this interval. But it is typical of the Friar's insinuating character and manner that he now tries to make as smooth a changeover as possible between the Wife's *Tale* and his own. In lines 10–18 he tries to show that it is not his own malice but the rules about entertainment and story-telling on the pilgrimage that make his 'joke about a summoner' necessary.

He suggests that if, however, this joke should happen to look rather pointed, he himself cannot be held to blame. For 'you all know' he explains suavely 'that nothing good can be said of a summoner'. He follows up too quickly, though, with a direct insult to his enemy (ll. 19–21). His smooth and polished mask slips here, and something of his real anger and vindictiveness is revealed. The Host is quick to notice this, and (probably with his tongue in his cheek) politely interrupts to remind him about his 'image' (ll. 22–4).

The Host himself gets into some trouble, however, when he goes on to ask the Friar to 'leave the Summoner alone' (l. 25). The Summoner is far from being in the mood to accept favours of this kind, and starts to give such strong evidence of his ability to look after himself (ll. 26–33) that, for a moment, it looks as if he is about to take over from the Friar. But the Host knows how to handle both types of character. At this point, as on a later occasion in the *Tale* itself (ll. 70–3), he manages to slap down the Summoner, whilst politely asking the Friar to continue. His politeness to the Friar doesn't, however, mean that he is under any illusions about his character. Here, as in lines 22–4, he probably has his tongue in his cheek.

The Friar's sly attempt to slide smoothly into his tale against the Summoner seems, then, to have ended in failure. And in the process of describing that failure, Chaucer has been able not only to expose his hypocrisy, but also to show something more of his relationship to the other characters involved in the battle. Even in such a short *Prologue* as this the poet shows skilfully just how anger and resentment can bubble up to the surface as a quarrel comes back to the boil.

The Friar's Tale

The Friar's malice and anger against the Summoner have spurred him on to tell his *Tale*. So it isn't surprising that the summoner in it is the central figure and the focal point for the satire. Nor is it particularly surprising that some of his characteristics, especially the ones described at the beginning of the *Tale*, are very like those of the pilgrim-Summoner.

The Friar loses no time in emphasizing this point. He introduces his summoner as the cat's paw of a grasping Archdeacon (see p. 6), and claims with a kind of grim pleasure that 'there was no craftier rogue in England' (ll. 57–8). He then challenges the pilgrim-Summoner himself to see if the cap fits – even going so far as to say that it is his enemy's own 'villainy' that is being described (l. 64). And after the Summoner's indignant interruption has been silenced (ll. 68–73) the Friar continues for a while to talk as if the two characters were more or less identical. He goes on to attack his mock-summoner with increased relish – calling him a 'false thief', and listing the various tricks that he uses for cheating both his victims and his employer.

The accusations that the Friar proceeds to make in lines 74–110 have some foundation in what we already know about the pilgrim-Summoner. In the *General Prologue* portrait (ll. 25–36) he has been seen as a link in the chain of bribery and corruption – and we are told that he takes care to know the secrets of the young people in the diocese, presumably in order to blackmail them. His counterpart here in the *Friar's Tale* is even more methodical. He keeps a complete network of spies – including blackmailed lechers (ll. 59–62), bawds (ll. 75–9) and prostitutes (ll. 91–4).

In the description of both summoners contempt for them is expressed partly through the imagery. The pilgrim-Summoner is compared to a lecherous sparrow and a chattering jay (ll. 4 and 20 of his portrait). The summoner in the *Friar's Tale* is compared to a hunting-dog and a venomous shrike (ll. 105–7 and 144). All of these suggest that the two summoners are seen as something less than human. The summoner in the *Friar's Tale*, for example, is like a dog in the way he sniffs out and hunts down the Archdeacon's victims.

The Friar continues in this vein at the beginning of the main narrative (ll. 111–14), where he shows his summoner riding out, 'keeping an eye open for his prey'. The comparison is given an ironic twist, though, when the summoner meets a 'yeoman' who also seems to be some kind of hunter (ll. 117–18). This yeoman is a devil in disguise, who, as he later declares, is himself on the watch for his 'prey' (ll. 190–1 and 207–8). So the summoner, having started out on his journey as a hunter, ends up as the one who is hunted.

The character of the summoner comes more to life with the appearance of the yeoman-devil. Up to this point the Friar has been rather obviously pulling the strings – using him as a kind of puppet, in order to challenge his enemy personally and make satirical points about summoners in general. But now, at the start of his story proper, the Friar himself steps back, allowing the character to develop more independently, through the similarities and contrasts that develop during the course of the relationship between him and his new-found 'brother'. Of course the scope of the satire still includes both the pilgrim-summoner and the profession as a whole. But it now becomes both broader and deeper – and the summoner comes near to being a kind of unredeemable Everyman as he rides along the road to damnation accompanied by his guardian-devil.

The fundamental satirical point about this relationship between devil and summoner is, of course, that it shows they have something in common. (In this way the Friar seems to be inviting his audience to draw the same general conclusion about summoners that the Summoner himself puts forward about friars later on in lines 8–10 of his *Prologue* – namely that there's little difference between them and devils.) Both the summoner and the devil in the *Tale* are the servants of hard masters (the grasping Archdeacon and Satan); both are liars; both pretend to be yeomen; both are seen as hunters – and both work by means of trickery and violence. In view of these similarities it doesn't seem surprising that the devil is able to lure the summoner into swearing an oath of brotherhood (ll. 131–42) – especially when he uses the bait of 'gold and silver'.

But although these similarities reflect ironically upon the summoner, the *differences* between him and the devil do so even more sharply. The devil is obviously much cleverer than his victim. He is quick to see that he doesn't need to make much of a mental effort to outwit the summoner. He feels able to reveal his true identity quite early on (l. 184) and shortly after this he also shows, in a contemptuously offhand way, that he has seen through his companion's attempt at disguise (l. 210). He even goes on to tell the summoner directly that his intelligence is inferior. In fact he is so confident in his victim's stupidity that he feels able to answer his naïve questions with a short and fairly truthful lecture on the motives and activities of devils like himself (ll. 218–56). Any wrongdoer who was even slightly less stupid than the summoner would be bound to take this kind of information as something of a warning. But the devil seems to be sure that there is no risk of this happening, and he seems to take a donnish pleasure in dropping hints that he knows the summoner will never pick up.

The stupidity of the summoner is shown to be closely connected with his particular kind of greed. Here again we can see an important difference between him and the devil. The summoner wants material things – like money, carthorses and cooking pans – and he seems to be unable to see beyond these, even when danger threatens. The devil, on the other hand, is mainly after something that is not material at all – the soul – and he obviously has much more insight into the workings of the human mind.

This difference between the two characters is illustrated by the episode in which they come across a carter cursing his horses (ll. 273–306). This scene, with its violent language and action, stands out as a reminder of everyday life in contrast to the abstract lecture and discussion that have been going on before. It serves also as a further practical test of the intelligences of the summoner and the devil. The summoner, though, sees the encounter simply as a test of the agreement that has just been struck (about sharing proceeds). All he seems to see here is a chance to get a share of the carter's three horses and load of hay, which have been wished to the devil. He eagerly urges the devil to take the carter's 'gift', without realizing that his companion has his eyes on a different kind of prey altogether. The devil, on the other hand, knows anyway that the carter doesn't mean what he says about his horses, and that this, according to common superstition, makes his cursing of them harmless. But he doesn't bother to explain this point in lecture-form, as he has done previously for other subjects that are beyond the summoner's 'meagre intelligence' (see ll. 216–58). He is content just to let events prove that things are not so simple as the materially minded summoner thinks, and that a person may 'say one thing, but think another'.

The summoner's stupidity is not just materialistic short-sightedness, however. There is also a kind of wild bravado to it which seems to go beyond the simple pursuit of 'profits'. He perversely insists on treating his companion as a 'brother' – and on sticking to the agreement about sharing proceeds – even when he knows that he is dealing with a devil. After the failure to get anything from the carter he even proceeds to turn this agreement into a kind of competitive game, in which he himself fixes the place for the next round, taunts the devil for his poor performance so far, and promises to show him 'how it's done' (ll. 309–16).

This kind of bravado reaches its high point in the final scene of the story, where the summoner tries to blackmail an old widow and is cursed by her. Here, without any prompting from the devil, he rushes forward along his path to destruction – oblivious to pleas, curses and warnings – until the ground is, almost literally, cut from beneath his feet. As he warms to the attack on the widow he becomes wildly extravagant in his language, demands and accusations. He even calls on the devil to take him if he lets her out of his clutches (l. 346) – thus perhaps suggesting to her the very form of the curse that she is to use against him (ll. 358–9). He himself, however, remains completely blind to the implications of both his oath and her curse. He gives no sign of being worried when the devil intervenes to make sure about the old woman's intentions. And even when she gives him a last chance to repent (l. 365) he defiantly rejects it. His last words before the devil takes him are characteristic; they show him grotesquely hankering after the very clothes off the widow's back (l. 369).

Since the summoner virtually damns himself in this last scene, there is very little left for the devil to do, except to step in and carry off his 'prey'. His last words, too, are characteristic; he makes one of his donnish little jokes about improving the summoner's knowledge of devils. And, being a stickler for detail (as medieval devils often were), he doesn't forget to take the pan that has been wished to him along with the summoner.

There is thus a strong contrast in this scene, as in the rest of the *Tale*, between the quietly confident devil and the noisily aggressive summoner. It could perhaps be seen as a kind of reflection here of a contrast we have already been presented with – between the smooth Friar and the violent pilgrim-Summoner.

Indeed, the Friar, as he steps forward at the end of his *Tale* (l. 378), seems to have a lot in common with the devil in it. Both are, morally speaking, as bad as the characters they are pitted against (and both, of course, make summoners their victims). Both also have a smooth and genial manner, which they use to mask their real intentions. The Friar is less successful in the *Prologue* to his *Tale*, where, as we have seen, he is eventually unable to disguise his personal malice against the Summoner. But in this epilogue he is able to use the preacher's pious tone of authority as a cloak, from behind which to take one last stab at his enemy. He does so by taking the summoner in his *Tale* as the main example for a miniature sermon about hell, temptation and repentance (ll. 378–400) – and by praying earnestly that summoners in general, and 'this Summoner' in particular, may repent before the Devil takes them too (ll. 380 and 399–400).

In this way the Friar's 'sermon' brings him to the fore again as a character at the end of his *Tale*. But although this is its most immediate effect, it is not the only one. Part of it at least (from lines 381 to 398) can be taken quite seriously as a comment on the story and an impartial verdict on the summoner. It may help to remind us that the *Tale* is not just a malicious joke with a grim conclusion.

The *Friar's Tale* as a whole can be seen as both the Friar's satire on summoners, and as Chaucer's satire on blind and violent greed.* Chaucer is able to achieve this broader effect by making the Friar less noticeable as narrator in the main part of the *Tale*. Between the point where he starts his actual narrative (l. 111) and the point where he steps forward to preach to his audience at the end (l. 378) the Friar's voice seems to be toned down, and as a character he withdraws into the background.

But this does not mean that the *Tale* ceases to belong to the Friar between these points. There are other, more indirect ways by which Chaucer makes his tales suit their tellers, whilst allowing scope for his broader effects. He often does so by making the plot and characterization *generally* appropriate to the narrator and his interests. In this case the Friar tells a folk-tale type of story, of the kind that medieval preachers often used as an 'exemplum' or illustration for their sermons (see Owst, pp. 162-3) As for the characters, we have seen that the summoner in it is fairly close to being an image of the Friar's enemy, and that the Friar himself has a lot in common with his devil, whom he uses as a kind of cat's paw. Finally, the fitting of tale to teller can also be done more dramatically by means of a style that may not echo the character's exact tone of voice as we know it, but is still broadly appropriate to him. The Friar's smooth performance, with its cool, often understated irony, is a very good example of this.

The Summoner's Prologue

As soon as the Friar has ended his *Tale* the Summoner's rage against him finds voice. Trembling with wrath (l. 3), and standing up in his stirrups to attract attention, he allows no time for the pilgrims or the Host to express any reaction to what the Friar has said. He is impatient to get on with his counter-attack, and, having briefly asked permission to start (ll. 4–7), he launches straight away into a vivid preliminary anecdote about a friar's vision of Hell.

At least as far as subject-matter is concerned, the Summoner seems to be taking his cue from his enemy. At the end of his *Tale*, the Friar has shown a summoner being taken off to Hell, and in his conclusion he has said a few piously horrified words about the

---

* For another treatment of this theme see Chaucer's *Canon's Yeoman's Tale* (also in this series).

impossibility of describing the pains of 'that cursed place' (ll. 381–8). But, as we might expect, the Summoner soon shows some marked differences in the way he treats such a subject. Referring back to the Friar's claims to know about Hell, he points out that, 'God knows, this isn't surprising; there's little difference between friars and devils' (ll. 9–10). This straightforward gibe is quite different in tone from the Friar's ironic implications about the similarities between the summoner and the devil in his *Tale* (see p. 13 of this Introduction). Likewise, showing friars imprisoned in 'the Devil's arse' is a much more violently mocking way of attacking an enemy than the Friar ever uses. The Summoner places his friars doubly low in Hell, by attaching them to Satan himself, and by putting them in the most unsavoury part of his body. His grotesque fantasy here sets the tone for a *Tale* in which the central episode will enact much the same kind of satirical mockery.

If the reference to Satan's arse shows the crude force of the Summoner's satire, the description of the friars swarming out of it like bees (ll. 28–34) shows some of its more imaginative and ironic qualities.* For, although only these friars in Hell are being compared to bees, the Summoner's comparison also caricatures the behaviour of busy, inquisitive friars in general. So, he tells us, when given the chance (ll. 25–32) these friars swarm about in Hell as they have done upon earth. This vivid kind of imagery has also characterized the Summoner's language earlier on, at the beginning of his quarrel with the Friar (see p. 9 of this Introduction).

At the end of his *Prologue* the Summoner turns his attention more particularly to the Friar and what he has said. His reference to Hell (l. 42) as a friar's 'natural heritage' could be taken as a reply to the Friar's description of Hell at the end of his *Tale* (l. 377) as the place 'where summoners have their heritage'. Likewise, his mock-blessing in the next line – 'God save all of you, *except* this cursed Friar!' – could be taken as a contemptuous reply to the Friar's pious wishes (*Friar's Tale*, ll. 380, 399–400) that summoners, and 'this Summoner' in particular, may mend their ways. The Summoner, for his part, scorns any such ironic 'concern' for his enemy when rounding off *his* cautionary tale, and seems here to be thumbing his nose at the Friar and his hypocrisy. Here, as elsewhere, his rough straight-forwardness contrasts strongly with his enemy's genial and in-sinuating manner.

This *Prologue* as a whole, then, does more than just lead in to the *Summoner's Tale*. The Summoner takes the offensive from the start,

* See also (again) the opening of the *Wife of Bath's Tale* (D 864–81).

and answers the Friar in terms of the tale he has just told. His tone in the final line of his *Prologue* suggests that he is very satisfied with the way things are going. He seems pleased with himself at having already chalked up a hit against the Friar, and is eager to get started on the next round of the contest.

The Summoner's Tale

Unlike the leisurely, 'ambling' Friar, the hot-blooded Summoner launches straight away into his actual story. The friar who is its central character and the focal point for its satire is directly shown in action earlier on than is the summoner in the *Friar's Tale*. The Summoner's opening presentation of his activities (unlike the Friar's general description of his summoner's corrupt practices) is part of the main plot of the *Tale* – and the activities themselves are from the start given more point by being seen as part of a single typical fund-raising campaign. This difference of approach between the *Friar's* and *Summoner's Tales* could be due simply to a desire on Chaucer's part for variety of treatment. But it could also perhaps reflect something of the difference between the characters of the two tellers.

Of course there are necessarily some similarities between the Friar's and Summoner's ways of introducing the main characters of their *Tales*. They both make these characters serve the purpose of their quarrel by giving them some personal and professional features in common with those we have seen in the *General Prologue* portraits of each. The Summoner's friar, like the pilgrim-Friar, has an oily, pious and genteel manner, which he uses throughout the *Tale* to mask his greed and his other vices. He tries hard in his sermons and elsewhere to discredit his rivals for the parishioners' money (see ll. 56–9 and 63–4, and the Commentary on ll. 60–7), as the pilgrim-Friar also does (ll. 11–13 of his portrait). The Summoner's friar is also shown to be an expert door-to-door beggar (see ll. 71–96), as Friar Hubert also is (l. 45 of his portrait) – and they are both said to take especial care to be well in with women and the local worthies. In view of all these challenging similarities it isn't surprising that the pilgrim-Friar is provoked into interrupting the Summoner here (l. 97), as the Summoner has done in the *Friar's Tale*.

But even at this early stage in the *Tale* the figure of Friar John is more than just a caricature of the Summoner's enemy. By showing him in the very act of preaching in the parish church and begging from door to door, the Summoner extends and makes more vivid the satirical view of fraudulent friars and their methods that we have already been given in the *General Prologue* portrait. Within about the first hundred lines of the Tale the Summoner's friar can be seen adopting a very wide range of tones and manners to suit the different stages of his fund-raising campaign. He moves rapidly from the lurid emotional blackmail that he uses to sell his 'trentals' in church (see ll. 60–8 and Commentary) to the wheedling 'how much shall I put you down for' tone of his doorstep begging (ll. 82–9). And in the process of begging itself his manner changes from one of busy, insect-like inquisitiveness (ll. 71–5) to one of soft-footed, ingratiating charm, as he sidles into the house 'where he was used to being made more comfortable than in a hundred other places' (ll. 101–3). By this time he has become less like a busy insect and more like the cat whose place he takes on the bench at the bedside of the sick householder, Thomas.

The satirical view of Friar John's fraudulence and hypocrisy is developed in detail through his relationships with Thomas's wife, Thomas himself, and the lord of the manor.

In his dealings with Thomas, Friar John seems to think that one way to the churl's purse is through his wife. This is suggested by the way he greets her with kissing and compliments (ll. 138–47) and takes advantage of her complaints about her husband when encouraging him to make his confession (ll. 159–71 and 319–40). The hypocrisy involved in this kind of exploitation is pointedly exposed at the end of the friar's conversation with the wife – where he is shown first accepting her invitation to stay to dinner and then reacting to the news of her child's death. In the space of a few lines here (ll. 174–86) he smoothly manages to accept the invitation appreciatively, to give the impression of being above such things as food, *and* to make the wife feel that she has been taken into his special confidence as well.* An even worse kind of hypocrisy is shown by Friar John when, on hearing of the child's death, he immediately launches into an account of the 'revelation' concerning it that was granted to himself and his fellows (ll. 190–204). Chaucer here emphasizes the slickness of the friar's pat response by rhyming

---

* A similar sort of hypocrisy can be seen in the way that the schoolmaster, Dr Skinner, orders supper in chapter 27 of Samuel Butler's *The Way of All Flesh* – and the way that the evangelist, Mr Chadband, discourses about food before converting it into 'preaching oil' in chapter 19 of Dickens's *Bleak House*.

the first line of his speech (l. 190) with the last of the wife's (l. 189). The satire is made much more bitter here by the virtual certainty that the friar is lying, and the sure fact that he is using the death of a child as an opportunity for self-advertisement. For, in a typically slick and opportunistic way, he goes on to claim that both the 'revelation' and the supposed effectiveness of his prayers are the results of the poverty and abstinence of friars.†

Friar John's slickness and opportunism are shown in action more fully during his direct approach to the churl Thomas which occupies most of the *Tale*. His main aim, of course, is simply to get money out of the sick man – but he has to make use of a very wide variety of tactics, arguments and ploys in the process. He begins by deftly turning his 'sermon' on abstinence (which started as an improvisation for the benefit of Thomas's wife) into a reminder to the churl about the amount of praying that the 'charitable, chaste and busy friars' are doing on his behalf (ll. 205–83). Thomas's answer to this, however (ll. 284–9), is brief and to the point – namely that the results of these much-vaunted prayers don't seem to justify the amount spent. The only way that the friar can deal with this kind of criticism is by launching out on another, even lengthier 'sermon' (ll. 290–429).

This second 'sermon' divides into several stages, which indicate the shifts in the friar's mental footwork as he searches out the best line of attack. He begins by replying quite directly to Thomas's objections – urging him to ignore other friars and concentrate his money where the praying is most diligent, namely in Friar John's own convent (ll. 290–316). Meeting here with what seems to be an obstinate silence, he starts out on another manoeuvre, which has been mapped out earlier on in his campaign – namely a long denunciation of the sin of anger (ll. 317–429), about which he has previously promised to say 'a word or two' for Thomas's benefit. The main purpose of this is to get the stubborn churl to confess himself of this sin, and accept the friar's absolution for a fee (ll. 425–9). Thomas's reply, however (ll. 430–4) is even briefer than the one he has made to the previous appeal – and the argument he uses (that he has already confessed to his parish priest) shows clearly and ironically that even the friar's attempts to discredit his rivals have failed. Faced with such shrewd obstinacy, Friar John changes his approach once again. Instead of launching out on yet another

---

† His gushing piety here has quite a lot in common with the 'soul-butter and hogwash' which the 'king' and the 'duke' use to exploit a death in chapter 25 of Mark Twain's *Huckleberry Finn*.

sermon, he now throws everything into a desperate hard-luck story about the convent building-fund (ll. 435–42), rounded off with an extravagant advertisement for the friars and their activities.

The irony of all this ingenuity is that, in several ways, it recoils upon Friar John himself. For, on the one hand, he sometimes overreaches himself while preaching, and reveals something of his basic hypocrisy – as when he follows one of his main examples of the sin of anger with a not very moral moral about not offending the rich and powerful by pointing out their vices (ll. 410–14). And, on the other hand, it eventually becomes clear that the main effect of all his moving appeals and of all his preaching about anger is simply to make Thomas angry. It is also ironic that the churl doesn't give vent to his anger immediately. Like the friar he practises 'dissimulation', and charms his victim with the same kind of smooth talk and assurances ('your holy convent . . .', 'my dear brother . . .') that he has received from him.

The main satirical pay-off for Friar John is, however, delivered by means of the bargain that Thomas traps him into. The churls 'gift' of a fart in the hand (to be divided equally among the members of the 'holy convent') is just the right kind of reward for the friar's long-winded hypocrisy and grasping greed. It not only expresses Thomas's pent-up resentment, but also reveals something more of the truth about Friar John's character. His basic motive of greed is underlined by the number of references to his groping hand (5 times in ll. 467–85) just before he receives the 'gift'. And his real viciousness and hypocrisy are emphasized by the way he reacts to the fart (ll. 488–97) – demonstrating exactly the same sin of anger that he has just preached against at such length.

Friar John's viciousness and hypocrisy are given their final satirical expression through his relationship with the lord of the manor, to whom he goes to complain about Thomas. The impression of spluttering indignation conveyed by his arrival and greeting (ll. 502–5) is brilliantly contrasted with the mild surprise and friendly concern of the lord as he sits quietly eating at his table. There cannot be many comic 'entrances', except in the theatre itself, that are as dramatically effective as this.*

At the start of this final scene Friar John's habitual hypocrisy and the need to maintain his religious 'image' prevent him from

---

* One of the few that could match it, in non-theatrical writing, is the appearance of the mud-bespattered Dr Slop at the door of Walter Shandy's drawing-room in Sterne's *Tristram Shandy* (Book II, chs. 8–10).

losing control completely. He is still able to respond with his usual bogus humility when the lord addresses him as 'master' (ll. 521–4) – and he puts up a show of piously unselfish indignation by presenting the insult he has suffered as one not only to himself but also to his convent and his order (ll. 519 and 527). In a moment of inspiration he even goes on to claim that Thomas's fart is directed at the whole Church as well. But remembrance of the grotesque and impossible bargain that he has been fooled by eventually brings out the real malice and viciousness in him – and, in reply to the lady's attempt to make light of the whole affair (ll. 541–5), he gradually lashes himself into a fury – threatening to denounce in public the 'false blasphemer' who has bound him 'to share out what cannot be shared (ll. 547–51). These violent threats, appropriately enough, are the last that we hear from the previously genteel and subtle friar.

This is not the last that we hear, however, of Friar John's bargain with Thomas. A spoken agreement of the kind that he has made was considered to be binding, and in the literature of the time there are several more serious examples of the kind of problem that a rash promise could give rise to (for instance, in Chaucer's own *Franklin's Tale*). So the question is first of all mulled over at length by the lord of the manor, who brings to it the kind of puzzled but scholarly approach that Walter Shandy also adopts towards similar problems that bother him in *Tristram Shandy*. It is then handed over to the lord's 'squire and carver', who reaches a grotesque but ingenious and concrete solution which is like something devised by Rabelais or Swift, or by the cunning scholar Nicholas in Chaucer's own *Miller's Tale*. This inflation of the churl's fart into a problem of mathematics and engineering may also provide something of an ironic reflection on the friar's own ingenuity and pretentiousness, especially in his 'glosing' (see the Commentary on ll. 126–30).

A further ironic effect of this discussion and of the final scene as a whole is that it increases Friar John's humiliation by making him an object of fun for his superiors. The judgment passed on him is a mock-judgment of course, but it has some weight of worldly authority behind it. By the end of the *Tale*, therefore, the friar has not only been paid out by someone of a class that he usually exploited, but he has also been ridiculed by members of a class that he had been accustomed to depend upon. This widening of the social setting in the final scene gives additional force to the conclusion of the Summoner's attack on friars, and could also amount to an encouragement – an appeal, even – to the educated people and the 'gentles' among Chaucer's pilgrims and in his audience to join in the laugh against them.

Looking back over the *Tale* as a whole, we can see that it enables its teller to 'play' his audience in other ways too. Like the *Friar's Tale*, it is much more dramatic in presentation than most of the other *Canterbury Tales* – allowing the narrator to entertain his audience with rapid changes of voice and tone.* In some ways, though, the *Summoner's Tale* is even more fully dramatic than the *Friar's*; the dialogue is more extensive, for example, and the personalities of the characters show through it in greater detail. In fact the *Tale* could quite easily be presented as a play. The two short scenes (in the parish church and the lord of the manor's hall) provide a good dramatic prologue and epilogue to the main one (in Thomas's house).† In the main scene, itself, from the moment when Friar John enters the house to the moment when he is chased out, there is hardly any straight narrative, except in the form of 'stage-directions'. When, for example, Thomas tells the friar that his wife is out in the yard and will come in presently (ll. 134-5). her 'entry-line' follows immediately (l. 136) without even an introduction from the narrator. In the central part of the scene straightforward questions and statements from the wife and bluntly obstinate replies from Thomas serve as 'feed-lines' for the friar's slick 'patter'. At the end of it the quicker exchange of dialogue between the churl and the friar helps to speed up the pace of the story as it reaches its climax.

In the final scene the contrast between the genial, musing tone of the lord and the brisk efficiency of his squire helps to keep the joke alive for the audience whilst further ridicule is being heaped upon the ruffled friar. The lord's words in praise of the churl's cleverness (ll. 554-78) are particularly good as an example of 'thinking aloud'. It even seems that, from lines 554 to 563, he is soliloquizing – and that he turns to address the company in his hall only in line 564. Throughout the whole speech Chaucer follows closely the loose, rambling style of someone turning over a puzzling problem in his mind – going over the terms in which it has been

---

* The need for this kind of performance is apparent from the structure of stories – especially of the comic, 'fabliau' (*OF*, orig. = 'fable') kind – long before Chaucer's time. See, for example, the tale of *Dame Sirith* (pp. 77-95 of *Early Middle English Verse & Prose*, ed. J. A. W. Bennett and G. V. Smithers).

† They also point to the social significance of the friar's method of exploitation in the main scene. He uses the spiritual authority of the Church as a base from which to work, and the secular authority of the lord of the manor as a refuge to fall back on.

stated, asking himself questions about it, expressing a kind of wry admiration for the person who posed it (ll. 554-5, 563 and 574-5), and finally giving the whole thing up in mock-despair.

The voice of the main character, Friar John, is, of course, reproduced in even greater detail. He varies his tone from stage to stage throughout the *Tale*, as he changes his tactics or responds to a new situation. We hear him at one moment threatening in his trentals-sermon, at another wheedling in his doorstep-manner – at one moment chatting roguishly with Thomas's wife, at another preaching solemnly to Thomas himself – at one moment on his knees pleading pathetically, at another on his feet spluttering threats.

It is the friar's preaching voice, however, that we hear most of. His sermons and appeals to Thomas together occupy over a third of the *Tale*, and help to illustrate both his professional skill as a preacher and his basic hypocrisy. Even within this 'register' he shows command of a wide range of tone – from self-righteous denunciation (ll. 260-73) to colloquial bluffness (ll. 297-307) – and from a plain narrative style (ll. 353-420) to extravagant emotional language (ll. 435-55).

But, although there is this degree of variety in Friar John's preaching, the great length of his 'sermons' might still make them run the risk of boring the audience of the *Tale* as they obviously bore Thomas. By comparison with Friar John, even the donnish devil in the *Friar's Tale* is fairly concise. His 'lecture' to the summoner (*Friar's Tale*, ll. 210-58) is altogether less than fifty lines long, and is broken in the middle by a question from his 'pupil'. So do Friar John's 240 lines of preaching overburden the middle of the *Summoner's Tale*? This is a question that each reader must settle for himself. Hearing the Tale read aloud, as if it were a play, will help to decide.

A final question that we might ask about the Summoner's Tale, as we have about the Friar's, is, how closely does it suit its teller, and how much does his presence as narrator make itself felt? If the Tale were being considered simply as an extension of the Summoner's character, it might be said that the range of knowledge displayed in it – in the friar's preaching and the lord of the manor's learned speculations – is a bit above the intellectual level of a man who, as Chaucer has told us, knew only a few words of Latin 'out of some decree' (Summoner's portrait, ll. 15-24). From this point of view it could also be shown that, unlike the Friar, the Summoner is not a very prominent narrator either after his *Prologue* or at the end of his *Tale* (he steps forward only very briefly in l. 630).

But, as already suggested (p. 16), Chaucer's apparent aims in the *Canterbury Tales* are not so simple or so limited as this. In the *Summoner's Tale* even more than in the *Friar's* he seems concerned to develop the story into an imaginative satire on greed (of the hypocritical kind here) rather than to tailor it exactly to the character of the teller. And, although the *Tale* is developed in a style which sometimes goes beyond the Summoner's probable limitations, this style still corresponds loosely to the kind of person that he is. Something of his violent, talkative and highly-coloured character can be seen reflected not only in the earthiness of the *Tale*'s plot, but also in the vividness of its dialogue and descriptive language.

The Pardoner

The Pardoner and his friend the Summoner are the last of the ordinary pilgrims to appear in the *General Prologue*. It may be that Chaucer reserved this place for them because he saw them as the worst of the various tricksters that he describes here. In any case they are among the most sinister-looking of all the Canterbury pilgrims.

The Pardoner is much paler in colouring than the Summoner – but he is just as grotesque in his own way. His straggling yellow hair, his bulging eyes and his bleating voice make his attempts to appear jaunty and fashionable (ll. 4 and 12–15) seem especially outlandish. As in the case of the Summoner (ll. 4 and 20–1 of the latter's portrait), images drawn from the animal-world emphasize this outlandishness: the Pardoner's eyes are compared with those of a hare, and his voice with that of a goat. Chaucer even goes on to say that his skin was so smooth that one might have thought he was a 'gelding or a mare' – that is, like a eunuch or a woman. This suggestion about the Pardoner's sexual nature is crudely developed by the Host at the end of the *Pardoner's Tale* (ll. 663–7).

The Pardoner contrasts with the Summoner, however, both by being further up in the hierarchy of the Church, and by being more sophisticated in his methods of extortion. Pardoners, unlike summoners, were usually members of the clergy, and would probably, therefore, have received some kind of education. Chaucer's Pardoner shows some evidence of this; he seems to be well-acquainted with the techniques of pulpit-rhetoric and well-provided, as he says, with a store of authoritative-sounding quotations and 'old stories', in order to impress his audience (see ll. 56–8 and 147–50 of his Tale).

But the Pardoner doesn't preach sermons simply to display his learning – still less for the good of his hearers' souls. Like the friar in the *Summoner's Tale* (ll. 49–70), he preaches in order to advertise. The pardoners dealt in two main commodities – indulgences and the power of relics. Indulgences were originally just a means of doing penance for a sin, through paying money to the Church. But by Chaucer's time the belief had grown up (encouraged by the authorities) that this kind of payment could also be a way of ensuring 'pardon' – in the form of salvation and a reduction of the number of years to be spent in Purgatory. A common way of obtaining indulgences was to go on pilgrimage – especially to Jerusalem or Rome. Failing this, they could be bought from a pardoner like Chaucer's, who claimed to have brought them, like cakes or pies, 'hot from Rome' (l. 19 of his portrait).

Relics were the pardoners' other main source of profit, and the pilgrim-Pardoner carries a varied selection of these in his luggage (ll. 26–32). He later describes at length the methods that he uses for exploiting them (ll. 59–100 of his *Prologue*). Both the Pardoner himself, and the narrator in the *General Prologue* make it clear that they are little more than rags and bones – and indeed in Chaucer's own time there were complaints from the Pope himself about travelling salesmen like the Pardoner who traded on the supposedly magical power of such bogus relics. There were also complaints from the highest level in the Church about those who sold pardons without the proper authorization from an archbishop or bishop (see p. 379 of *Chaucer's World* by E. Rickert). There were even at this time pardoners who pretended to be raising funds for the hospital of St Mary of Rouncivalle in London – which is the place that the pilgrim-Pardoner himself comes from (l. 2 of his portrait), and for which he would probably claim to be working.

As with friars and summoners, hostility to the pardoners was also voiced from the pulpit and in the poetry of Chaucer's contemporaries. The Lollards (the most active religious nonconformists of the day, who based their work on the ideas of Wyclif) attacked even the theory of indulgences, as well as those who sold them on false pretences. Other reformers of the time denounced the greed of the pardoners and the stupidity of people who trusted blindly in the indulgences that they bought from them (see Owst, pp. 372–4). Several popular poems of about this time also make some hostile remarks in passing about the activities of pardoners (see the *Commentary on the General Prologue* by M. Bowden, p. 282). The Prologue to Langland's *Piers Plowman* shows a pardoner busily hoodwinking people, and contemptuous references are made to the profession at several other points in the rest of the poem (see the Penguin translation, pp. 65, 79, 82 and 118). In general it can be said that pardoners are not attacked so frequently and vividly as friars are in the literature of Chaucer's time, but they seem to attract more of this kind of attention than summoners do.

Chaucer's Pardoner as we see him in the *General Prologue* might be said to combine some of the worst features of the Summoner and the Friar. Like both of them he represents active corruption within the Church and the poisoning of the relationship between it and ordinary people. Like his friend the Summoner, he reveals something of his inner corruptness through his unhealthy appearance. Like the smooth-tongued Friar, he is shown to be an expert in the arts of persuasion – particularly in the pulpit, and where money is concerned (ll. 37–46 of his portrait).

Later on in the *Canterbury Tales* the Pardoner shows that he also has a professional eye for a good performance by another orator. He interrupts the *Wife of Bath's Prologue* (D 163–87) in order, first of all, to compliment her on being such a 'noble preacher'. In this passage he seems to be playing up to the Wife by presenting himself as a young man on the threshold of marriage, respectfully seeking advice and instruction from an authority on the subject (D 184–7).

By the beginning of his own *Tale* the Pardoner seems to have become accepted as something of a 'character' by his fellow-pilgrims – and, between the end of the *Physician's Tale* and the beginning of his own, he shows something more of his skill as a performer in the different roles that he has to play for them. The Host (ll. 24–9) is in desperate need of some light relief after the Physician's pathetic story, and he turns to his 'fine friend' the Pardoner as being the most likely person to provide 'some entertainment or jokes'. The Pardoner cheerfully takes up the role of jester, and enters into the spirit of the occasion by taking on something of the Host's own tone – using the same non-existent saint to swear by (ll. 22 and 32), and saying that he must have a drink before going any further. This, however, displeases the 'respectable' pilgrims, who remind him of his position as a man of the Church by urging him to tell a moral tale instead (ll. 37–8). Without a moment's hesitation he takes up the second role just as cheerfully as the first – for, as we shall see in his *Prologue* and *Tale*, he can play both the clown and the clergyman with equal zest and conviction. Indeed, the Pardoner is such an accomplished performer that he appears to have developed his hypocrisy into something approaching the art of an illusionist. In the last lines of his exchange with the Host and the pilgrims (ll. 39–40) he almost makes it seem that there is nothing at all strange about seeking moral inspiration in a pot of ale.

The Pardoner's Prologue

The Pardoner takes much longer to lead into his *Tale* than either the Friar or the Summoner, since Chaucer is here using a rather different method in his treatment of the character.* For, instead of being given a satirical view of the swindler's activities by another pilgrim (as is the case with the Friar and Summoner), we are presented in this Prologue with the Pardoner's own quite full assessment of himself, his aims and methods. In this way the Pardoner's *Prologue* is more like the Wife of Bath's than the Friar's or Summoner's. Like the Wife he makes a frank declaration of his way of life here – and he does so with a mixture of irony, boastfulness and obstinate unrepentance which is very like what we find at some points in her *Prologue*.

The first main item of the Pardoner's confession concerns his trade in relics (ll. 59–100). The relics that he displays to the people in church are, as he cheerfully admits, nothing more than 'rags and bones' (l. 60) – just like the ones that have been described in his *General Prologue* portrait (ll. 26–32). But this is only part of the satirical point here. There is a good deal more irony in the way that he advertises such wares.

The kinds of motive that the Pardoner appeals to when publicizing the relics from the pulpit (ll. 64–100) are very far from being those which a conscientious preacher would be expected to encourage in his audience. He is shown here playing ruthlessly upon some of the basic fears and desires of the 'ignorant people'. He touches upon the insecurity, and the greed perhaps, of the peasant-farmer when he promises that use of his relics will heal sick animals and bring an increased yield of both livestock and crops (ll. 64–77

---

* Compare his presentation of the Canon's Yeoman in the long autobiographical introduction to the latter's *Tale*.

and 84–8). For his women customers he holds out the prospect of free adultery as a bait. In lines 78–83 he hints that any wife who uses the relic in the way he describes will be able, undetected, to cuckold her husband just as often as she likes. On the other hand he also uses the same idea a little later on as a *threat*. He suggests (ll. 90–8) that anyone who doesn't come forward and offer to the relics must have done some 'horrible sin', and especially that any wife who fails to do so will be virtually admitting in public that she has committed adultery.

The Pardoner himself doesn't seem to feel at all guilty, either about this 'trickery' (l. 101) or about its moral effects upon his victims. He shows an intense enjoyment of the whole performance (ll. 110–11) and a considerable pride in his sheer professionalism (ll. 41–4). He keenly relishes the idea of preaching against his congregation's greed in order to get them to satisfy his own (ll. 112–14 and 135–40). And he appreciates the irony of a situation in which a preacher, whose motive is solely avarice (ll. 136 and 145), 'and not at all to reprove sin' (ll. 115–16), can still 'make other people renounce avarice and repent deeply'.

But, although the Pardoner wryly admits that his preaching can have such unforeseen consequences, he hastens to point out that, in spite of these, he still remains at heart a grasping and ruthless swindler, who genuinely couldn't care less about what happens to his victims in this world or the next (ll. 115–18). He makes no secret of his contempt for such 'ignorant people' (ll. 104 and 149), and sees no reason why a poor widow shouldn't sacrifice a child or two in order to maintain him in comfort (ll. 159–65). Altogether, he seems to be even more unscrupulous than Friar Hubert, who had no conscience about taking money from a widow who 'hadn't so much as a shoe' (ll. 46–48 of his *General Prologue* portrait) – and even more coldhearted than Friar John in the *Summoner's Tale*, who uses the death of a child as an opportunity for self-advertisement. In this general lack of concern for ordinary people, as well as in the blatant hypocrisy of his preaching, the Pardoner here comes out as the polar opposite to Chaucer's Parson (see ll. 477–528 of the *General Prologue*).

The final admission that the Pardoner makes in this Prologue would perhaps be the most immediately damaging in the eyes of his fellow-pilgrims. In his usual frank and fearless way he makes the nature and purpose of his Tale quite clear to them in advance – telling them to expect an example of his hypocrisy in action, a 'moral tale' told by an immoral man (ll. 171–2). He even adds (l.

173) that it is also a standard example of his preaching for profit – thus hinting to the pilgrims that they themselves may be his next victims.

Why does the Pardoner take so much trouble in this Prologue to expose his own hypocrisy, reveal his own professional secrets and warn his audience about his intentions? Perhaps the professional pride and admiration for his own cleverness that he shows here, combined with the influence of the holiday atmosphere and the ale he has just drunk (l. 40), have made him say more than is wise. Perhaps some or all of the 'confession' here should be taken as a further example of the Pardoner's extravagant 'posing' and of the way in which such a performer 'plays' his audience. Or it may be that Chaucer is not expecting us to look for psychological motives, but is using the Pardoner's confession as a dramatic device for satirizing him without having to bring in another character as an intermediary.* All these possibilities could be borne in mind when considering the relationship in general between the Pardoner's character and his story, and in particular between this *Prologue* and the *Tale* which follows.

The Pardoner's Tale

The Pardoner in his *Prologue* has already shown something of his skill as a performer – especially in the brief sample that he has given of his advertising methods (ll. 64–100). He now proceeds to give a full-scale demonstration of his craft which creates a vivid and sometimes baffling impression of the variety of tones and techniques that he has at his command. In his *Tale* he deploys the full-blooded rhetoric of the preacher, the plain style of the storyteller, and the colloquial 'patter' of the salesman, all with equal confidence and effect.

Strictly speaking, nearly all of this *Tale* (ll. 175–627) is a sermon – as is emphasized by the lengthy and methodical denunciation of the main characters (the 'ryotoures'†) at the beginning of the

---

* A dramatically conventional confession of this kind is made in the thirteenth-century French *Roman de la Rose*, by an allegorical character called Faus Semblanz (False Appearance), who has something in common with both the Pardoner and the Friar in the *Canterbury Tales*. (Chaucer knew the *Roman* well, and translated at least some of it. See especially Fragment C of the *Romaunt of the Rose*, in Robinson – though it is not certain that Chaucer himself wrote this.)

† On the meaning of this word see the Commentary on line 373.

Pardoner's story (ll. 195–371). But even when going through this kind of pulpit routine the Pardoner shows a sure professional touch – taking care to mark changes of subject clearly for the benefit of his listeners (see the Commentary on ll. 301–2), and frequently varying his tone and treatment in order to hold their attention and interest.

In his attack on drunkenness and gluttony, for example, the Pardoner begins with a full-throated denunciation of the sins – with declamatory 'purple patches' effectively spaced out (ll. 210–16, 224–32 and 246–60) among passages of example or quotation. With the shift of subject to drunkenness alone the Pardoner changes key in his rhetoric – adopting the more colloquial tone of common-sense advice (ll. 261–84). He becomes only slightly more formal at the end of this section (ll. 285–300), where, through the use of brief examples, he directs the advice especially towards those who have ambitions or hold authority. And when he turns to the subject of gambling (ll. 301–40) he maintains the same formal but straight-forward and practical approach – thus helping to give these parts of his sermon more cohesion than they would otherwise have had.

In his treatment of swearing (ll. 341–71), which is the last vice in this group, the Pardoner continues to show skill, not only in varying his style, but also by linking his denunciation of the sin with its dramatization in his main story. He makes two approaches to the subject here. First he makes a formal condemnation of swearing, backed up by weighty references to the Old and New Testaments (ll. 341–59). Then he switches once again to a more practical approach and a more colloquial tone – warning the man who is 'too violent in his oaths' about God's vengeance, and mimicking the language of such a swearer as he sits at the gaming-table (ll. 360–7). This last brief sketch not only dramatizes the causes and violent consequences of swearing for the benefit of the Pardoner's audience, but also helps to lead back (l. 372) to his story of the three 'ryotoures', who speak much the same kind of language and are guilty of the same sin.

The Pardoner also draws attention to his skill as a performer in a conscious way. During the whole of this 'sermon' (ll. 175–627) he is addressing an imaginary congregation – of the kind of people that he usually exploits – for the benefit of his 'real' audience of pilgrims. This creates a kind of 'mirror-effect' within the Tale which might well help to cause confusion about the extent of the Pardoner's hypocrisy.

But all this sleight of hand doesn't alter the basic nature of the hypocrisy itself. For eventually it has to be noticed that, before starting to preach against swearing, gluttony and drunkenness in his *Tale*, the Pardoner has already in his own *Prologue* sworn roundly (ll. 32 and 169), and shown that for him food and drink are more than just the basic necessities of life (ll. 33–4, 39–40, 164 and 168). Lechery gets only a brief mention in his sermon (ll. 189–94), but even this can be set against his own passing acknowledgment of the sin in his *Prologue* (l. 165). Avarice is the main theme of the *Tale*, and, as the Pardoner has already admitted (ll. 139–43), he habitually preaches in this way against his own dominant vice. In fact, among the main sins that he denounces at the beginning of his 'sermon', gambling seems to be the only one that he hasn't already confessed to.

The power of the Pardoner's description of these sins and their consequences, however, helps to draw attention away from the hypocrisy that is involved. His main story about the three young men (ll. 373–606) is a kind of moral fable that effectively dramatizes his previous condemnation of their drunkenness, gambling, swearing and avarice. He shows drunkenness from the beginning as the almost natural state in which they and people like them begin and end their days (ll. 374–5, 386 and 417) – and it is perhaps meant as a fitting ending for two of them to be poisoned by their drink. Gambling is seen as one of their vices only at the beginning of the story (l. 177), but anger and the threat of violence, which the Pardoner has said to be the 'fruits' of the dice (ll. 368–9), seem to dominate their relationships throughout – to Death, to the Old Man, and eventually to each other. Swearing with 'many a terrible oath' colours their language at moments of anger and excitement (e.g. ll. 404–22 and 462–71) – and the self-destruction of the brotherhood that they have sworn to so solemnly could be seen as an appropriate 'vengeance' (already prophesied in ll. 360–2) for this particular sin. Avarice, finally (the Pardoner's chief sin and the main 'selling-point' of his sermon), comes to dominate the later part of the story – where the gold lying at the foot of a tree vividly illustrates the Pardoner's text that 'greed is the root of evil', and brings out a rapidly increasing amount of selfishness and treachery in the three 'brothers'.

The Pardoner's story about the three young men is, like the Friar's story about a summoner, a 'moral tale' mainly about the self-destructiveness of blind greed. But his portrayal of such characters is at least partly meant to exploit any feelings of guilt which his audience may have about the sins that they illustrate – especially the sin of avarice. So, whilst the summoner in the *Friar's Tale* starts off as a mirror for the pilgrim-Summoner to see his face in, and only later becomes a kind of unredeemable Everyman figure (see p. 13 of this Introduction) – the 'ryotoures', on the other hand, are broadly representative figures with whom the Pardoner's audience is meant to feel some guilty identification from the start.

This is probably why the Pardoner introduces his main characters first of all in a very general way as 'a company of young people that indulged themselves' (ll. 175–6). It is only after he has generalized at length about the various sins that are involved in this folly that he comes back to the story and tells us that it is about these three 'ryotoures' in particular (l. 373). And, although during the course of the story the motives of these three are very clearly shown and their dialogue is suitably colloquial and violent they are not very clearly distinguishable from each other as individuals. The Pardoner doesn't even go so far as to give them the titles of First, Second or Third. He does on occasion refer to 'the proudest' (l. 428), 'the worst of them' (l. 488) – and, of course, 'the youngest of them all' (l. 516) has a very important part to play at the end of the story. But all we can say for sure about these characters as individuals is that, on the one hand, there are the two elder 'brothers', one of whom tempts the other through avarice into murder (ll. 518–48) – and that, on the other, there is the youngest, who could be said to be the 'worst', since he ends up by being about twice as avaricious and murderous as his fellows.

The most important features of the 'ryotoures', therefore, are those which they have in common. As well as exemplifying the sins that the Pardoner has described, they also share a kind of defiant blind ignorance, and their deafness to advice and warning is (like that of the summoner in the *Friar's Tale*) wilful to the point of being suicidal – as is reflected in their obsessive quest for revenge upon Death. Their youth, which the Pardoner emphasizes at points throughout the *Tale*, obviously has nothing to do with innocence, simplicity or ability to learn. This point is underlined at the very beginning of their quest, when the child who is their servant expresses the simple traditional wisdom about Death, which, through their way of life, they have chosen to ignore: 'Always be ready to meet him; so my mother taught me – I say no more' (ll. 395–6).

This combined impression of youth and wilful ignorance is strengthened and developed by the scene in which the seekers for Death meet the wandering Old Man. The Old Man's main speech (ll. 433–61), in response to their jeering and contemptuous questions,

begins and ends with reminders about the real and proper relationship between youth and old age, and contains some further traditional wisdom about Death. Death, to him, is a figure of authority,
whose actions – far from being criminal, as the 'ryotoures' claim
(ll. 411 and 465) – are part of 'God's will' (l. 438). He sees the
process of dying not as an unjust cutting short of a life of pleasure
(as the young men see it), but as being 'at rest' with his 'mother
earth' – which, after the sufferings of old age, he has come to value
above all material possessions. All this not only emphasizse the
difference of attitude between him and the young men, but could
also be taken as advice to them not to interfere with a force that
they do not understand.

The 'ryotoures', however, will have nothing to do with this sort
of advice. The Old Man's view of old age and his recognition of
Death's authority serve only to convince them that he is in league
with Death, 'to kill us young folk' (ll. 470–1). This reminds us not
only of the great gap between his age and theirs, but also of their
obsession with violence, which acts as a bar to understanding.

But are they in any way right about the Old Man? He certainly
claims to know something about Death and his ways – and the
directions he gives do eventually lead the three to their deaths. But
this need not necessarily mean that he is actually in league with
Death against them – still less that he himself *is* Death in disguise
(as at least one critic has claimed). Taking into account his whole
description of himself, together with his relationship to the young
men, it would make more sense, perhaps, to see him as the em-
bodiment of Old Age. This would mean that they were right about
the closeness of his relationship to Death, but wrong to see anything
particularly sinister in it – for Old Age at this time was often
described as a messenger warning of the approach of Death. But it
would be wrong to see the Old Man just in this symbolic but
limited role, for much of the strength of his portrayal lies in the
mystery of his situation – his restless wanderings and his knowledge
of Death. His warning to the three seekers for Death (contained in
the description of his physical decay and mental suffering) is – like
the means Death uses to strike them down – indirect but powerful.

The 'ryotoures' quest itself could be seen, especially in its later
stages, as a kind of speeded-up journey through life. They not only
encounter a figure who seems in several ways to represent old age,
but they also follow a 'crooked way' (l. 473), at the end of which
they do in fact find Death. They themselves are not just embodi-
ments of certain Deadly Sins but also more generally representative

figures whose blind ignorance, deafness to advice, and sudden destruction are meant to make the audience of the *Tale* more aware of their own guilt and vulnerability and of the lurking presence of death all around them.

The presence of death in the *Tale* is all the more sinister for being presented indirectly, through its effects alone: the reported killing of the 'ryotoures'' friend – the Old Man's signs of suffering – and the rapid self-destruction of the 'brothers' themselves. The Pardoner's audience and Chaucer's would have been familiar enough with sudden death through violence or accident (see, for example, ll. 1995–2040 and 2453–69 of the *Knight's Tale*), or through an outbreak of plague such as the servant refers to here (l. 391) – without having or adopting many of the ways that are used today, both to evade the idea and to cushion the reality. Through religious lyrics, and the paintings, carvings and stained glass in churches they would also have been familiar enough with the figure of Death as a shrunken corpse, an armed skeleton, the leader in a grotesque dance or a chess-player (see the illustrations on pp. 140–1 of *Chaucer's World*, by M. Hussey). But the Pardoner's presentation of Death as a 'sly thief' is more subtly menacing than any of these. The tradition that it is based upon goes back at least as far as Revelation, xvi, 15: 'Behold, I come as a thief. Blessed is he that watcheth . . .' This combines the idea of a sudden loss of life with that of judgment and the need to be prepared for it. Both ideas are strikingly reflected not only through what the child (l. 387) and the Old Man actually say about Death, but also through the young men's own sudden ending.

The Pardoner achieves this effect with hardly any use of the stock paraphernalia of skeletons, worms and shrouds that were used to shock the guilty into an awareness of death and judgment. His story – with its simple characterization, plain dialogue, and rapid reversal of fortunes at the end – has more of the quality of a folk-tale, and it isn't surprising that very similar kinds of fable about death have been found in the traditions of, for example, India and West Africa. Like many good folk-tales it makes its effects in an unspectacular but compelling way. The view it presents of Death is not of a hollow-eyed pursuer but of an essential and inevitable part of the 'ryotoures'' way of life. What need is there, as the Pardoner says, to preach about it any more?

The Pardoner and the Pilgrims

The Pardoner's style becomes more vividly spectacular when he steps forward at the end of his 'sermon' to deliver the summing-up – which he handles with his usual skill and verve (ll. 607–27). In his most full-bloodedly rhetorical vein, he covers all the sins he has described with a final sweeping denunciation, and follows up with a highly-charged emotional appeal to the individual sinner. This, however, is just a preparation for his final appeal to his imaginary congregation – which begins with a warning against avarice (ll. 616–17), and continues with an even livelier and more inventive line of 'patter' than, for example, the Summoner's Friar John uses in his sermons and on his rounds (see especially ll. 49–89 of the *Summoner's Tale*). The Pardoner's sheer confidence and agility as a performer are revealed by his ability to switch his tone, within ten lines, from the preacher's heart-rending 'Alas, mankind! . . .' (l. 612) to the huckster's touting 'Come up, you wives! . . .' (l. 622). Even more than the rest of the *Tale*, this whole passage demands to be read aloud for the full range of its effects to be made.

But the Pardoner's confidence overreaches itself when he tries to treat his 'real' audience of pilgrims as if they were an extension of his imaginary congregation. For – having invited the pilgrims to admire his expertise, and having piously reminded them that, after all, there is such a thing as a genuine pardon to be looked for in the after-life (ll. 627–30) – he now seems to think he can go straight on to exploit them in the usual way. In his sales-talk to them (ll. 631–57) he uses a combination of 'soft sell' and 'hard sell' as he has done with his imaginary congregation in his *Prologue* and sermon – first pointing out to them their great good luck in having with them a pardoner who can dispense his wares 'all new and fresh at the end of every mile' (l. 640) – and then trying to exploit the fears of sudden and unexpected disaster, which his story of the three seekers after Death would probably have reawakened in them.

His final and fatal mistake is to call upon the Host, as the member of the company who is 'the most steeped in sin', to be the first to pay for the privilege of kissing his relics (ll. 653–7). The Host is a much tougher and solider customer than the meek but imaginary souls who have bowed their heads beneath the Pardoner's 'holy document' (ll. 618–21). His reply to the invitation (ll. 658–67) combines an outright rebuff with a crudely forceful nailing of the lie behind the relics, methods and character of the Pardoner – who is so completely discredited, isolated and infuriated (ll. 668–71) by the attack that the Knight has to intervene in order to bring him back into the company of the pilgrims (l. 678).

It isn't very surprising that the Pardoner fails in this attempt to hoodwink the Host and the other pilgrims. What *is* surprising is that he tries at all. In view of the demonstration of his methods in the *Prologue* and at the very end of his sermon, it seems unusually stupid of him to suppose that his 'real' audience – however great the impact of his 'serious' preaching had been – would trust him to the extent of buying his wares. On the face of it, he seems to be simply asking for the violent setting-down that the Host gives him.

It is possible, however (see p. 30 of this Introduction), that the Pardoner's 'confession' in his *Prologue* is simply a kind of 'stage convention' (like an 'aside' or a soliloquy), which does not need psychological motives, and which is intended mainly for our ears rather than the pilgrims'. But this convention does not seem to be operating at the end of the Pardoner's sermon – especially where he proudly turns to his immediate audience and says, 'Look . . . this is how I preach!' (l. 627). Here, whatever the reasons for it may be, he directly draws the pilgrims' attention to the very methods and style that he has just exposed and is about to use again, on them.

This might suggest that the Pardoner has been carried away by his own eloquence into supposing that he can now do anything he likes with his audience – though this would be uncharacteristic in such a crafty and skilful performer. Or it might suggest that he knows exactly how much he is risking and still thinks he can get away with it. If he is making this sort of calculated gamble, his whole sermon can then be seen as an example of the classic kind of confidence-trick, in which the 'operator' appears to show the victim exactly 'how it's done' – on the principle that no one is more easily deceived than somebody who thinks he is being let into a secret.* If, however, this *is* the ploy that the Pardoner is using here, the fact still remains that he has misjudged both his moment and his victim.

But there are other possible interpretations of what he is trying to do here. It may be, perhaps, that he means his offer to be taken as a final joke to round off his 'performance' – regardless of the bad taste involved. Or – in a more subtle way – he may be leaving open

---

* A very successful example of this kind of trick is described in chapters 27 and 28 of Dickens's *Martin Chuzzlewit* – where the racketeer Montague Tigg entraps the miserly Jonas Chuzzlewit through a clever combination of confession and flattery.

the possibility that he is joking, as a line of retreat in case his plans misfire. The tone of his 'patter' to the pilgrims here (ll. 631–57) could thus be at one of several points on the scale between jest and earnest – depending on how we interpret his aims. (Reading the passage aloud, together with the end of the sermon, may help to decide this question.) The same might be said of the way in which the Pardoner singles out the Host for special attention in lines 653–7. He may be just having a bit of fun here as he rounds off his *Tale*, and trying to get the Host to enter into the spirit of the occasion, as the Host has got him to do at the beginning (see ll. 30–40). He may, on the other hand, be seriously trying to exploit the guilt that he hopes the Host will feel after the sermon – especially after the denunciation of taverns and doctored wine in it. Or it may be that he is doing both these things, in order to exploit what he would hope to be a confused response on the part of his victim.

If there is some kind of 'doubletalk' going on here, then the Host's crude and violent mockery of the Pardoner (ll. 658–67) is a very effective way of responding to it and breaking through the atmosphere of confusion that it has created. An indignant response would not perhaps have been enough to stop the Pardoner – since he might than have claimed that he was only joking anyway, and bided his time until a better opportunity came along. One way of checkmating him completely, therefore, is to isolate and anger him by a mixture of insult and ridicule – as the Host proceeds to do. He not only reminds the pilgrims of the Pardoner's hypocrisy in the coarsest and most personal terms, so that it cannot fail to be understood by all of them – but he does so in a roughly humorous way that allows the Pardoner no easy chance of a 'comeback'. And when the Pardoner has been reduced to angry speechlessness by this attack (ll. 668–9), the Host completes his humiliation and the turning of the tables by claiming (ll. 670–1) that he himself has just been having a bit of a joke.

This violent rebuff for the Pardoner can also be seen as necessary from the point of view of Chaucer's own audience. The Pardoner's thoughts about himself and his way of life have been presented to us at much greater length than those of any of the other pilgrims except the Wife of Bath. The danger is, then, that the readers or hearers of the Tale may have become so fascinated by the Pardoner and his 'performance' that by the end of it they will be nearly as confused by his 'doubletalk' as he would like his immediate victims to be. The Host's rough treatment here may thus have the effect of breaking the spell on *both* audiences and reminding us as well as the pilgrims of the Pardoner's real corruptness.

But there is yet one more reversal to come. The ending of the *Tale* (ll. 672–80) shows the Pardoner and the Host obeying the Knight's command to kiss and be friends, and riding off together along the road to Canterbury. This re-admittance of the Pardoner into the ranks of the pilgrims could be taken as reflecting a pessimistic or even cynical view of his corruptness within the society of Chaucer's time. But, on the other hand, it could help to remind us that the pilgrimage to Canterbury represents, not society as a whole to be generalized about and set to rights – but a number of individual souls winding along the road towards judgment. The Knight's encouragement to the pilgrims to 'laugh and joke as we did before' (l. 679) would in this case warn us not to expect a quick solution here to the whole problem of the Pardoner's corruptness, or demand to see him immediately damned as well as exposed. Nevertheless, this does not allow room for complacency. It may well make us feel uneasy to see the Host, who has resolutely refused to kiss the Pardoner's relics, being politely made to kiss the Pardoner himself (ll. 676–7). And the reconciliation that rounds off the *Tale* is also given a rather hollow ring by the terseness of the final couplet:

'And, as we diden, lat us laughe and playe.'
Anon they kiste, and riden forth hire waye.

The Three Tales

Violence and anger play a leading part in all these Tales and in their dramatic framework. The *Friar's* and *Summoner's Tales* themselves grow out of the quarrel between the two pilgrims. In the *Friar's Tale* the summoner is shown to be both aggressive and self-destructive – and his wild and grotesque threats against the old widow result almost directly in his being spirited off to Hell. In the *Summoner's Tale* the friar preaches long-windedly about anger – and is totally and comically deflated by his furious reaction to a fart. The *Pardoner's Tale*, on the other hand, explores the causes and effects of violence more fully than either of the other two, and shows powerfully how it recoils upon the violent 'ryotoures' – though the irony of this – unlike that of the reversals in the *Friar's* and *Summoner's Tales* – is far from comic in its effects. And at the end of this Tale the scathing mockery of the Host enacts a further violent judgment, upon the Pardoner himself.

Greed is also a major concern in the three *Tales*. The irony of the summoner's extortion in the *Friar's Tale* and the friar's begging in the *Summoner's Tale* is pointed and often subtle. But Chaucer does not try to give it a further dimension by making the two narrators remind us, in the process, of the greed that (according to their *General Prologue* portraits) they themselves are guilty of. On the other hand, this is exactly what happens when the Pardoner tells his *Tale* (immediately after the confession in his *Prologue*), and gives his treatment of the 'ryotoures'' greed a point that can be turned ironically against himself.

The main characters in these *Tales* – through whom such themes are embodied and developed – themselves show considerable variety. But, from this sample at least, it seems that Chaucer's irony finds more potential in the 'smooth' characters than in the 'rough' ones. This impression is given partly by the way in which, as we have seen (p. 16), the slick Friar is made more prominent in his *Tale* than the angry Summoner is in his – and partly by the richer characterization of the Summoner's friar, compared with that of the Friar's summoner. The noisy but naïve summoner in the *Friar's Tale* is given much less space to express himself than is the quiet but clever devil who accompanies him. The cunning friar in the *Summoner's Tale*, on the other hand, dominates the story, not only because of the sheer length of his preaching, but also because of the dexterity and persistence with which he probes for profitable responses from his various audiences, and the variety of tones which, intentionally or unintentionally, he adopts.

A similar kind of contrast can be seen *within* the *Pardoner's Tale*. The violent 'rioters' who are the main characters of the story are, like the Friar's summoner, presented in a broadly powerful way as doomed 'Everyman' figures (see p. 33). But it is the figure of the crafty Pardoner himself – with, like the Summoner's friar, a wide range of persuasive tones and techniques at his command – who dominates the stage (to a greater degree than either the Friar or Summoner in their *Tales*) and is himself the main focus for the satire.

Chaucer's irony in these tales seems, then, to be at its most fully effective in the treatment of these three characters (the Friar, the Summoner's friar and the Pardoner). This fullness is achieved mainly through the precise presentation of their subtle and persuasive methods of fraud. But an important part of the satirical effect is also gained by the suitably crude responses that they all eventually meet with. The pilgrim-Friar's hypocrisy is exposed first through the mimicking of his arguments in the *General Prologue* – then through the mixture of geniality and piousness with which he tries to mask his malice against the Summoner in his Tale – and finally through the rough scorn with which the Summoner treats him. The friar in the *Summoner's Tale* is discredited from the start by his own words and actions – and he is totally humiliated by the fart which is the sole product of all his appeals and ploys.

But it is the Pardoner who experiences the most telling reversal of all. He has shown himself to be even more expert than the two friars in the arts of persuasion and confusion – and the violent insults of the Host are, as we have seen (pp. 38–9), probably necessary to break through his 'doubletalk' at the end of the *Tale*. Chaucer's irony has revealed the Pardoner's vices in a richly complex and often humorous way – but this does not mean that we can rest comfortably in some illusion of the poet as 'gentle Geoffrey', genially 'accepting' such characters as part of 'God's plenty'. Its dramatic explosion into violent mockery here and elsewhere in these Tales should help to remind us that, although such hypocrites may seem just fascinating and comic, they are nonetheless both morally corrupt and socially poisonous.

Opinions for Discussion

The following opinions may be found useful to take into account when the Tales are being discussed. I have chosen them not because they agree with each other or with what I have said, but in the hope that they will give some impression of the range of possible approaches to Chaucer's work.

Chaucer's Pilgrims

The characters of Chaucer's Pilgrims are the characters which compose all ages and nations: as one age falls, another rises, different to mortal sight, but to immortals only the same; for we see the same characters repeated again and again, in animals, vegetables, minerals, and men; nothing new occurs in identical existence; Accident ever varies, Substances can never suffer change or decay.

Of Chaucer's characters, as described in his *Canterbury Tales*, some of the names or titles are altered by time, but the characters themselves for ever remain unaltered, and consequently they are the physiognomies or lineaments of universal human life, beyond which Nature never steps. Names alter, things never alter.

William Blake, *A Descriptive Catalogue of Pictures, Poetical and Historical Inventions* (1809), quoted in *Geoffrey Chaucer* (Penguin critical anthologies), ed. J. A. Burrow (1969), p. 77

The Friar

The Friar is a character . . . of a mixed kind . . . he is a complete rogue, with constitutional gaiety enough to make him a master of all the pleasures of the world.

William Blake, op. cit., p. 79

The quarrel between the Friar and Summoner

The Friar's degradation begins when he becomes involved with so low a fellow as the Summoner, and it is completed when he is permitted no rebuttal to the Summoner's scurrility. This is the harshest judgment visited by the author on any pilgrim except the Pardoner.

E. T. Donaldson, *Chaucer's Poetry* (1958), p. 917

Nowhere in the pilgrimage is the dramatic interplay of character more remarkable.

G. L. Kittredge, *Chaucer and His Poetry* (1915), p. 192

Theirs is a conflict not of men, but of professions. . . .

F. Tupper, *Types of Society in Medieval Literature* (1926), p. 56

The Friar's Tale

Elsewhere he [Chaucer] takes an amusing incident and builds it up by accretion of more or less relevant matter. . . . Here in the Friar's Tale the incident is a functional part of the whole, which he has imagined as a setting for it, and which beautifully complements the description of the Friar in the General Prologue.

P. F. Baum, *Chaucer: A Critical Appreciation* (1958), p. 135

The Summoner's Tale

The *Summoner's Tale* is altogether richer [than the *Friar's Tale*]. . . . The core of the Tale . . . is in the portrayal of the Friar and his winning ways. . . . In the end the figure of the friar is so completely filled out that we have quite forgotten the flyting.

D. A. Pearsall, *The Canterbury Tales*, in vol. I of the *Sphere History of Literature in the English Language*, ed. W. F. Bolton (1970), pp. 190–1

The Summoner and Pardoner

. . . the Pardoner, the Age's Knave . . . always commands and domineers over the high and low vulgar. This man is sent in every age for a rod and scourge, and for a blight, for a trial of men, to divide the classes of men; he is in the most holy sanctuary, and he is suffered by Providence for wise ends, and has also his great use, and his grand leading destiny.

His companion, the Sompnour, is also a Devil of the first magnitude, grand, terrific, rich and honoured in the rank of which he holds the destiny. The uses to Society are perhaps equal of the Devil and of the Angel, their sublimity, who can dispute.

William Blake, op. cit., p. 80

The Pardoner

The depth of his depravity is symbolized in his physical disability – in the fact that he is a eunuch . . . it is the one fact about himself that he conceals in the amazingly candid confession of his viciousness. His desire to hide this one fact later becomes the means by which the seemingly triumphant evil of one who has set his heart against man and God is rendered impotent.

E. T. Donaldson, op. cit., p. 900

It is amusing to fancy that Chaucer really knew that his Pardoner was a eunuch and took pleasure in saying so with a metaphor, but it is only an amusing fancy. Harry Bailey the Host (who of course had not read the General Prologue) did not think so.

P. F. Baum, op. cit., p. 54

The Pardoner's Prologue and Tale

The 'confession' should simply be accepted as a convention like those soliloquies in Elizabethan plays in which the villain comes to the front of the stage and, taking the audience entirely into his confidence, unmasks

43

himself. . . . The consideration that the rogue is here apparently giving away to his fellow pilgrims the secrets he lives by will only intervene when we refuse (incapacitated, perhaps, by modern 'naturalistic' conventions) to accept the convention.

J. Speirs, *Chaucer the Maker* (1951), p. 169

There is in his [the Pardoner's] sermon . . . a sly yielding to what for him is the grotesque fascination of the flesh.

J. Speirs, op. cit., p. 173

The Pardoner has not always been an assassin of souls. He is a renegade, perhaps, from some holy order. Once he preached for Christ's sake; and now under the spell of the wonderful story he has told and of recollections that stir within him, he suffers a very paroxysm of agonized sincerity. It can last but a moment. The crisis passes, and reaction follows. He takes refuge from himself in a wild orgy of reckless jesting. . . .

G. L. Kittredge, op. cit., pp. 216–17

Chaucer's satire

Chaucer's Monk, his Canon, and his Friar, took not from the character of his Good Parson. A satirical poet is the check of the laymen on bad priests. . . . But they will tell us, that all kind of satire, though never so well deserved by particular priests, yet brings the whole order into contempt. Is then the peerage of England anything dishonoured when a peer suffers for his treason? . . . They who use this kind of argument, seem to be conscious to themselves of somewhat which has deserved the poet's lash, and are less concerned for their public capacity than for their private; at least there is pride at the bottom of their reasoning.

John Dryden, Preface to *Fables* (1700), quoted in *Geoffrey Chaucer* (Penguin critical anthologies), ed. J. A. Burrow (1969), p. 65

Read Chaucer's description of the Good Parson, and bow the head and knee to him, who, in every age, sends us such a burning and a shining light. Search, O ye rich and powerful, for these men and obey their counsel, then shall the golden age return: But alas! you will not easily distinguish him from the Friar or the Pardoner; they, also are 'full solemn men', and their counsel you will continue to follow.

William Blake, op. cit., p. 81

For Reference

The full titles and details of books referred to more than once in the Introduction (apart from those listed under Abbreviations, p. vi) are as follows:

Langland, *Piers the Ploughman*, translated by J. F. Goodridge (Penguin Classics, 1959)

R. T. Davies (ed.), *Medieval English Lyrics* (Faber, 1963 – paperback edition, 1966)

J. J. Bagley and P. B. Rowley, *The Pelican Documentary History of England*, vol. I (1066–1540) (Penguin, 1966)

E. Rickert, *Chaucer's World* (Columbia University Press, 1948 – paperback edition, 1962)

M. Hussey, *Chaucer's World*, A Pictorial Companion (Cambridge University Press, 1967)

C. S. Lewis, *Studies in Words* (Cambridge University Press, 1960 – paperback edition, 1967)   N.R.H.

Biographical Note

Geoffrey Chaucer, the son of John Chaucer, a well-to-do vintner, was born in London about 1343. Little is known about his formal education, but this most widely read of medieval English poets probably got his knowledge of French and Latin at one of the London schools, and he may also have had a general as well as legal education at the Inner Temple during the years from 1361 to 1367. He did not go to either university, though in later life he was in touch with Oxford scholars like Ralph Strode. But as a poet he acquired most of his knowledge of men and manners through his experience of court life. He was a page in the household of the Countess of Ulster and then in that of Prince Lionel, from about the age of fourteen to twenty (1357–63), and a squire of the Royal Household from 1367 to 1378. During these years he became a friend of John of Gaunt, the death of whose wife Blanche was the occasion of Chaucer's first long poem, *The Book of the Duchess* (1369–70). These were formative years for Chaucer: he went on diplomatic missions to France, Flanders and Italy, learnt Italian and read the works of Dante and Boccaccio, which deeply influenced his own poems written after about 1380. As a very young man he had served in the English army in France, where he was captured and ransomed (1360), and he took part in Gaunt's French expedition nine years later. In 1366 he married Philippa, one of the Queen's ladies; but nothing is known of their life together. They may have had two sons, Thomas and Lewis, and a daughter Elizabeth, who became a nun, but the evidence is not certain that these Chaucers were the poet's children.

In the last twenty-five years of his life, Chaucer held a succession of administrative appointments which brought him into contact with businessmen and merchants. Between 1374 and 1386 he was the King's senior customs official for wools, skins and hides in the port of London, and in 1382 he took over the Petty Customs for wine, etc. In his later years he was Clerk of the King's Works (1389–91, a post which included responsibility for the upkeep of the royal palaces) and in 1391 he became Deputy Forester of the King's Somersetshire forest of North Petherton. He eked out the income from these offices with exchequer grants received from his royal masters Edward III, Richard II and Henry IV. During the politically disturbed later years of the fourteenth century, Chaucer managed to avoid making enemies in high places and, while never becoming a rich man (like Shakespeare in his last years), he avoided poverty. His poetry, written for and circulated among the court circle and his friends, was highly successful but did not bring him much financial reward. After 1385 Chaucer left London and lived in Kent, where he was justice of the peace for four years and, in 1386, knight of the shire (member of Parliament) for Kent. In 1399 he leased a house in the garden of Westminster Abbey. He died in 1400, and tradition has it that he was buried in the Abbey.

During his years as a customs official Chaucer was hard-worked and had little leisure for poetry, though one of his finest earlier poems *The Parliament of Fowls* (and possibly also the unfinished comic fantasy *The House of Fame*) belong to this period. But after 1382 he had the help of deputies, and in the 1380s he translated the *Consolation of Philosophy* of Boethius and wrote his great narrative poem *Troilus and Criseyde*. The increase of leisure which came with his move to Kent may have stimulated him to begin *The Canterbury Tales*, the crowning work of his maturity and the greatest work of medieval English literature. The *General Prologue* is dated about 1387 but between this work and *Troilus* he wrote the unfinished collection of tales called *The Legend of Good Women*, the *Prologue* of which is an exquisite semi-autobiographical love-vision in which the heroic couplet appears for the first time. The *Tales* (some of which Chaucer had written years before) occupied the remaining years of his life and remained unfinished at his death in 1400. Nevertheless the twenty-four tales and fragments, together with the *Prologue*, cover a wide spectrum of literary forms, styles and themes, and they constitute, with the earlier poems and *Troilus*, a body of work second in range and quality only to that of Shakespeare.

Suggestions for Further Reading

Of the many books on Chaucer's life and times the best still remains G. G. Coulton's pungently-written study *Chaucer and his England* (Methuen, University Paperback edn, 1963), although D. S. Brewer's *Chaucer in his Time* (Nelson, 1963), is also very readable and there are many pictorial companions and guides of varying quality. The court-culture in which Chaucer produced his mature work is well studied in the opening chapters of Gervase Mathew's *The Court of Richard II* (John Murray, 1968) and the most entertaining 'background' book for *The Canterbury Tales* is still J. J. Jusserand's *English Wayfaring Life in the Middle Ages* (Benn, 1950). Useful introductions to Chaucer's work as a whole are John Speirs's *Chaucer the Maker* (Faber paperback, 1964) (which quotes lavishly from the text) and the Pelican *Age of Chaucer* (ed. Boris Ford). But the classic introduction to Chaucer's early work (including *Troilus*) is C. S. Lewis's *The Allegory of Love* (Galaxy paperback, 1958), a study of Courtly Love, and the best book on the tales themselves is W. W. Lawrence's *Chaucer and The Canterbury Tales* (Columbia University Press, reprinted 1969). The standard edition of the poems is F. N. Robinson's *The Complete Works of Geoffrey Chaucer* (Oxford University Press, 2nd edition, 1957), but also useful are the 'Everyman' editions of the tales (ed. by A. C. Cawley) and of *Troilus and Criseyde* (ed. John Warrington) with marginal glosses and footnote-paraphrases of difficult lines which make for easier reading.   A.V.C.S.

The Friar's, Summoner's and Pardoner's Tales

Abbreviations

(c) after a word or phrase, means 'See Commentary' (at the back of the book), for further discussion of the point

OF Old French

Lat. Latin

GP the *General Prologue* to the *Canterbury Tales*

FT the *Friar's Tale*

ST the *Summoner's Tale*

PT the *Pardoner's Tale*

The Portrait of the Friar

(from the **General Prologue** to the **Canterbury Tales**, A 208–69)

A FRERE there was, a wantown and a merye,
A limitour, a ful solempne man.
In alle the ordres foure is noon that can
So muchel of daliaunce and fair langage.
He hadde maad ful many a mariage   5
Of yonge wommen, at his owne cost.
Unto his ordre he was a noble post.
Ful wel biloved and famulier was he
With frankeleyns overal in his contree,
And eke with worthy wommen of the town;   10
For he hadde power of confessioun
(As sayde himself) moore than a curat –
For of his ordre he was licenciat.
Ful swetely herde he confessioun,
And plesaunt was his absolucioun.   15
He was an esy man to yive penaunce

---

[1] *Frere*, friar.   *wantown*, high-spirited.   *merye*, pleasant.

[2] *limitour*, a mendicant (begging) friar who was licensed to beg for alms within a specified *limit* (district).   *solempne*, festive (a difficult word to translate – it here means virtually the opposite of the modern 'solemn' ('grave')).

[3] *the ordres foure*. (The 'four orders' of Friars were the Dominicans, the Franciscans, the Carmelites and the Augustinians).   *can*, knows.

[4] *daliaunce and fair langage*, idle gossip and flattering talk.

[7] *post*, pillar (support).

[9] *frankeleyns*, well-to-do country landowners below the rank of the aristocracy (see the portrait of the Franklin in the *GP*).

[10] *worthy*, either 'wealthy' or 'respectable' or both.

[12] *curat*, parish priest.

[13] *licenciat*, licensed (i.e. he was a representative of his order licensed to hear confessions without being authorized by the local bishop, as were parish priests, who were not empowered to grant absolution in all cases. The Friar *was*).

49

There as he wiste to han a good pitaunce.
For unto a povre ordre for to yive
Is signe that a man is wel y-shrive:
For 'if he yaf', he dorste make avaunt,   20
'He wiste that a man was repentaunt';
(For many a man so hard is of his herte,
He may nat wepe, although him soore smerte;
Therefore, in stede of weping and prayeres,
Men moot yive silver to the povre freres.)   25
His tipet was ay farsed ful of knyves
And pinnes, for to yiven faire wyves.
And certaynly he hadde a murye note:
Wel koude he singe and playen on a rote;
Of yeddinges he bar outrely the prys.   30
His nekke whyt was as the flour-de-lys;
Therto he strong was as a champioun.
He knew the tavernes wel in every town,
And everich hostiler and tappestere
Bet than a lazar or a beggestere;   35
For unto swich a worthy man as he
Acorded nat, as by his facultee,
To have with sike lazars aqueyntaunce.
(It is nat honest, it may nat avaunce,
For to delen with no swich poraille,   40
But al with riche and sellers of vitaille.)

---

¹⁷ 'In cases where he knew it would be made worth his while.' (*Pitaunce* here means a gift or 'extra' of any kind, not necessarily food, as Skeat suggests.)

¹⁸ 'For to give (gifts) to a poor order. . . .'

¹⁹ *wel y-shrive*, has made a good confession (lit.: 'is well shriven').

^{20–1} 'For "if a man gave" – he dared avow – "he could know [for sure] that he was repentant".'

²³ 'He is unable to weep, even if he should feel sharp remorse.'

²⁵ *men moot yive*, people ought to give.

²⁶ *tipet*, hood (often used as a pocket).   *farsed*, stuffed.

²⁷ *wyves*, women generally (though it could mean 'wives').

²⁸ *murye note* – i.e. an agreeable voice.

²⁹ *rote*, fiddle.

³⁰ 'He was the best of ballad-singers' (*yeddinges* were stories set to music). *outrely*, utterly, absolutely.

³¹ *flour-de-lys*, lily-flower.

³² *champioun*, a professional fighter in judicial combats ('champion').

³⁴ *hostiler*, innkeeper, publican.   *tappestere*, barmaid, female tapster (the '-ster' ending here denotes femininity – as in present day English 'spinster').

³⁵ *Bet*, better (the adverb).   *lazar*, leper (from the leper Lazarus in the parable of Dives and Lazarus – see *ST*, l. 213).

³⁷ 'It was not fitting (*acorded nat*), considering his position (*facultee*).'

^{39–40} 'It is not becoming (*honest*) or profitable to have anything to do with such poor wretches (*poraille*).'

⁴¹ 'But wholly (or "exclusively") with rich [people] and with food-merchants.'

And overal, there as profit sholde aryse,
Curteys he was and lowely of servyse –
There nas no man nowhere so vertuous.
He was the beste beggere in his hous;   45
For though a widwe hadde noght a sho,
So plesaunt was his 'In principio',
Yet wolde he have a ferthing, er he wente.
His purchas was wel bettre than his rente.
And rage he koude, as it were right a whelp.   50
In love-days, there koude he muchel help –
For there he was nat lyk a cloisterer
With a thredbar cope, as is a povre scoler;
But he was lyk a maister or a pope:
Of double worsted was his semicope,   55
That rounded as a belle out of the presse.
Somwhat he lipsed, for his wantownesse,
To make his Englissh sweete upon his tonge.
And in his harping, whan that he hadde songe,
His eyen twinkled in his heed aright,   60
As doon the sterres in the frosty night.
This worthy limitour was cleped Huberd.

---

[42] *overal, there as*, everywhere that. . . .
[43] 'He was courteous, and offered his services humbly.'
[44] *vertuous*, either 'energetic, efficient' (Skeat), or 'virtuous' (said ironically).
[46] *widwe*, widow.   *sho*, shoe.
[47] 'In principio', in the beginning (the opening words of St John's Gospel, which the Friar quoted as he went from house to house. Chaucer may intend a pun: 'So pleasant were his *opening words* . . .').
[48] 'He would still manage to get a farthing before leaving.'
[49] *purchas*, what he picked up by begging.   *rente*, (regular) income.
[50] *rage*, frisk about.   *as it were right a whelp*, just like a puppy.
[51] *love-days*, 'days appointed for settlement of disputes out of court . . . the clergy took an active part as arbiters, at first with the approval of the Church. Later, when the institution became corrupt, they were forbidden to take part' (Robinson).
[53] *cope*, cloak (worn by priests).
[54] *maister*, Master (of Arts, Theology).
[55] *semicope*, half-cope (short cloak).
[56] *rounded*, fell into a round shape.   *presse*, mould.
[57] *lipsed*, lisped.   *for his wantownesse*, as a playful affectation.
[60] *aright*, really, indeed.

The Portrait of the Summoner

(from the **General Prologue** to the **Canterbury Tales,** A 623–68)

A SOMNOUR was there with us in that place,
That hadde a fyr-reed cherubinnes face –
For sawcefleem he was, with eyen narwe.
As hoot he was and lecherous as a sparwe
With scalled browes blake and piled berd: 5
Of his visage children were aferd!
There nas quiksilver, litarge, ne brimstoon,
Boras, ceruce, ne oille of tartre noon,
Ne oynement that wolde clense and byte,
That him mighte helpen of his whelkes whyte,   10
Nor of the knobbes sitting on his chekes.
Wel loved he garleek, oynons, and eke lekes,
And for to drinken strong wyn, reed as blood –
Thanne wolde he speke and crye as he were wood.
And whan that he wel dronken hadde the wyn,   15
Thanne wolde he speke no word but Latyn.
A fewe termes hadde he, two or three,
That he had lerned out of som decree –
(No wonder is, he herde it al the day!) –
And eke ye knowen wel, how that a jay   20
Kan clepen 'Watte' as wel as kan the pope.
But whoso koude in other thing him grope,
Thanne hadde he spent al his philosophye:
Ay '*Questio quid iuris*' wolde he crye.
He was a gentil harlot and a kynde;   25
A bettre felawe sholde men noght fynde.

---

[1] *Somnour,* Summoner.
[2] 'A fire-red face, like one of the cherubim.'
[3] *sawcefleem,* with a red pimpled face (thought to be caused by too much salt phlegm (Lat.: *salsum phlegma*) in the constitution).   *eyen narwe,* narrow, slitted eyes.
[4] *sparwe,* sparrow.
[5] *scalled,* scabby.   *piled,* scanty (with the hair falling out).
[7] *litarge,* litharge (lead oxide).
[8] *Boras,* borax.   *ceruce,* ceruse, white lead.   *oille of tartre,* cream of tartar.
[9] *oynement,* ointment.
[10] 'That might help him [to remove] his white pimples (*whelkes*).'
[12] 'garlic, onions, leeks.'
[21] *clepen,* call out.   *Watte,* Wat (Walter) – as parrots are taught to say 'Poll'.
[22] *in other thing him grope,* examine him in any other matter.
[24] *Questio quid iuris,* a stock Latin phrase meaning: 'The question is, what is the aw on this matter?'
[25] *gentil harlot,* nice fellow.
[26] *felawe,* companion (the word could imply rascality, as in l. 28, below).

He wolde suffre, for a quart of wyn,
A good felawe to have his concubyn
A twelf-month, and excuse him atte fulle;
Ful prively a finch eke koude he pulle.   30
And if he foond owhere a good felawe,
He wolde techen him to have noon awe,
In swich cas, of the erchedekenes curs,
But if a mannes soule were in his purs –
For in his purs he sholde y-punisshed be.   35
'Purs is the erchedeknes helle', sayde he.
But wel I woot he lyed right in dede!
Of cursing oghte ech gilty man him drede –
For curs wol slee, right as assoilling savith –
And also war him of a *Significavit.*   40
In daunger hadde he at his owne gyse
The yonge girles of the diocyse,
And knew hir counseil, and was al hir reed.
A gerland hadde he set upon his heed,
As grete as it were for an ale stake;   45
A bokeler hadde he maad him of a cake.

[27–9] 'In return for a quart of wine he was willing to allow one of his rascally companions to keep his concubine for a year, and entirely excuse him.'

[30] *pulle*, pluck (the feathers). The phrase probably means that the Summoner was accomplished in the same sin for which he excused others – as well as that he could 'deceive simpletons'.

[31] *owhere*, anywhere.

[32–3] 'He would teach him not to stand in awe of the archdeacon's excommunication (*curs*), if he was keeping a concubine (*in swich cas*, lit. = "in such circumstances").'

[34–6] The Summoner maintained that there was no need to fear excommunication unless a man's soul resided in his purse, because that was where he would suffer – i.e. by having to pay a fine to be released.

[39] 'Excommunication will slay, just as absolution will save.'

[40] 'And he should also beware of a writ enabling him to be put in prison' (the opening word of such a writ being *Significavit*).

[41] 'He had within his control (*daunger*), just where he wanted them (*at his owne gyse*) the young people (*girles*) of the diocese.'

[43] *was al hir reed*, 'was wholly their adviser' (Skeat).

[45] *ale-stake*, the support for a garland outside an ale-house.

The Beginning of the Quarrel between the Friar and Summoner

(from the end of the **Wife of Bath's Prologue,** D 829–56)

Biholde the wordes bitwene the Somnour and the Frere

The Frere lough whan he hadde herd al this.
'Now, dame,' quod he, 'so have I joye or blis,
This is a long preamble of a tale!'
And whan the Somnour herde the Frere gale,
'Lo!' quod the Somnour, 'Goddes armes two!   5
A frere wol entremette him evermo.
Lo, goode men! a flye and eke a frere
Wol falle in every dissh and eke matere.
What spekestow of preambulacioun?
What! amble, or trotte, or pees, or go sit down!   10
Thou lettest oure disport in this manere.'
    'Ye, woltow so, sir Somnour?' quod the Frere.
'Now, by my feith, I shal, er that I go,
Telle of a somnour swich a tale or two
That alle folk shal laughen in this place.'   15
    'Now elles, Frere, I bishrewe thy face,'
Quod this Somnour, 'and I bishrewe me,
But if I telle tales two or thre
Of freres, er I come to Sidingbourne,
That I shal make thyn herte for to morne;   20
For wel I woot thy pacience is goon!'
    Oure Hooste cryde: 'Pees! and that anon!'
And sayde: 'Lat the womman telle hire tale;

---

[1] *lough,* laughed.
[2] *so have I joye or blis,* as I may know the joy and (lit.: or) blessedness (of Heaven).
[4] *gale,* complain.
[5] *Goddes armes two,* by the two arms of God.
[6] *entremette him evermo,* always thrust himself in.
[8] 'Will fall in every dish [of food] and also every thing that's going on.'
[9] 'Why are you talking of preambles?'
[10] *amble, or trotte, or pees,* go and amble, or trot, or shut up.
[11] *lettest,* are hindering.   *disport,* entertainment.
[12] *Ye, woltow so,* Oh yes, is that what you'd like?
[16-19] *Now elles . . . Sidingbourne,* 'I defy you to do your worst, Friar – I curse your face . . . and I curse myself if I don't (*but if,* lit. = "unless") tell two or three tales about friars before we reach Sittingbourne.'
[20] *make thyn herte for to morne,* make you very sorry.
[21] 'For I can see very well (*woot,* lit. = "know") that you're already getting rattled.'
[22] *Pees . . . anon,* be quiet at once.

Ye fare as folk that dronken ben of ale!
Do, dame, tel forth youre tale, and that is best.'   25
   'Al redy, sire,' quod she, 'right as yow lest –
If I have licence of this worthy Frere?'
   'Yis, dame,' quod he, 'Tel forth, and I wol here.'

Here endeth the Wyf of Bathe hire Prologe

[24] 'You're behaving like people drunk on beer.'
[25] *Do, dame,* go ahead, madam.
[26] *right as yow lest,* just as you please (lit.: 'as it pleases you').
[27] *licence,* permission.
[28] *Yis,* yes (emphatic).

The Prologue to the Friar's Tale

This worthy limitour, this noble Frere,
He made alway a maner louring cheere
Upon the Somnour, but for honestee
No vileyns word as yet to him spak he.
But atte laste he sayde unto the Wyf,   5
'Dame,' quod he, 'God yive yow right good lyf!
Ye han here touched, also moot I thee,
In scole-matere grete difficultee –
Ye han sayd muche thing right wel, I saye.
But, dame, here as we ryden by the waye,   10
Us nedeth nat to speken but of game,
And lete auctoritees, on Goddes name,
To preching and to scoles of clergye!
But, if it lyke to this compaignye,
I wol yow of a somnour telle a game.   15
Pardee! ye may wel knowe by the name
That of a somnour may no good be sayd.
I praye that noon of yow be yvel apayd.
A somnour is a renner up and doun
With mandements for fornicacioun,   20
And is y-bet at every townes ende –'
   Our Hoost tho spak, 'A, sire! ye sholde be hende
And curteys, as a man of your estat;
In compaignye we wol have no debat!

---

[1] *limitour*, limiter (c) – a friar who raised funds by begging within a 'limited' area.
[2] *a maner louring cheere*, a sort of glowering look.
[3] *the Somnour*, the Summoner.   *for honestee*, for good manners' sake.
[4] *vileyns* (adjective), churlish, rude (c).
[5] *atte laste*, at last (lit.: 'at *the* last').   *the Wyf*, the Wife of Bath (who has just ended her Tale).
[6] *God yive yow right good lyf*, God bless you (lit.: 'give you a very good life').
[7] *han here touched*, have here touched on.   *also moot I thee*, so help me (lit.: 'so may I thrive').
[8] *scole-matere*, academic questions (c).
[10] *ryden*, ride (pl.).
[11] 'We need speak only for entertainment's sake' ('nedeth' is an impersonal verb, taking an indirect object – see also ll. 14 and 198).
[12] *lete auctoritees*, leave (the quoting of) authorities (c).
[13] *clergye*, learning.
[14] *if it lyke to* (impersonal verb), if it pleases.
[15] *wol*, will.   *game*, an entertaining story.
[16] *Pardee*, by God.
[18] *yvel apayd*, ill-pleased.
[19] *renner*, runner.
[20] *mandements*, summonses.   *or*, relating to, on account of.
[21] *y-bet*, beaten up (c).
[22] *tho*, then.   *hende*, polite.
[23] *estat*, rank, 'position'.
[24] *debat*, quarrelling.

Telleth your tale, and lat the Somnour be.'   25
   'Nay,' quod the Somnour, 'lat him saye to me
What so him list. Whan it comth to my lot –
By God! – I shal him quyten every grot!
I shal him telle which a grete honour
It is to be a flatering limitour –   3
And eke of many another maner cryme
Which nedeth nat rehercen at this tyme.
And his offyce I shal him telle, y-wis!'
   Our Hoost answerde, 'Pees, namoore of this!'
And after this he sayde unto the Frere,   35
'Tel forth your tale, my leeve maister deere.'

The Tale

HERE BIGINNETH THE FRERES TALE

'Whilom there was dwelling in my contree
An erchedekene, a man of heigh degree,
That boldely dide execucioun
In punisshing of fornicacioun,   40
Of wicchëcraft, and eke of bawderye,
Of diffamacioun, and avoutrye,
Of chirche-reves, and of testaments,
Of contractes, and of lakke of sacraments,
Of usure, and of symonye also.   45

<hr>

25 *Telleth*, tell (2nd person plural imperative – the polite form).   *lat the Somnour be*, leave the Summoner alone.

27 *What so him list*, whatever he pleases. (lit.: 'it pleases him').   *my lot*, my turn.

28 *him quyten every grot*, pay him back every bit.

29 *which* (in this context), what.

31 *maner cryme*, kind *of* crime (see also l. 174).

32 *Which nedeth nat rehercen*, which doesn't need to be gone over.

33 'And I'll tell him his business, indeed.'

36 *leeve*, beloved.

37 *Whilom*, once.

38 *erchedekene*, archdeacon (c).   *degree*, rank.

39 *boldely dide execucioun*, energetically enforced the law.

41 *eke*, also.   *bawderye*, procuring, prostitution.

42 *diffamacioun*, slander.   *avoutrye*, adultery (c).

43 *chirche-reves*, robbing of churches.   *testaments*, (interfering with) wills.

44 *contractes*, breaking of marriage-contracts.   *lakke of sacraments*, failure to take sacraments.

45 *usure*, money-lending (usury).   *symonye*, simony (buying and selling church-offices, especially livings).

But certes, lecchours dide he grettest wo:
They sholde singen if that they were hent;
And smale tytheres weren foule y-shent,
If any persone wolde upon hem pleyne.
There mighte asterte him no pecunial peyne.   50
For smale tythes and for smal offringe
He made the peple pitously to singe –
For, er the bisshop caughte hem with his hook,
They weren in the erchedeknes book;
Thanne hadde he, thurgh his jurisdiccioun,   55
Power to doon on hem correccioun.
He hadde a somnour redy to his hond;
A slyer boy nas noon in Engelond,
For subtilly he hadde his espiaille,
That taughte him where him mighte availle.   60
He koude spare of lecchours oon or two,
To techen him to foure-and-twenty mo. –
For, though this Somnour wood were as an hare,
To telle his harlotrye I wol nat spare;
For we been out of his correccioun;   65
They han of us no jurisdiccioun,
Ne never shullen, terme of alle hire lyves –'
    'Peter! so been wommen of the styves',
Quod the Somnour, 'y-put out of our cure!'
    'Pees! with mischance and with misaventure!'   70

⁴⁶ 'But certainly he inflicted the greatest suffering upon lechers.'
⁴⁷ *singen* (euphemism), cry out (because of the archdeacon's extortions).   *if that*, if.   *hent*, caught.
⁴⁸ 'And those who paid small tithes (i.e. in short measure) had a hard time of it (lit.: "were badly damaged").'
⁴⁹ 'If any parson wanted to complain about them.'
⁵⁰ 'No fine (lit.: "financial punishment") could escape him.'
⁵³ *er*, before.   *hem*, them (c).
⁵⁵ *Thanne*, then.   *thurgh his jurisdiccioun*, because of his legal authority.
⁵⁶ *doon*, do, carry out.   *correccioun*, punishment.
⁵⁷ *redy to his hond*, ready to hand.
⁵⁸ *boy*, rogue (c).   *nas noon*, there was no.
⁵⁹ 'For he cunningly kept a body of spies.'
⁶⁰ *taughte*, informed.   *where him mighte availle*, where there might be profit for him.
⁶¹ *of lecchours oon or two*, one or two lechers.
⁶² *techen him to*, put him on to.   *mo*, more.
⁶³ *wood were*, should become mad, angry (c).
⁶⁴ *harlotrye*, villainy (c).
⁶⁵ *been*, are.   *correccioun*, sphere of authority (a different sense from that in l. 56).
⁶⁷ *Ne*, nor.   *terme of alle hire lyves*, throughout all their lives.
⁶⁸ *Peter*, by St Peter.   *styves*, brothel-quarters (c).
⁶⁹ *y-put*, put (past participle).   *cure*, jurisdiction, control.
⁷⁰ ' "Quiet – God rot you!" ' (lit.: 'with bad luck and misfortune').

58

Thus sayde our Hoost, 'and lat him telle his tale!
Now telleth forth, though that the Somnour gale.
Ne spareth nat, myn owene maister dere.'
    'This false theef, this somnour,' quod the Frere,
'Hadde alway bawdes redy to his hond,   75
As any hauk to lure in Engelond,
That tolde him al the secree that they knewe;
For hire acqueyntance was nat come of newe;
They weren his approwours prively.
He took himself a grete profit therby;   80
His maister knew nat alway what he wan.
Withouten mandement a lewed man
He koude somne, on peyne of Crystes curs,
And they were glade for to fille his purs
And make him grete feestes atte nale.   85
And, right as Judas hadde purses smale,
And was a theef, right swich a theef was he;
His maister hadde but half his duëtee.
He was, if I shal yiven him his laude,
A theef, and eke a somnour, and a bawde.   90
He hadde eke wenches at his retenue,
That whether that Sir Robert or Sir Huwe,
Or Jakke, or Rauf, or whoso that it were,
That lay by hem, they tolde it in his ere.
Thus was the wenche and he of oon assent,   95

[72] *though that the Somnour gale*, although the Summoner may rage.
[73] *Ne spareth nat*, don't hold anything back (2nd person plural imperative, as in l. 25).
[74] *quod*, said.
[75] *bawdes*, procurers, procuresses.
[75–6] 'As ready to hand as any hawk in England is to its lure' (c).
[77] *secree*, secrets.
[78] *hire*, their.   *nat come of newe*, not newly made – i.e. was of long standing.
[79] *approwours*, agents (from OF: *approuver*, to cause to profit).   *prively*, confidentially.
[80] *took himself*, took for himself.
[81] *wan*, got, earned.
[82] *lewed*, ignorant ((c) on l. 264 of *ST*)—or, possibly, 'lay'.
[83] 'He could summon on pain of excommunication' (*coude*, knew how to).
[84] *for to*, to.
[85] *atte nale*, at the ale house (from: 'atten ale').
[86] *smale*, small (here, as often in Chaucer's verse, the adjective comes after the noun).
[87] *swich*, such.
[88] *duëtee* (3 syllables), due (noun) (c).
[89] *his laude*, the praise due to him.
[91] *at his retenue*, in his service.
[92] *whether that*, whether.   *Sir Huwe*, Sir Hugh (c).
[93] 'Or Jack, or Ralph, or whoever it might be.'
[95] *of oon assent*, of one mind, hand in glove.

And he wolde fecche a feyned mandement,
And somne hem to chapitre bothe two,
And pile the man, and lete the wenche go.
Thanne wolde he saye, "Freend, I shal for thy sake
Do stryken hir out of our lettres blake –   100
Thee thar namoore as in this cas travaille.
I am thy freend, there I thee may availle."
Certayn, he knew of bryberyes mo
Than possible is to telle in yeeres two;
For in this world nis dogge for the bowe   105
That kan an hurt deer from an hool knowe
Bet than this somnour knew a sly lecchour,
Or an avouter, or a paramour;
And, for that was the fruit of al his rente,
Therfore on it he sette al his entente.   110
    And so bifel, that ones on a day
This somnour, ever waiting on his prey,
Rood for to somne an old widwe, a ribybe,
Feyning a cause, for he wolde brybe.
And happed that he saugh bifore him ryde   115
A gay yeman, under a forest syde.
A bowe he baar, and arwes brighte and kene;
He hadde upon a courtepy of grene,
An hat upon his heed, with frenges blake.

⁹⁶ *feyned*, forged, faked.
⁹⁷ *chapitre*, the ecclesiastical court (held in the chapter-house of the cathedral).
⁹⁸ *pile*, 'fleece'.
¹⁰⁰ 'Get her struck out of our black books' (c).
¹⁰¹ 'There's no need for you to bother any more about this matter.'
¹⁰² *there I thee may availle*, wherever I can be of use to you.
¹⁰³ *Certayn*, certainly.   *bryberyes*, swindling.
¹⁰⁵ 'For there is no hunting-dog (lit.: "dog for the bow" – cf. the modern "gun-dog") in the world.'
¹⁰⁶ 'That can tell a hurt animal from a sound one.'
¹⁰⁸ *avouter*, adulterer.   *paramour*, concubine, lover.
¹⁰⁹ *for*, because.   *the fruit of al his rente*, the most substantial part of (lit.: 'the fruit of') his whole income.
¹¹⁰ *he sette al his entente*, he concentrated (on it).
¹¹¹ 'And so it happened, that one day.'
¹¹² *ever waiting on*, always keeping an eye open for.
¹¹³ *Rood*, rode.   *a ribybe*, an old stick (lit.: 'a fiddle' (c)).
¹¹⁴ 'Inventing a charge, as he wanted to blackmail (her).'
¹¹⁵ 'And it happened that he saw riding in front of him.'
¹¹⁶ *gay*, smart.   *yeman*, yeoman (c).   *under a forest syde*, by the edge of a forest.
¹¹⁷ *baar*, carried.   *kene*, sharp.
¹¹⁸ 'He had a short green jacket on.'
¹¹⁹ 'A hat with black borders, on his head.'

"Sire," quod this somnour, "hayl, and wel atake!"   120
"Welcome," quod he, "and every good felawe.
Where rydestow, under this grene-wode shawe?"
Sayde this yeman, "wiltow fer to-day?"
    This somnour him answerde, and sayde, "Nay;
Here faste by", quod he, "is myn entente   125
To ryden, for to reysen up a rente
That longeth to my lordes duëtee."
    "Artow thanne a baillif?" "Ye", quod he.
He dorste nat, for verray filthe and shame,
Saye that he was a somnour, for the name.   130
    "*Depardieux!*" quod this yeman, "deere brother –
Thou art a baillif, and I am another!
I am unknowen as in this contree;
Of thyn acqueyntance I wolde praye thee,
And eke of bretherhede, if that yow leste.   135
I have gold and silver in my cheste;
If that thee happe to comen in our shyre,
Al shal be thyn, right as thou wolt desyre."
    "Grantmercy," quod this somnour, "by my feith!"
Everich in otheres hand his trouthe leith,   140
For to be sworne bretheren til they deye.
In daliance they ryden forth and playe.
    This somnour, which that was as ful of jangles
As ful of venim been thise wariangles,
And ever enquering upon every thing –   145
    "Brother," quod he, "where is now your dwelling,

120 *wel atake*, well met (lit.: 'well overtaken').
121 *good felawe*, good companion (c).
122 *rydestow*, are you riding (c).   *shawe*, wood.
123 *wiltow fer*, will you be going far . . .?
126 *reysen up a rente*, to collect a rent.
127 'Which is one of my lord's dues.'
128 *Artow* (art thou), are you.   *Ye*, yes.
129 'He dared not, because of the sheer sordidness and shamefulness [of his occupation].'
130 *for*, because of, on account of.
131 *Depardieux* (OF) By God.
133 *as in*, in.
134 *Of* (here and in l. 135), for.
135 *bretherhede*, brotherhood.   *if that yow leste*, if you were willing.
137 'If you chance to come into our part of the country.'
138 *right as thou wolt desyre*, just as you would wish.
139 *Grantmercy*, many thanks (Fr. *grand merci*).
140 'Each gives the other his hand on it (as a pledge).'
141 *for to*, to.
142 'They ride on and amuse themselves (*pleye*) with gossip (*daliance*).'
143 *jangles*, chatter.
144 'As these butcher-birds (shrikes) are full of venom' (c).
145 *enquering*, poking his nose into.

Another day if that I sholde yow seche?"
This yeman him answerde in softe speche,
   "Brother," quod he, "fer in the north contree,
Where-as, I hope, some tyme I shal thee see.   150
Er we departe, I shal thee so wel wisse,
That of myn hous ne shaltow never misse."
   "Now, brother," quod this somnour, "I yow praye,
Teche me, whyl that we ryden by the waye
(Sin that ye been a baillif as am I)   155
Som subtiltee, and tel me feithfully
In myn offyce how I may moost winne.
And spareth nat for conscience ne sinne,
But as my brother tel me, how do ye?"
   "Now, by my trouthe, brother deere," sayde he,   160
"As I shal tellen thee a feithful tale:
My wages been ful streite and ful smale;
My lord is hard to me and daungerous,
And myn offyce is ful laborous,
And therfore by extorciouns I live.   165
For soothe, I take al that men wol me yive!
Algate, by sleighte or by violence,
Fro yeer to yeer, I winne al my dispence.
I kan no bettre tellen feithfully."
   "Now, certes," quod this somnour, "so fare I!"   170
I spare nat to taken, God it woot,
But-if it be to hevy or to hoot!
What I may gete in conseil prively,

[147] 'If I were to look for you another day.'
[150] *where-as*, where.   *hope*, hope, or, possibly, expect (both meanings were current in Chaucer's time).
[151] *departe*, part company.   *wisse*, direct.
[152] 'That you'll never miss my house.'
[155] *Sin that*, since.
[156] *subtiltee*, tricks.   *feithfully*, truthfully.
[157] *offyce*, job, business.
[158] *for*, for fear of.
[159] *how do ye*, what kind of methods you use.
[160] *by my trouthe*, upon my word.
[161] 'To tell you the truth.'
[162] *ful streite*, very scanty (lit.: 'narrow, tight').
[163] *daungerous*, grudging, hard to please (c).
[164] *laborous*, hard, troublesome.
[166] *For soothe*, indeed.   *wol*, are willing to.
[167] *Algate*, anyway.   *sleighte*, trickery.
[168] *I winne al my dispence*, I earn all my living.
[170] *fare*, proceed.
[171] *God it woot*, God knows.
[172] *But-if it be*, unless it is.   *to hoot*, too hot (to hold).
[173] *in conseil prively*, secretly, on the quiet.

No maner conscience of that have I.
Nere myn extorcioun I mighte nat liven –   175
Ne of swiche japes wol I nat be shriven.
Stomak ne conscience ne knowe I noon –
I shrewe thise shrifte-fadres everichoon!
Wel be we met, by God and by Seint Jame!
But, leeve brother, tel me thanne thy name",   180
Quod this somnour. In this mene whyle
This yeman gan a litel for to smyle.
    "Brother," quod he, "woltow that I thee telle?
I am a feend – my dwelling is in helle.
And here I ryde aboute my purchasing,   185
To wite where men wol yive me anything.
My purchas is th'effect of al my rente.
Looke how thou rydest for the same entente,
To winne good – thou rekkest never how.
Right so fare I, for ryde wolde I now   190
Unto the worldes ende for a preye."
    "A!" quod this somnour, "*benedicite*! what say ye?
I wende ye were a yeman trewely;
Ye han a mannes shap as wel as I!
Han ye a figure thanne determinat   195
In helle, there ye been in your estat?"
    "Nay, certeinly," quod he, "there have we noon.
But whan us lyketh, we kan take us oon,
Or elles make yow seme we been shape

174 'I've no kind of scruples about that.'
175 *Nere*, if it weren't for.
176 'And I don't want to be absolved of such tricks.'
177 'Pity and remorse aren't my concern.'
178 'Damn all these father-confessors, say I.'
179 *Jame*, James.
181 A 'headless' line; the stress falls on the first syllable of the line rather than the second.   *In this mene whyle*, meanwhile.
182 *gan a litel for to smyle*, began to smile a little.
183 *woltow that I thee telle*, do you want me to tell you.
185 *purchasing*, picking up what I can.
186 *To wite where*, to see whether.
187 'What I can pick up by the way is the substance of my whole income' (compare l. 109, and the *GP*, A 256).
188 *entente*, purpose.
189 'To get what you can, you don't care how.'
190 *for ryde wolde I now*, for I would ride now, at once.
192 *benedicite* (Lat.), (God) bless (me), pronounced here: 'bén'dic'te').
193 'I thought you were really a yeoman.'
195 'Do you have a definite shape then.'
196 'In hell, where you are at home [in your natural habitat.]'
198 'But when it pleases us, we can take one for ourselves.'
199 'Or else make it seem to you that we are shaped.'

Somtyme lyk a man, or lyk an ape;   200
Or lyk an angel kan I ryde or go.
It is no wonder thing though it be so;
A lousy jogelour kan deceyve thee,
And, pardee, yet kan I moore craft than he."
    "Why," quod this somnour, "ryde ye thanne or goon   205
In sondry shap, and nat alway in oon?"
    "For we", quod he, "wol us swich formes make
As moost able is our preyes for to take."
    "What maketh yow to han al this labour?"
    "Ful many a cause, leeve sire somnóur –"   210
Sayde this feend, "but alle thing hath tyme.
The day is short, and it is passed pryme –
And yet ne wan I nothing in this day.
I wol entende to winning, if I may,
And nat entende our wittes to declare.   215
For, brother myn, thy wit is al to bare
To understonde, although I tolde hem thee.
But, for thou axest why labouren we –
For somtyme we been Goddes instruments,
And meenes to doon his comandements,   220
Whan that him list, upon his creatures,
In dývers art and in dyvérse figures.
Withouten him we han no might, certayn,

201 *go* (here and in l. 205), go on foot, walk.
202 *no wonder thing*, nothing surprising.
203 *jogelour*, magician, conjurer (c).
204 *kan I moore craft*, I know more tricks.
206 *In sondry shap*, in different shapes.
207 *For*, because.
208 'As are most convenient for catching our prey.'
209 *to han al this labour*, to take all this trouble.
210 *somnour* is here stressed on the second syllable (c).
211 *alle thing hath tyme*, all in good time.
212 *it is passed pryme*, it's past nine o'clock (a.m.). 'Prime' was the time appointed by the Church for the first part of the daily service (at 6 a.m. or sunrise). Here the word is applied to the period between 6 a.m. and the next 'canonical hour' (9 a.m.).
213 *ne wan I nothing*, I've earned nothing (the double negative is common in Chaucer – see also ll. 355 and 357).
214 *entende to*, pay attention to, concentrate upon.
215 'And not try to explain (the workings of) our minds.'
216 *thy wit is al to bare, your* intelligence is much too meagre.
217 *although I tolde hem thee*, even if I told you about them (i.e. about the 'causes' referred to in l. 210).
218 *for thou axest*, since you ask.
219 *For*, (this is) because.
220 *meenes to doon*, the means for doing.
221 *Whan that him list*, when it pleases him.
222 'In various ways and in various shapes.'
223 *certayn*, certainly.

If that him list to stonden ther-agayn.
And somtyme at our prayere han we leve   225
Oonly the body and nat the soule greve –
Witnesse on Job, whom that we diden wo.
And somtyme han we might of bothe two –
This is to sayn, of soule and body eke.
And somtyme be we suffred for to seeke   230
Upon a man, and doon his soule unreste,
And nat his body – and al is for the beste.
Whan he withstondeth our temptacioun
It is a cause of his salvacioun,
Al-be-it that it was nat our entente   235
He sholde be sauf, but that we wolde him hente.
And somtyme be we servant unto man –
As to the erchebisshop Seint Dunstan,
And to the Apostles servant eke was I.”
    “Yet tel me”, quod the somnour, “feithfully –   240
Make ye yow newe bodies thus alway
Of elements?” The feend answerde, “Nay;
Somtyme we feyne, and somtyme we aryse
With deede bodies in ful sondry wyse,
And speke as renably and faire and wel   245
As to the Phitonissa dide Samuel
(And yet wol som men saye it was nat he –
I do no fors of your divinitee).
But oo thing warne I thee – I wol nat jape –
Thou wolt algates wite how we been shape.   250

224 *to stonden ther-agayn*, to oppose this (i.e. any plan or activity of ours).
225-7 'And sometimes at our request we have permission
        To harm only the body and not the soul –
        Take, for example, Job, whom we tormented' (see the Book of Job).
228 *might of*, power over.
230-1 *for to seeke/Upon*, to trouble, molest.
231 *doon his soule unreste*, cause trouble in his soul.
233 *temptacioun*, testing.
235 *Al-be-it that*, although.
236 'That he should be saved, but rather that we should catch him.'
239 *servant eke was I*, I was also servant (C).
241 'Do you always make yourselves new bodies like this?'
242 *Of elements*, out of the (four) elements (i.e. earth, water, fire and air).
243-4 'Sometimes we make likenesses, and sometimes we rise up [as zombies]
        With dead bodies in many different ways.'
245 *renably*, eloquently, readily ('re[aso]nably').
246 'As Samuel did to the Pythoness' (i.e. the Witch of Endor (C)).
248 'I set no store by your [humans'] theology.'
249 *oo thing warne I thee*, I'll tell you one thing.   *jape*, joke.
250 'You will in any case come to know what our shape is like.' Or the line could
read – with altered punctuation: '(Since you want nevertheless to know what our
shape is like).'

Thou shalt herafterward, my brother deere,
Come there thee nedeth nat of me to lere;
For thou shalt, by thyn owene experience,
Konne in a chayer rede of this sentence
Bet than Virgýle, whyl he was on lyve,   255
Or Dant also. Now lat us ryde blyve –
For I wol holde compaignye with thee,
Til it be so that thou forsake me."
    "Nay," quod this somnour, "that shal nat bityde!
I am a yeman, knowen is ful wyde –   260
My trouthe wol I holde as in this cas.
For, though thou were the devel Sathanas,
My trouthe wol I holde to my brother,
As I am sworn, and ech of us til other,
For to be trewe brother in this cas;   265
And bothe we goon abouten our purchas.
Take thou thy part, what that men wol thee yive,
And I shal myn – thus may we bothe live.
And if that any of us have moore than other,
Lat him be trewe, and parte it with his brother."   270
    "I graunte," quod the devel, "by my fay."
And with that word they ryden forth hire way.
And right at the entring of the townes ende,
To which this somnour shoop him for to wende,
They saugh a cart that charged was with hay,   275
Which that a carter droof forth in his way.

---

251 *herafterward*, after this.
252 'Come (to a place) where there won't be any need for you to learn from *me*.'
254 'Be able to lecture authoritatively on this point of doctrine' (c).
255 *Virgýle*, Vergil (c).   *on lyve*, alive.
256 *Dant*, Dante (c).   *blyve*, quickly.
257 *holde*, keep.
258 *Til it be so that*, until such time as.
259 *bityde*, happen.
260 *knowen is ful wyde*, as is very widely known.
261 *as in this cas*, as far as this matter is concerned.
262 *Sathanas*, Satan.
263 *wol I*, I mean to (as in l. 261).
264 *ech of us til other*, either of us towards the other ('any' in l. 269 also means 'either').
265 *For to be*, to be a.
266 'And we are both going about on the make.'
267 *what that*, whatever.
270 *trewe*, faithful (to his word).   *parte*, share (verb).
271 *I graunte*, I agree.   *by my fay*, upon my word (cf. French: *foi*).
272 *forth hire way*, on their way.
273 'And just at the beginning of the outskirts of the town.'
274 *shoop him for to wende*, was aiming to go.
275 *charged*, loaded.
276 *droof forth in his way*, was driving along.

Deep was the way, for which the carte stood.
The carter smoot and cryde as he were wood:
"Heyt, Brok! heyt, Scot! – what spare ye for the stones?
The feend", quod he, "yow fecche, body and bones,   280
As ferforthly as ever were ye foled –
So muche wo as I have with yow tholed!
The devel have al – bothe hors and cart and hay!"
    This somnour sayde, "Here shal we have a play!"
And neer the feend he drough, as nought ne were,   285
Ful prively, and rowned in his ere:
"Herkne, my brother, herkne by thy feith!
Heerestow nat how that the carter saith?
Hent it anon, for he hath yive it thee –
Bothe hay and cart, and eke his caples three!"   290
    "Nay," quod the devel, "God woot, never a del!
It is nat his entente, trust me wel.
Axe him thyself, if thou nat trowest me –
Or elles stint a whyle, and thou shalt see."
    This carter thakketh his hors upon the croupe,   295
And they bigonne to drawen and to stoupe.
"Heyt, now!" quod he, "there Jesu Cryste yow blesse,
And al his handwerk, bothe moore and lesse!
That was wel twight, myn owene lyard boy!
I pray God save thee, and Sëint Loy!   300
Now is my cart out of the slow, pardee!"
    "Lo, brother!" quod the feend, "what tolde I thee?
Here may ye see, myn owene deere brother,

[277] 'The road was deep [with stones and mud], and so the cart got stuck.'
[278] *smoot and cryde as he were wood*, whipped and shouted as if he were mad.
[279] 'Hey, Brock! Hey, Scot! [names of horses] what are you letting the stones stop you for?' ('*Brock*' ('badger') is a name for a grey horse.)
[280] *The feend yow fecche*, devil take you.
[281-2] 'As surely as ever you were foaled –
    For all the trouble I've stood from you.'
[284] *have a play*, have fun.
[285] 'And he came up to the devil as if nothing were happening.'
[286] *rowned*, whispered.
[287] *herkne*, listen ('hearken').
[288] *Heerestow nat how that*, Don't you hear what . . .?
[289] *hent it anon*, take it at once.
[290] *caples*, horses.
[291] *God woot, never a del*, not a bit of it, God knows.
[293] *if thou nat trowest me*, if you don't believe *me*.
[294] *stint a whyle*, wait a bit.
[295] *thakketh*, smacks.   *hors*, horses.   *croupe*, rump (croup).
[296] 'And they begin to buckle to (*stoupe*) and pull.'
[298] *moore*, greater.
[299] 'That was well heaved, my old grey rascal.'
[300] *Sëint Loy* ('Sëint' pronounced as 2 syllables), St Eligius (c).
[301] *slow*, slough, mud.

The carl spak oo thing, but he thoghte another.
Lat us go forth abouten our viage –   305
Here winne I nothing upon cariage."
    Whan that they comen somwhat out of towne,
This somnour to his brother gan to rowne:
"Brother," quod he, "here woneth an old rebekke,
That hadde almoost as leef to lese hir nekke   310
As for to yive a peny of hir good.
I wol han twelf pens, though that she be wood,
Or I wol somne hir unto our offyce.
And yet, God woot, of hir knowe I no vyce.
But, for thou kanst nat, as in this contree,   315
Winne thy cost, take here ensample of me!"
    This somnour clappeth at the widwes gate.
"Com out," quod he, "thou olde viritrate!
I trowe thou hast som frere or preest with thee!"
    "Who clappeth?" sayde this wyf, "*benedicite*!   320
God save yow, sire, what is your sweete wille?"
    "I have", quod he, "of somonce a bille.
Up peyne of cursing, looke that thou bes
To-morn bifore the erchedeknes knee,
T'answere to the court of certayn thinge!"   325
    "Now, Lord," quod she "Cryst Jesu, king of kinges,
So wisly helpe me, as I ne may!
I have been sik, and that ful many a day.
I may nat go so fer," quod she, "ne ryde,
But I be deed – so priketh it in my syde!   330

---

[304] *carl*, fellow.
[305] *viage*, journey.
[306] 'I'll get nothing here by claiming on the tenant's horse and cart' (c).
[307] *comen somwhat*, had come a little distance.
[309] *woneth*, lives.   *rebekke*, old stick ((c) on l. 113).
[310] 'Who would almost prefer to lose her neck' (*leef* = 'preferable').
[311] *As for*, rather than.   *hir good*, her money.
[312] *wol*, mean to.   *wood*, furious.
[313] *offyce*, court (c).
[314] *of hir knowe I no vyce*, I don't know anything bad about her.
[315-6] 'But since, as far as this area is concerned, you aren't able to cover your expenses – look, take your example from me.'
[317] *clappeth*, knocks.
[318] *viritrate*, dodderer.
[319] *I trowe*, I think, reckon.
[320] *benedicite*, see l. 192 (pronounced here: 'ben'dícite').
[322] *of somonce a bille*, a writ of summons.
[323-4] 'On pain of excommunication, see that you are
    in the archdeacon's presence tomorrow.'
[325] *T'answere* = to answere.   *of*, about.
[327] 'I can't, so help me (Jesus Christ, king of kings – l. 326).'
[330] 'Without it killing me – such a pain I've got in my side.'

May I nat axe a lybel, sire somnour,
And answere there by my procuratour
To swich thing as men wol opposen me?"
   "Yis", quod this somnour. "Pay anon – lat see –
Twelf pens to me, and I wol thee acquyte.   335
I shal no profit han therby but lyte.
My maister hath the profit, and nat I.
Com of, and lat me ryden hastily.
Yif me twelf pens – I may no lenger tarie."
   "Twelf pens!" quod she. "Now, lady Seinte Marie   340
So wisly help me out of care and sinne –
This wyde world though that I sholde winne,
Ne have I nat twelf pens withinne myn hold!
Ye knowen wel that I am povre and old;
Kythe your almesse on me povre wrecche!"   345
   "Nay thanne," quod he, "the foule feend me fecche
If I th'excuse, though thou shul be spilt!"
   "Allas!" quod she, "God woot, I have no gilt!"
   "Pay me," quod he, "or, by the sweete Seinte Anne,
As I wol bere away thy newe panne   350
For dette, which thou owest me of old,
Whan that thou madest thyn housbond cokewold!
I payde at hoom for thy correccioun."
   "Thou lixt!" quod she, "by my salvacioun!
Ne was I never er now, widwe ne wyf,   355
Somoned unto your court in al my lyf –

[331] *axe a lybel*, ask for a copy of the charge.
[332] *by my procuratour*, through my lawyer.
[333] *as men wol opposen me*, as they want to charge me with.
[334] *Yis*, yes (emphatic).   *lat see*, let me see.
[335] *I wol thee acquyte*, I'm prepared to let you off.
[336] '*I* shall get very little profit out of it.'
[338] 'Get on with it, and let me ride off quickly.'
[339] *I may no lenger tarie*, I can't wait any longer.
[341] 'As surely as may [the Virgin Mary] preserve me from harm and sin.'
[342] 'Even if I were to win this whole wide world [by it].'
[343] *ne have I not*, I simply don't have (emphatic negative).   *withinne myn hold*, in my possession.
[345] 'Show some charity to a poor wretch like me' (*almesse* = (lit.) 'alms').
[347] 'If I let you off ("*th'excuse*" = "*thee excuse*"), even though it breaks you' (*spilt* = (lit.) 'destroyed').
[348] *I have no gilt*, I'm not guilty.
[350] *As I wol bere away*, I mean to carry off (*as* is redundant here, as in l. 161).
[351] *For dette*, on account of a debt.
[352] *madest thyn housbond cokewold*, cuckolded your husband (c).
[353] 'I paid in full for [getting you off] your punishment.'
[354] *Thou lixt*, you're lying. (As the old woman gets angry she addresses the summoner contemptuously in the 2nd person singular, the form *he* has used to her all along. She, however, has till now been addressing *him* in the polite (*plural*) form.)

Ne never I nas but of my body trewe!
Unto the Devel blak and rough of hewe
Yive I thy body and my panne also!"
   And whan the devel herde hir cursen so   360
Upon hir knees, he sayde in this manere,
"Now, Mabely, myn owene moder deere,
Is this your wil in ernest that ye saye?"
   "The Devel", quod she, "so fecche him er he deye,
And panne and al, but he wol him repente!"   365
   "Nay, olde stot, that is nat myn entente,"
Quod this somnour, "for to repente me
For any thing that I have had of thee! –
I wolde I hadde thy smok and every clooth!'
   "Now, brother," quod the devel, "be noght wrooth;   370
Thy body and this panne been myne by right.
Thou shalt with me to helle yet to-night,
Where thou shalt knowen of our privitee
Moore than a maister of divinitee."
   And with that word this foule feend him hente –   375
Body and soule he with the devel wente
Where-as that somnours han hire heritage.
And God, that made after his image
Mankinde, save and gyde us, alle and some,
And leve thise somnours goode men bicome!   380
     Lordinges, I koude han told yow,' quod this Frere –
'Hadde I had leyser for this Somnour here –
After the text of Cryst, Poul and John,
And of our othere doctours many oon,

[357] 'Nor was I ever anything but faithful' (lit.: 'true in body').
[358] *of hewe*, in looks.
[361] *in this manere*, thus.
[362] *Mabely*, Mabel.
[363] 'Do you seriously mean what you say?'
[365] *but he wol him repente*, unless he will repent.
[366] *olde stot*, you old cow.
[367] *for to*, to (*for* is redundant here, as in l. 265).
[369] 'I wish I had your smock and all your clothes.'
[370] *be noght wrooth*, don't be annoyed.
[372] *Thou shalt with me*, you shall come with me.   *yet to-night*, this very night.
[373] *of our privitee*, about our secrets.
[374] *a maister of divinitee*, a Doctor of Divinity (c).
[375] *him hente*, grabbed him.
[377] *Where-as that*, to the place where.
[378] *after his image*, in his image, likeness.
[379] *gyde us, alle and some*, guide us one and all.
[380] 'And grant that these summoners may become good men.'
[381] *Lordinges*, ladies and gentlemen.
[382] 'If this Summoner here had given me the chance.'
[383] *Poul* (pronounced as 2 syllables), St Paul (c).
[384] 'And many a one of our other great teachers.'

Swiche peynes that your hertes mighte agryse;   385
Al-be-it so no tonge may devyse –
Though that I mighte a thousand winter telle –
The peynes of thilke cursed hous of helle.
But, for to keepe us fro that cursed place,
Waketh, and prayeth Jesu for his grace   390
So keepe us fro the temptour Sathanas.
Herketh this word (beth war as in this cas):
"The leoun sit in his await alway
To slee the innocent, if that he may."
Disposeth ay your hertes to withstonde   395
The feend, that yow wolde make thral and bonde.
He may nat tempte yow over your might,
For Cryst wol be your champion and knight –
And prayeth that this Somnour him repente
Of his misdedes, er that the Feend him hente!'   400

Here endeth the Freres Tale

385 *peynes*, torments.   *agryse*, shudder.
386 *Al-be-it so*, although.   *devyse*, describe.
388 *thilke*, that.
389 *for to*, in order to.
390 *Waketh, and prayeth*, keep watch and pray.
391 *So keepe us*, that he may protect us.
392-3 'Give heed to this text (be on your guard in this matter): The lion
ceaselessly lies in wait' (c) (*sit* = *sitteth* (3rd person).
394 *slee*, slay.   *if that*, if.
395-6 'Prepare yourselves always to withstand the Devil, who wants to make you
his slave and bondman.'
397 *over your might*, beyond your strength (1 Corinthians, x, 13).
399 *him repente*, may repent.
400 *er that*, before.

The Prologue to the Summoner's Tale

This Somnour in his stiropes hye stood;
Upon this Frere his herte was so wood
That lyk an aspen leef he quook for yre.
    'Lordinges!' quod he, 'but oo thing I desyre –
I yow biseke that of your curteisye,   5
Sin ye han herd this false Frere lye,
As suffereth me I may *my* tale telle!
This Frere bosteth that he knoweth helle,
And God it woot that it is litel wonder –
Freres and feendes been but lyte asonder!   10
    For, pardee, ye han ofte-tyme herd telle
How that a frere ravisshed was to helle
In spirit ones by a visioun.
And as an angel ladde him up and doun,
To shewen him the peynes that there were,   15
In al the place saugh he nat a frere.
Of other folk he saugh ynough in wo.
Unto this angel spak the frere tho:
    "Now, sire," quod he, "han freres swich a grace
That noon of hem shal come to this place?"   20
    "Yis," quod this angel, "many a millioun!"
And unto Sathanas he ladde him doun.
"And now hath Sathanas", seith he, "a tayl
Brodder than of a carrik is the sayl.
Hold up thy tayl, thou Sathanas!" quod he,   25
"Shewe forth thyn ers, and lat the frere see
Where is the nest of freres in this place!"
And, er that half a furlong way of space,
Right so as bees out swarmen of an hyve,

---

[1] *hye stood*, stood high up.
[2] *Upon*, against.   *wood*, furious.
[3] *quook for yre*, shook with anger.
[4] *Lordinges*, ladies and gentlemen.   *but oo thing*, just one thing.
[5] *biseke*, beg.   *of*, through.
[6] *Sin*, since.   *han*, have.
[7] 'Allow me to tell *my* tale.'
[9] *God it woot*, God knows.
[10] 'There's little difference between friars and devils.'
[11] *pardee*, by God.   *ofte-tyme*, often.
[12] *ravisshed was*, was transported (c).
[13] *ones*, once.
[14] *ladde*, led.
[16] *saugh he nat*, he didn't see.
[18] *tho*, then.
[19] *swich a grace*, such mercy.
[20] *noon of hem*, none of them.
[21] *Yis*, yes indeed.
[24] '[Which is] broader than the sail of a galleon.'
[26] *ers*, arse.
[28] 'And within a short space of time' (c).

Out of the develes ers there gonne dryve   30
Twenty thousand freres on a route,
And thurghout helle swarmeden al aboute –
And comen agayn as faste as they may goon,
And in his ers they crepten everichoon.
He clapte his tayl agayn, and lay ful stille.   35
This frere, whan he looked hadde his fille
Upon the torments of this sory place,
His spirit God restored of his grace
Unto his body agayn, and he awook.
But nathelees for feere yet he quook,   40
So was the develes ers ay in his mynde,
That is his heritage of verray kynde.
God save yow alle – save this cursed Frere!
My prologe wol I ende in this manere.'

The Tale

HERE BIGINNETH THE SOMNOURS TALE

'Lordinges, there is in Yorkshyre, as I gesse,   45
A mersshy contree called Holdernesse,
In which there went a limitour aboute,
To preche, and eke to begge, it is no doute.
And so bifel that on a day this frere
Hadde preched at a chirche in his manere,   50
And specially, aboven every thing,
Excyted he the peple in his preching

30 *gonne dryve*, began to shoot (out).
31 *on a route*, in a rush.
33 *agayn*, back again.   *may goon*, could go.
34 *everichoon*, each one (of them).
35 'He clapped his tail back [into position], and lay very quietly.'
37 *sory*, wretched (C).
38 *of*, through.
40 'But nonetheless he still shook with fear.'
41 'The Devil's arse was still so much in his mind.'
42 *of verray kynde*, because of (his) very nature (C).
43 *save*, except.
44 *wol I*, I will.
45 *as I gesse*, I think.
46 *contree*, region (C).
47 *limitour*, begging friar ((C) on l. 1 of *FT*).
48 *eke*, also.   *it is no doute*, there is no doubt, you can be sure.
49 *so bifel*, it so happened.
50 *in his manere*, after his fashion.
52 *Excyted*, urged.

To trentals, and to yive, for Goddes sake,
Wherwith men mighten hooly houses make,
There as divyne service is honoured –   55
Nat there as it is wasted and devoured,
Ne there it nedeth nat for to be yive,
As to possessioners that mowen live
(Thanked be God) in wele and habundaunce.
"Trentals", sayde he, "deliveren fro penaunce   60
Hire freendes soules, as wel olde as yonge,
Ye, whan that they been hastily y-songe,
Nat for to holde a preest joly and gay –
He singeth nat but oo masse in a day!
Delivereth out", quod he "anon the soules!   65
Ful hard it is with flessh-hook or with oules
To been y-clawed, or to brenne or bake!
Now speede yow hastily, for Crystes sake!"
And whan this frere hadde sayd al his entente,
With "*Qui cum patre* . . ." forth his way he wente.   70
    Whan folk in chirche hadde yive him what hem leste,
He wente his way – no lenger wolde he reste.
With scrippe and tipped staf, y-tukked hye,
In every hous he gan to poure and prye,
And beggeth mele and chese, or elles corn.   75
His felawe hadde a staf tipped with horn,

---

53 *trentals* ((c) on ll. 60–7).
54 'The wherewithal for building "holy houses" (i.e. friars' convents)' (c).
55 *honoured*, conducted.
56 'Not where it [the money given] is wasted and squandered.'
57 *for to be yive*, to be given.
58 *possessioners*, monks (c).   *mowen*, can.
59 *wele and habundaunce*, wealth and prosperity.
60 *penaunce*, penance in Purgatory (c).
61 'Their friends' souls (i.e. the souls of the friends of those who buy trentals) both the old ones and the young.'
62 'Yes, when they are sung quickly.'
63 'Not in order to keep a priest merry and gay (i.e. prosperous).'
64 *nat but oo*, only one.
65 *Delivereth out*, set free (plural imperative).   *anon*, at once.
66 *Ful hard*, very painful.   *oules*, awls, spikes.
67 *to been y-clawed*, to be scratched.   *brenne*, burn (c).
68 *speede yow hastily*, hurry up.
69 *al his entente*, everything he had to say.
70 'He went on his way with, "Who with the Father . . ." ' (part of the Latin formula used for ending sermons).
71 *What hem leste*, what they pleased.
72 *lenger*, longer.
73 *y-tukked hye*, with his habit tucked up high (so as to walk more easily).
74 *gan to poure*, proceeded to peer.
75 *mele*, meal, flour.
76 *felawe*, colleague.

A paire of tables al of yvory,
And a poyntel polisshed fetisly,
And wroot the names alway, as he stood,
Of alle folk that yaf hem any good,   80
Ascaunces that he wolde for hem praye.
    "Yif us a busshel whete, malt or reye,
A Goddes kechil or a trip of chese,
Or elles what yow list – we may nat chese;
A Goddes halfpenny or a masse-peny,   85
Or yif us of your brawn, if ye have any;
A dagoun of your blanket, leeve dame,
Our suster deere – lo! here I wryte your name –
Bacoun or beef, or swich thing as ye fynde!"
    A sturdy harlot went hem ay bihynde,   90
That was hir hostes man, and baar a sak,
And what men yaf hem layde it on his bak.
And, whan that he was out atte dore, anon
He planed away the names everichoon,
That he biforn hadde writen in his tables.   95
He served hem with nifles and with fables! – '
    'Nay, there thou lixt, thou Somnour!' quod the Frere.
    'Pees!' quod our Hoost, 'for Crystes moder deere!
Tel forth thy tale, and spare it nat at al.'
    'So thryve I,' quod this Somnour, 'so I shal!   100
    So longe he wente, hous by hous, til he
Cam til an hous there he was wont to be
Refresshed moore than in an hundred placis.
Sik lay the goode-man whos that the place is;

---

77 *tables*, tablets of wax in ivory frames, used as notebooks.
78 'And a finely polished stylus' (for writing on wax).
80 *good*, goods.
81 *Ascaunces that*, pretending that.
82 *reye*, rye.
83 'A little cake for God's sake, or a small piece of cheese.'
84 *what yow list*, what you please.   *chese*, choose.
85 'A halfpenny for God's sake, or a penny for saying Mass.'
87 'A scrap of your woollen cloth, dear lady.'
89 *swich*, such.
90 *harlot*, ruffian (c).   *hem ay bihynde*, always behind them.
91 *hostes man*, servant to the guests (at the friars' covent).
92 *men*, people.
93 *he* – i.e. one of the friars (see ll. 76–81).   *out atte dore*, out of doors.
94 *everichoon*, every one (of the names).
96 *nifles*, fibs.
97 *thou lixt*, you're lying.
99 'Go on with your tale and don't pull any punches.'
100 *So thryve I*, So help me (lit.: 'so may I thrive').
102 *til*, to.   *there*, where.
104 'The householder whose home it was lay ill.'

Bedred upon a couche lowe he lay.   105
   "*Deus hic!*" quod he, "O Thomas, freend, good day!"
Sayde this frere curteisly and softe.
"Thomas," quod he, "God yelde yow ful ofte!
Have I upon this bench faren ful wel;
Here have I eten many a mery meel!"   110
And fro the bench he droof away the cat,
And leyde adoun his potente and his hat,
And eke his scrippe, and sette him softe adoun.
His felawe was go walked into town
Forth with his knave, into that hostelrye   115
Where-as he shoop him thilke night to lye.
   "O deere maister," quod this syke man,
"How han ye fare sith that March bigan?
I saugh yow noght this fourtenight or moore."
   "God woot," quod he, "laboured have I ful soore! 120
And specially, for thy salvacioun,
Have I sayd many a precious orisoun,
And for our othere freendes, God hem blesse!
I have to-day been at your chirche at messe,
And sayd a sermon after my simple wit –   125
Nat al after the text of hooly writ,
For it is hard to yow, as I suppose,
And therfore wol I tel yow al the glose.
Glosing is a glorious thing, certayn,
For lettre sleeth, so as we clerkes sayn.   130
There have I taught hem to be charitable,

105 *Bedred*, bedridden.
106 *Deus hic*, God be here (c).
108 *God yelde yow ful ofte*, may God reward you very often.
109 'I have fared very well upon this bench.'
111 *fro*, from.   *droof*, drove.
112 *leyde adoun his potente*, laid down his staff.
113 *sette him*, sat himself.
114 *was go walked*, had gone on foot (c).
115 *Forth with his knave*, along with his servant (c).
116 'Where he proposed to sleep that night.'
118 'How have you been since March began?' (c)
119 *I saugh yow noght*, I haven't seen you.
120 ' "God knows," said he, "I've been working very hard!" '
122 *precious orisoun*, valuable (i.e. effective) prayer.
124 *messe*, Mass.
125 *after my simple wit*, according to my humble capacity (c).
126 'Not completely following the text of the Holy Scriptures.'
127 *to*, for.
128 *glose*, commentary, interpretation (c).
129 *certayn*, certainly.
130 'For the letter (i.e. the literal interpretation) kills [the meaning], as we learned men say' (c).
131 *hem*, them (the congregation).

And spende hire good there it is resonable;
And there I saugh our dame – a! where is she?"
   "Yond in the yerd I trowe that she be,"
Sayde this man, "and she wol come anon."   135
   "Ey, maister, welcome be ye, by Seint John!"
Sayde this wyf, "how fare ye hertely?"
   The frere aryseth up ful curteisly,
And hir embraceth in his armes narwe,
And kiste hir swete, and chirketh as a sparwe   140
With his lippes: "Dame," quod he, "right wel,
As he that is your servant every deel.
Thanked be God that yow yaf soule and lyf –
Yet saugh I nat this day so fair a wyf
In al the chirche, God so save me!"   145
   "Ye, God amend defautes, sire!" quod she,
"Algates, welcome be ye, by my fay."
   "Graunt mercy, dame, this have I founde alway.
But of your grete goodnesse, by your leve –
I wolde pray yow that ye nat yow greve –   150
I wol with Thomas speke a litel throwe.
Thise curats been ful necligent and slowe
To grope tendrely a conscience
In shrift. In preching is my diligence,
And studie in Petres wordes and in Poules.   155
I walke, and fisshe Cristen mennes soules,
To yelden Jesu Cryst his propre rente;
To sprede his word is set al myn entente."
   "Now, by your leve, O deere sire," quod she,
"Chydeth him wel, for seinte Trinitee!   160

[132] *good*, wealth.   *there*, where.
[133] *our dame* – i.e. Thomas's wife.
[134] *trowe*, believe.
[137] *how fare ye hertely?* How are you indeed?
[139] *narwe*, tightly.
[140] *sweete*, sweetly.   *chirketh as a sparwe*, chirps like a sparrow (c).
[142] 'As one who is your servant in every way.'
[146] *God amend defautes*, may God mend (my) blemishes.
[147] *algates*, anyway.
[148] *Graunt mercy*, thank you (formal – see *FT*, l. 139).
[150] *that ye nat yow greve*, that you don't take it amiss.
[151] *throwe*, space of time.
[152] *curats*, parish-priests (*not* curates).
[153] *grope tendrely*, probe delicately into (c).
[154] 'When hearing confession. *My* efforts are concentrated on preaching.'
[155] *studie in*, the study of.
[156] Compare Matthew, iv, 19.
[157] 'In order to give Jesus Christ his true returns' (c).
[158] 'My mind is completely set on spreading his word.'
[160] *Chydeth*, chide, rebuke (plural imperative – the polite form).   *for seinte Trinitee*, for (the sake of) the holy Trinity.

He is as angry as a pissemyre,
Though that he have al that he kan desyre –
Though I him wrye a-night, and make him warm,
And on him leye my leg other myn arm,
He groneth lyk our boor, lyth in our sty!   165
Other disport right noon of him have I;
I may nat plese him in no maner cas."
    "O Thomas, *Je vous dy*, Thomas, Thomas!
This maketh the feend – this moste been amended!
Yre is a thing that hye God defended –   170
And therof wol I speke a word or two."
    "Now, maister," quod the wyf, "er that I go,
What wol ye dyne? I wol go theraboute."
    "Now, dame," quod he, "now *Je vous dy sanz doute*,
Have I nat of a capon but the livere,   175
And of your softe breed nat but a shivere,
And after that a rosted pigges heed
(But that I nolde no beest for me were deed) –
Thanne hadde I with yow hoomly suffisaunce.
I am a man of litel sustenaunce;   180
My spirit hath his fostring in the Byble;
The body is ay so redy and penyble
To wake, that my stomak is destroyed.
I pray yow, dame, ye be nat anoyed,
Though I so freendly yow my conseil shewe;   185
By God, I wolde nat telle it but a fewe."

161 *pissemyre*, ant.
163 *wrye*, cover up.
164 *other*, or.
165 *our boor, lyth*, our boar which lies.
166 'I get no other pleasure from him at all.' (Here and elsewhere in ll. 162–7 she is hinting at the lack of sexual pleasure.)
167 'I can't please him in any way.'
168 *Je vous dy* (OF), I tell you (c).
169 'The Devil is responsible for this – it must be corrected.'
170 *Yre*, anger.   *defended*, forbade (c).
172 *er that*, before.
173 'What will you have for dinner? I'll get started on it.'
174 *Je vous dy sanz doute* (OF), I tell you plainly (c).
175 'If I have just the liver of a capon.'
176 *nat but a shivere*, just a slice.
178 'Except that I wouldn't like any animal to die on my account.
179 'Then I would have had simple sufficiency with you.'
180 *litel sustenaunce*, small appetite (lit.: 'little food').
181 *hath his fostring in*, gets its nourishment from.
182–3 *so redy and penyble/To wake*, so eager and careful to keep awake.
183 *destroyed*, disturbed.
184 *ye be nat*, not to be.   *anoyed*, offended.
185 'Although I'm telling you my secrets in such a friendly way.
186 'By God, I would tell it to only a few [persons].'

"Now, sire," quod she, "but oo word er I go:
My child is deed withinne thise wykes two,
Soone after that ye wente out of this town."
"His deeth saugh I by revelacioun",   190
Sayde this frere, "at hoom in our dortour.
I dar wel sayn that, er that half an hour
After his deeth, I saugh him born to blisse
In myn avisioun, so God me wisse!
So dide our sexteyn and our fermerer,   195
That han been trewe freres fifty yeer.
(They may now, God be thanked of his lone,
Maken hire jubilee and walke allone.)
And up I roos, and al our covent eke,
With many a teere trilling on my cheke,   200
Withouten noyse or clatering of belles;
Te deum was our song, and no-thing elles —
Save that to Cryst I sayde an orisoun,
Thanking him of his revelacioun.
For, sire and dame, trusteth me right wel,   205
Our orisouns been moore effectuel,
And moore we seen of Cristes secree thinges
Than burel folk, although they weren kinges.
We live in poverte and in abstinence,
And burel folk in richesse and dispence   210
Of mete and drinke, and in hire foul delyt.
We han this worldes lust al in despyt.
Lazar and Dyves liveden diversly,

187 *but oo*, just one.
188 'My child died within the last two weeks.'
189 *after that*, after.
190 *revelacioun*, revelation, visionary dream.
191 *dortour*, dormitory.
192 *er that*, before.
194 'In my vision — may God guide me.'
195 *sexteyn*, sexton.   *fermerer*, infirmarer, friar in charge of the infirmary.
197 *of his lone*, for his favour.
198 *Maken hire jubilee*, celebrate their jubilee (c).
199 *roos*, rose.   *covent*, convent.
200 *trilling on*, streaming down.
202 *elles*, else.
203 *Save*, except.   *orisoun*, prayer.
204 *of*, for.
205 *trusteth me right wel*, believe me truly.
206 *effectuel*, effective.
207 'And we see more of Christ's hidden matters.'
208 *burel*, lay, not clerical.
210 *dispence*, extravagance.
211 *delyt*, pleasure.
212 'We hold the pleasure of this world in absolute contempt.'
213 *diversly*, in different ways. (For the story of Dives and Lazarus see Luke, xvi, 19–31.)

And diverse guerdon hadden they therby.
Whoso wol praye, he moot faste and be clene,   215
And fatte his soule, and make his body lene.
We fare as saith th' apostle – clooth and foode
Suffysen us, though they be nat ful goode.
The clennesse and the fasting of us freres
Maketh that Christ accepteth our prayeres.   220
    Lo, Moyses fourty dayes and fourty night
Fasted, er that the hye God of might
Spak with him in the mountain of Sinay.
With empty wombe fasting many a day,
Receyved he the lawe that was writen   225
With Goddes finger. And Elye, wel ye witen,
In mount Oreb, er he hadde any speche
With hye God, that is our lyves leche –
He fasted longe, and was in contemplaunce.
    Aaron, that had the Temple in governaunce,   230
And eke the othere preestes everichoon,
Into the Temple whan they sholde goon,
To praye for the peple, and do servyse,
They nolde drinken in no maner wyse
No drinke which that mighte hem dronke make,   235
But there in abstinence praye and wake,
Lest that they deyden. Take heede what I saye:
But they be sobre that for the peple praye –
War that I saye – namoore, for it suffyseth!
    Our lord Jesu, as hooly writ devyseth,   240

214 *guerdon*, reward.
215 'Anyone who wants to pray must fast and be pure.'
216 *fatte*, fatten.
217 *We fare as saith th' apostle*, We live as the apostle (Paul) instructs (I Timothy, vi, 8).
218 *Suffysen us*, are enough for us.
220 'Makes Christ accept our prayers.'
221 *Moyses*, Moses (see Exodus, xxxiv, 28).
224 *wombe*, stomach (c).
226 *Elye*, Elijah (see I Kings, xix, 8).   *witen*, know.
228 *our lyves leche*, our spiritual physician (lit.: 'the physician for our lives').
229 *contemplaunce*, contemplation.
230 *in governaunce*, under his control.
232 'When they had to go into the temple.'
233 *do servyse*, conduct services.
234 *in no maner wyse*, in no way at all.
235 *which that*, which
236 *wake*, keep awake.
237 'For fear of death (lit.: 'in case they died'). Pay heed to what I say.'
238 'Unless those who pray for the people are sober' (c).
239 'Note what I say – no more, for this is enough (i.e. clear enough)!'
240 *as hooly writ devyseth*, as the Holy Scriptures tell.

Yaf us ensample of fasting and prayeres;
Therfore we mendinants, we sely freres,
Been wedded to poverte and continence,
To charitee, humblesse and abstinence,
To persecucioun for rightwisnesse,   245
To weping, misericorde and clennesse;
And therfore may ye see that our prayeres
(I speke of us, we mendinants, we freres)
Been to the hye God moore acceptable
Than youres, with your feestes at the table.   250
Fro Paradys first, if I shal nat lye,
Was man out chaced for his glotonye –
And chaste was man in Paradys, certayn.
    But herkne now, Thomas, what I shal sayn.
I ne have no text of it, as I suppose,   255
But I shal fynde it in a maner glose –
That specially our sweete lord Jesus
Spak this by freres, whan he sayde thus:
    'Blessed be they that povre in spirit been.'
And so forth al the gospel may ye seen,   260
Wher it be likker our professioun,
Or hirs that swimmen in possessioun.
Fy on hire pompe and on hire glotonye!
And for hire lewednesse I hem diffye!
    Me thinketh they been lyk Jovinian,   265
Fat as a whale, and walking as a swan –
Al vinolent as botel in the spence.
Hire prayere is of ful grete reverence:
Whan they for soules saye the psalm of Davit,

241 *ensample*, an example.
242 *mendinants*, mendicants, begging friars.   *sely*, blessed innocent (C).
244 *humblesse*, humility.
245 *for*, on account of.
246 *misericorde*, compassion.
251–2 'If I'm not mistaken, Man was originally driven out of Paradise on account of his gluttony' (C).
254 *herkne*, listen.   *what*, to what.
255 *as I suppose*, I believe.
256 'But I shall establish it through a kind of commentary.'
257 *specially*, especially, particularly.
258 *by*, about, concerning.
259 Matthew, v, 3.
260 *forth al*, throughout.
261 'Whether it (i.e. the teaching of the Gospels) is closer to our profession.'
262 'Or that of those who wallow in their endowments' (C).
264 'And I despise them for their ignorance' (C).
265 'It seems to me that they are like Jovinian' (C).
267 'All full of wine, like a bottle in the buttery.'
268 *of ful grete reverence*, of very great piety.
269 *for soules*, for the souls (of the dead).

Lo, 'buf!' they saye, '*cor meum eructavit!*'   270
Who folweth Crystes gospel and his foore,
But we that humble been, and chaste and poore –
Werkers of Goddes word, nat auditours?
Therfore, right as an hauk up at a sours
Up springeth into th' air – right so prayeres   275
Of charitable and chaste bisy freres
Maken hire sours to Goddes eres two.
Thomas, Thomas, so moot I ryde or go,
And by that lord that clepid is Seint Yve –
Nere thou our brother, sholdestou nat thryve!   280
In our chapitre praye we day and night
To Cryst, that he thee sende heele and might
Thy body for to weelden hastily."
    "God woot," quod he, "nothing therof feele I!
As help me Cryst, as I in fewe yeeres   285
Have spended upon diverse maner freres
Ful many a pound, yet fare I never the bet.
Certayn, my good have I almoost biset.
Farewel, my gold, for it is al ago!"
    The frere answerde, "O Thomas, dostou so?   290
What nedeth yow diverse freres seche?
What nedeth him that hath a parfit leche
To sechen other leches in the town?
Your inconstance is your confusioun.
Holde ye than me, or elles our covent,   295
To praye for yow been insufficient?

270 *cor meum eructavit*, my heart has brought forth (c).
271 *foore*, footsteps, way of life.
272 *But*, except.
273 *Werkers*, doers (c).   *auditours*, hearers (c).
274 'Therefore just as a hawk soars up on the wing.'
277 *maken hire sours*, soar up.
278 *so moot I ryde or go*, as (sure as) I may ride or walk.
279 *that clepid is Seint Yve*, who is called St Yves (c).
280 'If you weren't our brother you wouldn't prosper' ((c) on ll. 462–4).
281 *chapitre*, chapter, assembly.
282 'To Christ that he may send you health and strength.'
283 'Quickly to regain the use of your limbs (lit.: "body")' (c).
284 ' "God knows," said he, "I feel nothing [the better] for that!" '
286 *diverse maner freres*, various kinds of friars.
287 *fare I never the bet*, I get no better.
288 *good*, goods.   *biset*, spent.
289 *ago*, gone.
290 *dostou so*, is that what you do.
291 'Why do you need to look for different friars?'
292 'Why does he who has a perfect physician need. . . .?'
294 'Your inconstance is [the reason for] your trouble.'
295–6 'Do you think that I, or else our convent, aren't good enough to pray for you?'

Thomas, that jape nis nat worth a myte –
Your maladye is for we han to lyte!
'A, yif that covent half a quarter otes!'
'A, yif that covent four-and-twenty grotes!'   300
'A, yif that frere a peny and lat him go!'
Nay, nay Thomas – it may no-thing be so!
What is a ferthing worth parted in twelve?
Lo, ech thing that is oned in him selve
Is moore strong than whan it is to-scatered.   305
Thomas, of me thou shalt nat been y-flatered;
Thou woldest han our labour al for nought!
The hye God, that al this world hath wrought,
Saith that the werkman worthy is his hyre.
Thomas, noght of your tresor I desyre   310
As for myself, but that al our covent
To praye for yow is ay so diligent –
And for to builden Crystes owene chirche.
Thomas, if ye wol lernen for to wirche,
Of building up of chirches may ye fynde,   315
If it be good, in Thomas lyf of Ynde!
Ye lye here full of anger and of yre,
With which the Devel set your herte a-fyre –
And chyden here this sely innocent,
Your wyf, that is so meeke and pacient.   320
And therfore, Thomas, trowe me if thee leste –
Ne stryve nat with thy wyf as for thy beste,
And bere this word away now, by thy feith.

---

297 'Thomas, that excuse isn't worth a ha'penny.'
298 'The reason for your illness is that we get too little.'
299 *half a quarter otes*, 4 bushels of oats (a 'quarter' = about 8 bushels).
300 *grotes*, groats (coins worth fourpence).
302 *it may no-thing be so*, that won't do at all.
303 *parted in*, divided into.
304 *oned in him selve*, united, single in itself.
305 *to-scatered*, scattered around.
306 *of me*, by me.
308 *wrought*, made, created.
309 *worthy is his hyre*, deserves his wages (Luke, x, 7).
311 *but that*, but because.
312 *is ay so diligent*, is always so conscientious.
314 'Thomas, if you want to learn about doing good.'
316 *in Thomas lyf of Ynde*, in the life of St Thomas of India (c). (This is a common construction with a double genitive in Middle English and later.)
318 *a-fyre*, on fire.
319 'And scold this harmless innocent here' (c).
321 *trowe me if thee leste*, believe me if you will.
322 'Don't quarrel with your wife for your own sake.'
323 'And take this advice to heart now, by all that you hold holy.'

Touching swich thing – lo, what the wyse man saith:
  'Withinne thyn hous ne be thou no leoun;   325
To thy subgits do noon oppressioun,
Ne make thyne aqueyntaunce nat for to flee.'
And, Thomas, yet eftsoones I charge thee –
Be war from hir that in thy bosom slepeth –
War fro the serpent that so slyly crepeth   330
Under the gras, and stingeth subtilly!
Be war, my sone – and herkne paciently –
That twenty thousand men han lost hire lyves
For stryving with hir lemmans and hire wyves.
Now, sith ye han so hooly meeke a wyf,   335
What nedeth yow, Thomas, to maken stryf?
There nis y-wis no serpent so cruel,
Whan man tret on his tayl, ne half so fel,
As womman is whan she hath caught an yre;
Vengeance is thanne al that they desyre.   340
Yre is a sinne, oon of the grete of sevene,
Abhominable unto the God of hevene;
And to himself it is destruccioun.
This every lewed viker or persoun
Kan saye – how Yre engendreth homicyde.   345
Yre is in sooth executour of pryde.
I koude of Yre saye so muche sorwe,
My tale sholde laste til to-morwe;
And therfore praye I God bothe day and night,

---

[324] 'Hear what the wise man says about such matters' (Ecclesiasticus, iv, 30).
[325] *ne be thou no leoun*, do not be (like) a lion.
[326] 'Do not be harsh to your dependants.'
[327] 'And do not make your acquaintances run away.'
[328] *eftsoones*, moreover, also.   *charge*, tell, warn.
[329] *war from*, wary of, careful about.
[331] *subtilly*, treacherously.
[332-3] *Be war . . . that*, be warned that.
[335] 'Now, since you have such a holy, meek wife.'
[336] *What nedeth yow*, why do you need.
[337] *There nis y-wis*, there isn't, indeed.
[338] *tret* (contracted form of *tredeth*), treads.   *fel*, vicious.
[339] *caught an yre*, flown into a rage.
[341] *oon of the grete of sevene*, one of the greatest of the seven (c).
[342] *abhominable* – spelling reflects mistaken derivation (as if from Lat. *ab homine* (man), rather than *abominari* (from *omen*)).
[343] *to himself* – i.e. to the angry man.
[344] *lewed*, ignorant ((c) on ll. 60–7, 238–9 and 264).
[345] *engendreth*, begets, results in.
[346] 'Anger is truly the henchman of pride' (c).
[347] 'I could say so much about the trouble caused by anger.'
[349] *praye I God*, I pray to God.

An yrous man, God sende him litel might!   350
It is grete harm and certes grete pitee
To sette an yrous man in hye degree.
   Whilom there was an yrous potestat
(As saith Senec), that during his estat,
Upon a day out ryden knightes two –   355
And, as fortune wolde that it were so,
That oon of hem cam hoom, that other noght.
Anon the knight bifore the juge is broght,
That sayde thus: 'Thou hast thy felawe slayn,
For which I deeme thee to the deeth certayn.'   360
And to another knight comanded he,
'Go, lede him to the deeth, I charge thee.'
And happed, as they wente by the waye
Toward the place there he sholde deye,
The knight com which men wenden had be deed.   365
Thanne thoghten they it were the beste reed
To lede hem bothe to the juge agayn.
They sayden, 'Lord, the knight ne hath nat slayn
His felawe; here he standeth hool alyve.'
'Ye shul be deed,' quod he, 'so moot I thryve –   370
This is to sayn, bothe oon, and two, and three!'
And to the firste knight right thus spak he:
'I dampned thee – thou most algate be deed.
And thou also most nedes lese thyn heed,
For thou art cause why thy felawe deyth.'   375
And to the thridde knight right thus he seyth:
'Thou hast nat doon that I comanded thee.'
And thus he dide do sleen hem alle three.

[350] *yrous*, wrathful.
[351] *certes*, certainly.
[352] *degree*, rank, position.
[353] *Whilom*, once.   *potestat*, ruler, chief magistrate.
[354] '(As Seneca says), during whose term of office' (c).
[356] 'And, as luck would have it.'
[358] *Anon*, at once.
[359] *That*, who (i.e. the judge).
[360] *deeme*, sentence (c).
[362] *charge*, order.
[363] *happed*, it chanced.
[365] '[that] the knight who they thought was dead came back.'
[366] *reed*, plan, course of action.
[369] *hool alyve*, alive and well (c).
[370] *so moot I thryve*, so help me (lit.: 'so may I thrive').
[371] 'I mean all three of you.'
[373] 'I condemned you – you must die in any case.'
[374] *thou* – i.e. the knight thought to have been murdered (see ll. 357 and 365).
nedes lese, necessarily lose.
[377] *that*, what.
[378] *dide do sleen hem*, had them killed.

Yrous Cambyses was eke dronkelewe,
And ay delyted him to been a shrewe.   380
And so bifel, a lord of his meynee,
That lovede vertuous moralitee,
Sayde on a day bitwix hem two right thus:
'A lord is lost if he be vicious –
And dronkenesse is eke a foul record   385
Of any man, and namely in a lord.
There is ful many an eye and many an ere
Awaiting on a lord, and he noot where.
For Goddes love drink more attemprely;
Wyn maketh man to lesen wrecchedly   390
His mynde and eke his limes everichoon.'
   'The revers shaltou see', quod he, 'anon,
And preve it by thyn owene experience,
That wyn ne dooth to folk no swich offence.
There is no wyn bireveth me my might   395
Of hand ne foot, ne of myn eyen sight.'
And for despyt he drank ful muchel moore,
An hundred part, than he had doon bifore.
And right anon this yrous cursed wrecche
Leet this knightes sone bifore him fecche,   400
Comanding him he sholde bifore him stonde.
And sodeynly he took his bowe in honde,
And up the streng he pulled to his ere,
And with an arwe he slow the child right there.
'Now whether have I a siker hand or noon?'   405
Quod he, 'is al my might and mynde agoon?

379 *eke dronkelewe*, a drunkard also.
380 'And always enjoyed being vicious' (c).
381 'And it so happened that a lord of his household.'
383 *bitwix hem two*, between the two of them.
385 *a foul record*, a filthy blot on the reputation.
386 *namely*, especially, above all.
388 *Awaiting*, spying.   *noot*, does not know.
389 *attemprely*, temperately, moderately.
390 *lesen*, lose control over.
391 *mynde*, reason.   *his limes everichoon*, all his limbs.
394 'That wine does no such harm to people.'
395 *bireveth me*, deprives me of.
396 *of myne eyen sight*, of the sight of my eyes.
397 'And out of spite he drank very much more.'
398 *An hundred part*, a hundred times more.
400 'Had this knight's son brought before him.'
403 *up the streng he pulled*, he pulled back the (bow-)string.
404 *slow*, killed.
405 'Now, do I have a steady hand or not?'
406 *mynde*, concentration.   *agoon*, gone.

Hath wyn bireved me myn eyen sight?'
  What sholde I telle th' answere of the knight?
His sone was slayn, there is namoore to saye.
Beth war therfore with lordes how ye playe;   410
Singeth *Placebo* and 'I shal if I kan',
But if it be unto a povre man.
To a povre man men sholde his vyces telle,
But nat to a lord, though he sholde go to helle.
  Lo, yrous Cyrus, thilke Percien,   415
How he destroyed the river of Gysen,
For that an hors of his was dreynt therinne,
Whan that he wente Babiloyne to winne.
He made that the river was so smal,
That wommen mighte wade it over al.   420
  Lo, what sayde he that so wel teche kan?
'Ne be no felawe to an yrous man,
Ne with no wood man walke by the waye,
Lest thee repente.' I wol no ferther saye.
  Now, Thomas, leeve brother, leve thyn yre;   425
Thou shalt me fynde just as is a squyre.
Hold nat the develes knyf ay at thyn herte –
Thyn anger dooth thee al to soore smerte –
But shewe to me al thy confessioun!"
  "Nay," quod the syke man, "by Seint Simoun!   430
I have be shriven this day at my curat.
I have him told al hoolly myn estat.
Nedeth namoore to speke of it," saith he,

408 *What*, why.
410 'Be careful, therefore, how you deal with lords.'
411 *Singeth*, '*Placebo*', Sing 'I shall please' (c).
412 *But if*, unless.   *povre*, poor.
414 *he* – i.e. the lord.
415 *thilke Percien*, that Persian (c).
416 *Gysen*, Gyndes (c).
417 'Because one of his horses had been drowned in it.'
418 *Whan that*, when.
419 *made that*, succeeded in making.
420 *wade it over al*, wade through all of it.
421 *that so wel teche kan*, who can teach so well (see Proverbs, xxii, 24 and 25).
422 *felawe*, companion.
423 *wood*, mad, furious.
424 *Lest thee repente*, in case you regret it.
425 *leeve*, dear.
426 'You'll find me as just as a carpenter's square.'
427 'Don't be always pointing the Devil's knife at your heart' (c).
428 'Your anger is making you suffer much too much.'
429 'But make your full confession to me.'
431 'I have been absolved today by my parish-priest' (c).
432 *hoolly*, fully, completely.   *estat*, (spiritual) condition.
433 *Nedeth namoore*, it's no longer necessary.

"But if me list, of myn humilitee."
"Yif me thanne of thy gold to make our cloistre," 435
Quod he, "for many a muscle and many an oystre,
Whan othere men han been ful wel at eyse,
Hath been our foode, our cloistre for to reyse.
And yet, God woot, unnethe the fundement
Parfourmed is – ne of our pavement 440
Nis nat a tyle yet withinne our wones;
By God, we owen fourty pound for stones!
  Now help, Thomas, for him that harwed helle!
Or elles moste we our bookes selle;
And if yow lakke our predicacioun, 445
Thanne gooth the world al to destruccioun.
For whoso fro this world wolde us bireve,
So God me save, Thomas, by your leve,
He wolde bireve out of this world the sonne.
For who kan teche and werchen as we konne? 450
And that is nat of litel tyme," quod he,
"But sith Elye was, or Elise,
Han freres been, that fynde I of record,
In charitee, y-thanked be our Lord.
Now Thomas, help – for seinte Charitee!" 455
And doun anon he set him on his knee.
  This syke man wex wel neigh wood for yre;
He wolde that the frere hadde been a-fyre,
With his false dissimulacioun.
"Swich thing as is in my possessioun", 460
Quod he, "that may I yive and noon other.

434 'Unless I want to, out of humility.'
435 of, some of.
436 muscle, mussel (c).
437 eyse, ease.
438 our cloistre for to reyse, in order to build our convent.
439–41 'And yet, God knows, the foundation is hardly finished, nor is there yet a [single] tile on the floor within our dwelling.'
442 owen, owe.
443 for him that harwed Helle, for the sake of him (i.e. Christ) who plundered Hell (c).
445 'And if our preaching is denied you.'
447 'For whoever wanted to remove us from this world.'
450 werchen, do (good deeds).
451 of litel tyme, since a short time ago.
452 sith, since.   Elye, Elijah.   Elise, Elisha ((c) on ll. 451–4).
453 of (here), on.
455 for seinte Charitee, in the name of holy charity.
456 'And at once he threw himself down on his knees.'
457 'The sick man [Thomas] grew well nigh mad with rage.'
458 wolde, wished.
459 dissimulacioun, dissimulation, hypocrisy.

Ye say me thus, how that I am your brother?"
    "Ye, certes," quod the frere, "trusteth wel;
I took our dame our lettre with our seel."
"Now wel," quod he, "and somwhat shal I yive   465
Unto your hooly covent whyl I live –
And in thyn hand thou shalt it have anon,
On this condicioun – and other noon –
That thou departe it so, my deere brother,
That every frere have as much as other.   470
This shaltou swere on thy professioun,
Withouten fraude or cavelacioun."
    "I swere it", quod this frere, "upon my feith!"
And therwithal his hand in his he leith,
"Lo here my feith; in me shal be no lak."   475
    "Now thanne, put thyn hand doun by my bak,"
Sayde this man, "and grope wel bihynde;
Binethe my buttok there shaltou fynde
A thing that I have hid in privitee."
    "A!" thoghte this frere, "that shal go with me!"   480
And doun his hand he launcheth to the clifte,
In hope for to fynde there a yifte.
And whan this syke man felte this frere
Aboute his tuwel grope there and here,
Amidde his hand he leet the frere a fart.   485
There nis no capul, drawing in a cart,
That mighte have lete a fart of swich a soun.
    The frere up stirte as dooth a wood leoun:
"A! false cherl!" quod he, "for Goddes bones –
This hastou for despyt doon, for the nones!   490

---

462 *say*, tell.   *how that*, that.
463 *trusteth wel*, (you can) depend on it completely.
464 'I gave your good lady our letter of fraternity with our seal' (c).
465 *Now wel*, fair enough.
468 *and other noon*, and no other.
469 *departe it so*, share it out in such a way.
471 *shaltou* (= 'shalt thou'), you must.   *on*, by.
472 *cavelacioun*, cavilling, quibbling.
474 'And with that he [Friar John] lays his hand in his [Thomas's].'
475 'Look, here is my pledge; there will be no failing on my part.'
476 *doun by*, underneath.
479 *in privitee*, in secret.
481 *launcheth*, shoves.   *clifte*, cleft (between the buttocks).
482 *for to*, to.   *yifte*, gift.
484 *tuwel*, anus (lit.: 'pipe' or 'chimney').
485 'He let off a fart straight into the friar's hand.'
486 *capul*, cart-horse.
487 *swich a soun*, such a sound.
488 *up stirte*, leapt up.
490 'You've done this expressly in defiance of me.'

Thou shalt abye this fart, if that I may!"
    His meynee, which that herden this affray,
Cam leping in and chaced out the frere;
And forth he gooth with a ful angry cheere,
And fette his felawe, there-as lay his stoor.   495
He looked as it were a wilde boor;
He grinte with his teeth, so was he wrooth.
A sturdy paas doun to the Court he gooth,
Where-as there woned a man of grete honour,
To whom that he was alway confessour.   500
This worthy man was lord of that village.
This frere cam as he were in a rage,
Where-as this lord sat eting at his bord.
Unnethe mighte the frere speke a word,
Til atte laste he sayde, "God yow see!"   505
    This lord gan looke, and sayde, "*Benedicitee*!
What, frere John, what maner world is this?
I see wel that som thing there is amis;
Ye looken as the wode were ful of thevis.
Sit doun anon, and tel me what your grief is,   510
And it shal been amended, if I may."
    "I have", quod he, "had a despyt to-day –
God yelde yow – adoun in your village,
That in this world there nis so povre a page,
That he nolde have abhominacioun   515

⁴⁹¹ 'You'll pay dearly for that fart, if I have anything to do with it.'
⁴⁹² 'His [Thomas's] household servants who heard this uproar.'
⁴⁹³ *leping*, rushing.
⁴⁹⁴ 'And away he goes with a very angry expression.'
⁴⁹⁵ 'And fetched his companion from the place where his luggage was' (see ll. 114–16).
⁴⁹⁶ *as it were*, like.
⁴⁹⁷ 'He gnashed his teeth, so angry was he.'
⁴⁹⁸ *a sturdy paas*, furiously striding.   *Court*, manor-house (c).
⁴⁹⁹ *Where-as there woned*, where there lived.
⁵⁰⁰ *was alway*, had always been.
⁵⁰³ *Where-as*, to where.   *bord*, table.
⁵⁰⁴ *Unnethe*, scarcely, hardly.
⁵⁰⁵ *atte*, at the.   *God yow see*, God protect you.
⁵⁰⁶ *gan looke*, proceeded to look (up).
⁵⁰⁷ *what maner world is this*, what on earth is going on (lit.: 'what kind of world is this').
⁵⁰⁸ *amis*, wrong ('amiss').
⁵⁰⁹ 'You look as if the wood were full of thieves' (proverb, which seems to mean, 'You look as if something were badly wrong').
⁵¹⁰ *grief*, *trouble*, grievance.
⁵¹¹ *amended*, righted, remedied.   *if I may*, if I can (do anything about it).
⁵¹² *had a despyt*, received an insult.
⁵¹³ *God yelde yow*, may God reward you.
⁵¹⁴⁻¹⁵ '[Of such a kind] that there's no menial so poor who wouldn't be disgusted.'

Of that I have receyved in your town.
And yet ne greveth me nothing so soore,
As that this olde cherl with lokkes hoore
Blasphemed hath our hooly covent eke."
   "Now maister," quod this lord, "I yow biseke –"   520
"No maister, sire," quod he, "but servitour.
Though I have had in scole that honour,
God lyketh nat that Raby men us calle,
Neither in market ne in your large halle."
   "No force," quod he, "but tel me al your grief."   525
   "Sire," quod this frere, "an odious meschief
This day bitid is to myn ordre and me,
And so, *per consequens*, to ech degree
Of hooly chirche, God amende it soone!"
   "Sire," quod the lord, "ye woot what is to doone.   530
Distempre yow noght; ye be my confessour;
Ye been the salt of the erthe and the savour;
For Goddes love, your pacience ye holde.
Tel me your grief", and he anon him tolde,
As ye han herd biforn – ye woot wel what.   535
   The lady of the hous ay stille sat,
Til she had herd what the frere sayde.
"Ey, Goddes moder," quod she, "blisful mayde!
Is there aught elles? tel me feithfully."
   "Madame," quod he, "how thinketh yow therby?"   540
   "How that me thinketh?" quod she, "so God me speede –
I saye, a cherl hath doon a cherles deede!
What sholde I saye? God lat him never thee!

516 *Of that*, at what.   *town*, village, manor (here).
517 'And yet nothing troubles me so much.'
518 *lokkes hoore*, hoary locks, grey hair.
519 *covent*, convent, friary.
520 *I yow biseke*, I beg you.
521 *servitour*, servant.
522 *in scole*, in the Schools – i.e. at university (c).
523 'God does not like men to call us Rabbi' (see Matthew, xxiii, 7–8).
525 *No force*, no matter.
526 *meschief*, injury.
527 *bitid is*, has happened to, come upon.
528 'And so, in consequence, to every rank.'
530 *ye woot what is to doone*, you know what must be done.
531 *Distempre yow noght*, don't be upset (c).
532 See Matthew, v, 13 (c).
533 *your pacience ye holde*, keep your temper (lit.: patience).
536 *ay stille sat*, remained sitting quietly.
538 *blisful mayde*, blessed Virgin.
539 *aught elles*, anything else.
540 *how thinketh yow therby*, what do you think of it.
541 *so God me speede*, so help me God.
543 *thee*, thrive, prosper.

His syke heed is ful of vanitee.
I holde him in a maner frenesye!"
   "Madame," quod he, "by God I shal nat lye,   545
But I on other wyse may be wreke;
I shal diffame him over-al where I speke,
The false blasphemour that charged me
To parte that wol nat departed be,   550
To every man y-liche – with meschaunce!"
   The lord sat stille as he were in a traunce,
And in his herte he rolled up and doun:
   "How hadde this cherl imaginacioun
To shewe swich a probleme to the frere?   555
Never erst er now herde I of swich matere –
I trowe the Devel putte it in his mynde!
In Ars-Metryke shal there no man fynde
Biforn this day of swich a questioun.
Who sholde make a demonstracioun   560
That every man sholde have y-lyke his part
As of the soun or savour of a fart?
O nyce proude cherl – I shrewe his face!
Lo sires," quod the lord, "with harde grace!
Who ever herde of swich a thing er now?   565
'To every man y-lyke' – tel me how?
It is an inpossible – it may nat be . . .
Ey, nyce cherl, God lat him never thee!
The rumbling of a fart, and every soun,
Nis but of air reverberacioun,   570

[544] *vanitee*, foolishness.
[545] *a maner frenesye*, a kind of delirium (c).
[547] 'But I may be avenged in another way' (c).
[548] *diffame*, denounce.   *over-al where*, everywhere that.
[550–1] 'To share what cannot be shared, with every man [of the convent] equally – devil take it!'
[552] *as*, as if.
[553] *rolled up and doun*, pondered, chewed it over.
[555] *shewe*, present.
[556] *Never erst er now*, never before now.
[557] *trowe*, think, believe.
[558] *Ars-Metryke*, arithmetic (c).
[559] *of swich a questioun*, (anything) about such a problem.
[560] 'Who could put it to the proof?'
[561] *sholde*, might.
[562] *savour*, smell.
[563] *nyce*, precise (c).   *I shrewe his face*, God rot him (lit.: 'I curse his face') (c).
[564] *with harde grace*, devil take it (lit.: 'with misfortune').
[567] *an inpossible*, an impossibility.
[569] *every soun*, each sound (of any kind).
[570] 'Is nothing but shock-waves in the air.'

And ever it wasteth litel and litel away.
There nis no man kan deeme, by my fay,
If that it were departed equally.
What, lo my cherl! lo, yet how shrewedly
Unto my confessour to-day he spak!   575
I holde him certayn a demoniak!
Now ete your mete, and lat the cherl go playe;
Lat him go hang himself a devel waye!"

*The Wordes of the lordes Squyer and his kerver
for departing of the fart on twelve*

Now stood the lordes Squyer at the bord,
That carf his mete, and herde word by word   580
Of alle thing of which I have yow sayd.
    "My lord," quod he, "be ye nat yvel apayd;
I koude telle, for a gowne-clooth,
To yow, sire frere, so ye be nat wrooth,
How that this fart sholde even y-deled be   585
Among your covent, if it lyked me."
    "Tel," quod the lord, "and thou shalt have anon
A gowne-clooth, by God and by Seint John!"
    "My lord," quod he, "whan that the weder is fair,
Withouten wind or perturbing of air,   590
Lat bring a cartwheel here into this halle;
But looke that it have his spokes alle –
Twelve spokes hath a cartwheel comunly.

571 'And it always fades away, little by little.'
572 'Upon my word, there is no man that can judge' (c).
573 'Whether it had been shared out equally.'
574 *What, lo,* now, indeed.
576 'I definitely consider him to be possessed (by a devil).'
577 *mete* (here), food.   *go playe,* have his fun (or perhaps equivalent to 'go hang').
578 *a devel waye,* in the Devil's name.
Title: 'The words of the lord's squire and carver about dividing the fart into twelve.'
580 *That carf,* who was carving (c).
581 'About everything that I have told you of.'
582 *yvel apayd,* displeased.
583 *for a gowne-clooth,* in exchange for a length of cloth (enough to make a gown) (c).
585 *even y-deled,* evenly shared out.
586 *if it lyked me,* if I pleased.
589 *whan that,* when.   *weder,* weather.
590 *perturbing,* disturbance.
591 *Lat bring a cartwheel,* have a cartwheel brought.
592 'But see that it has all its spokes' (*his* was the standard form for the possessive of 'it' until the early seventeenth century, when 'its' began to be used regularly).
593 *comunly,* usually.

And bring me thanne twelve freres – woot ye why?
For thrittene is a covent, as I gesse. 595
Your confessour here, for his worthinesse,
Shal perfourne up the nombre of this covent.
Thanne shal they knele adoun, by oon assent,
And to every spokes ende, in this manere,
Ful sadly leye his nose shal a frere. 600
Your noble confessour, there God him save,
Shal holde his nose upright under the nave.
Thanne shal this cherl, with bely stif and toght
As any tabour, hider been y-brought;
And sette him on the wheel right of this cart, 605
Upon the nave, and make him lete a fart.
And ye shul seen, up peril of my lyf,
By preve, which that is demonstratyf,
That equally the soun of it wol wende,
And eke the stink, unto the spokes ende – 610
Save that this worthy man, your confessour,
By-cause he is a man of grete honour,
Shal have the firste fruit, as reson is.
The noble usage of freres yet is this,
The worthy men of hem shal first be served. 615
And certaynly he hath it wel disserved;
He hath to-day taught us so muche good,
With preching in the pulpit there he stood,
That I may vouche-sauf, I saye for me,
He hadde the firste smel of fartes three; 620

594 *woot ye why*, do you know why.
595 'For thirteen is a convent, I believe' (C).
596 *for*, because of.
597 *perfourne up*, complete, fill up.
598 *by oon assent*, all together, as one man.
599 *in this manere*, in this way.
600 'Each friar shall firmly set his nose' (C).
601 *there God him save*, may God preserve him.
602 *nave*, hub.
603 *toght*, taut.
604 *tabour*, drum.
605 *on the wheel right*, right on the wheel.
607 *up peril of my lyf*, upon my life.
608 'By logical proof.'
609 *wende*, go.
613 *as reson is*, as is right and proper.
614 *usage*, custom.
615 *worthy* – also used of the Friar in the *GP* (l. 62 of portrait).　*of hem*, among them.
618 *there*, where.
619–20 'That I can guarantee that, as far as I'm concerned, he ought to have the first smell of *three* farts.'

And so wolde al his covent hardily,
He bereth him so fair and hoolily."
 The lord, the lady, and ech man, save the frere,
Sayden that Jankin spak in this matere
As wel as Euclide or [as] Ptholomee.   625
Touching the cherl, they sayde – subtiltee
And hye wit made him speken as he spak;
He nis no fool ne no demoniak.
And Jankin hath y-wonne a newe gowne.
My tale is doon – we been almost at towne.'   630

Here endeth the Somnours Tale

[621] *hardily*, certainly.
[622] *bereth him*, bears himself, behaves.
[625] *Euclide or Ptholomee*, Euclid or Ptolemy (Ancient Greek mathematicians, well known in the Middle Ages).   [*as*], see Textual Notes.
[626] *Touching*, concerning, about.   *subtiltee*, subtlety, cleverness.
[627] *wit*, intelligence (c).
[628] *demoniak*, see l. 576.
[630] *doon*, finished.

The Portrait of the Pardoner

(from the **General Prologue** to the **Canterbury Tales**, A 669–714)

With him there rood a gentil PARDONER
Of Rouncival, his freend and his compeer,
That streight was comen fro the court of Rome.
Ful loude he song 'Com hider, love, to me!'
This Somnour bar to him a stif burdoun –   5
Was never trompe of half so greet a soun!
This Pardoner hadde heer as yelow as wex,
But smothe it heng, as dooth a stryke of flex;
By ounces heng his lokkes that he hadde,
And therwith he his shuldres overspradde;   10
But thinne it lay, by colpons oon and oon.
But hood, for jolitee, wered he noon,
For it was trussed up in his walet.
Him thoghte he rood al of the newe jet –
Dischevelee, save his cappe, he rood al bare.   15
Swiche glaring eyen hadde he as an hare.
A vernicle hadde he sowed upon his cappe;
His walet lay biforn him in his lappe,
Bretful of pardoun comen from Rome al hoot.
A vois he hadde as smal as hath a goot.   20
No berd hadde he, ne never sholde have –
As smothe it was as it were late y-shave.
I trowe he were a gelding or a mare!
But of his craft, fro Berwik into Ware,
Ne was ther swich another pardoner: 25

[1] *him* – i.e. the Summoner (subject of the previous portrait – see pp. 52–53).
[2] *Rouncival*, the hospital of St Mary of Rouncivalle, in London, a 'cell' (subsidiary convent) of the Priory at Roncesvalles, in Navarre.   *compeer*, comrade.
[3] *the court* – i.e. the Papal Court.
[4] *hider*, hither (the opening line or refrain of a popular song).
[5] *bar to him a stif burdoun*, accompanied him with a strong (*stif*) ground bass.
[7] *wex*, wax.
[8] *stryke of flex*, hank (or bunch) of flax.
[9] *ounces*, thin clusters.
[11] *colpons*, portions.   *oon and oon*, one by one, singly.
[12] *for jolitee*, 'for greater comfort' (Skeat). But perhaps Chaucer's point is that the Pardoner wears no hood as a *sartorial* sport (see also l. 14, below).
[13] *trussed*, wrapped.   *walet*, wallet.
[14] *al of the newe jet*, in the very latest fashion.
[15] *Dischevelee*, with hair hanging loose (cf. French, *cheveux*).
[17] *vernicle*, a little 'Veronica' (*Veronike*), the handkerchief with which St Veronica (according to tradition) wiped the face of Christ on the way to Calvary, and which was thought to have received the imprint of his face.
[19] *Bretful of pardoun*, brim-full of pardons (indulgences).
[20] *smal*, high-pitched.   *goot*, goat.
[24] *But of his craft*, but, as regards his profession. . . .   *fro Berwik unto Ware*, a way of saying 'from North to South of England, the whole length of the country'. Probably Ware in Hertfordshire is meant.

For in his male he hadde a pilwe-beer,
Which that he sayde was Oure Lady veyl;
He sayde he hadde a gobet of the sayl
That Seinte Peter hadde whan that he wente
Upon the see, til Jesu Cryst him hente,   30
He hadde a crois of latoun ful of stones,
And in a glas he hadde pigges bones.
But with thise relikes, whan that he fond
A povre person dwelling upon lond,
Upon a day he gat him moore moneye   35
Than that the person gat in monthes tweye;
And thus, with feyned flaterye and japes,
He made the person and the peple his apes.
But trewely to tellen, atte laste,
He was in chirche a noble ecclesiaste.   40
Wel koude he rede a lessoun or a storie,
But alderbest he song an offertorie;
For wel he wiste, whan that songe was songe,
He moste preche, and wel affyle his tonge,
To winne silver, as he ful wel koude.   45
Therefore he song the murierly and loude.

The Wordes of the Hoost to the Phisicien and the Pardoner

Our Hoost gan to swere as he were wood.
'Harrow!' quod he, 'by nayles and by blood!

26 *male*, bag.   *pilwe-beer*, pillow-case.
27 *Oure Lady veyl*, Our Lady's veil.
28 *gobet*, a small piece.
30 *him hente*, caught hold of him (see Matthew, xiv, 29f.).
31 *a crois of latoun*, a cross made of latten (an alloy of copper and zinc).
34 'A poor country parish-priest.'
35 *a day*, one day.
36 *tweye*, two.
37 *japes*, deceitful tricks.
38 *He made . . . his apes*, he made fools ('monkeys') of.
40 *ecclesiaste*, churchman. The Pardoner was at least in minor orders (i.e. not an ordained priest or deacon, but a cleric of some kind).
41 *lessoun*, the Lesson.   *storie*, the *historia*. Both may be parts of the Canonical Office or (more likely) the Epistle and Gospel sections of the Mass (see next line).
42 *alderbest*, best of all.   *offertorie*, the Offertory of the Mass, beginning after the Creed, which would be said or sung (i.e. intoned).
44 *affyle*, file down (i.e. speak smoothly or plausibly).
45 *as he*, etc. as he well knew how to.
46 *the murierly and loude*, the more merrily and (the more) loudly (*murierly* = lit.: 'merrierly').

1 *gan to*, began to.   *as he were wood*, as if he were mad.
2 ' "Alas!" he said, "by [Christ's] nails and blood!" '

This was a fals cherl and a fals justyse!
As shameful deeth as herte kan devyse
Come to thise juges and hire advocats!
Algate this sely mayde is slayn, allas!
Allas – to deere boughte she beautee!
Wherfore I saye al day that men may see
That yiftes of Fortune and of Nature
Been cause of deeth to many a creature.
Of bothe yiftes that I speke of now
Men han ful ofte moore for harm than prow.
   But, trewely, myn owene maister deere,
This is a pitous tale for to heere!
But nathelees, passe over – is no fors.
I pray to God so save thy gentil cors,
And eke thyne urinals and thy jurdones,
Thyn Ipocras, and eke thy Galiones,
And every boist ful of thy letuarie –
God blesse hem, and our lady Seinte Marie!
So moot I theen, thou art a propre man –
And lyk a prelat, by Seint Ronyan!
Sayde I nat wel? – I kan nat speke in terme,
But wel I woot thou doost myn herte to erme,
That I almoost have caught a cardinacle.

5

10

15

20

25

---

³ *cherl*, villain ((c) on l. 542 of the *ST*).   *ustyse*, judge (c).
⁵ *hire advocats*, their advocates, lawyers.
⁶ *Algate*, anyway.   *sely*, innocent, pitiable ((c) on l. 242 of the *ST*).
⁷ 'Alas, she paid too dearly for her beauty!' (see l. 215 also).
⁸ 'Because of this I say that men can always see'.
⁹ *yiftes*, gifts, blessings (c).
¹⁰ *Been*, are.
[Most editors print an extra couplet here (see the Textual Notes on this tale).]
¹¹ *Of bothe*, from both.
¹² 'Men very often get more harm than benefit'.
¹³ *myn owene maister deere*, my own dear master.
¹⁴ *pitous*, pitiful.
¹⁵ 'But, nonetheless, let it be – it doesn't matter.'
¹⁶ 'I pray that God may preserve your good self (lit.: "your noble body")' (c).
¹⁷ 'And also your urine-bottles and your chamber-pots.'
¹⁸ *Ipocras*, cordial (named after Hippocrates, a Greek physician of the fifth century B.C.).   *Galiones*, medicines (named after Galen, a Greek physician of the second century A.D.).
¹⁹ *boist ful*, boxful.   *letuarie*, medicaments.
²¹ *So moot I theen*, so help me (lit.: 'so may I prosper').   *propre*, fine.
²² *Ronyan* – three syllables (c).
²³ 'Did I say the right thing? I can't speak in learned terms.'
²⁴ 'But well I know, you're making my heart ache.'
²⁵ 'That I have almost had a heart-attack.' (The proper word is 'cardiacle' (c), but the Host seems to be confusing it with 'cardinal'.)

By Corpus bones! but I have triacle,
Or elles a draughte of moist and corny ale,
Or but I heere anon a mery tale –
Myn herte is lost for pitee of this mayde!
Thou *beel amy*, thou Pardoner,' he sayde,   30
'Tel us som mirthe or japes right anon!'
    'It shal be doon,' quod he, 'by Seint Ronyon!
But first,' quod he, 'here at this ale stake
I wol bothe drinke, and eten of a cake.'
    But right anon thise gentils gonne to crye: 35
'Nay – lat him telle us of no ribaudye!
Telle us som moral thing, that we may lere
Som wit – and thanne wol we gladly heere!'
    'I graunte, y-wis,' quod he, 'but I moot thinke
Upon som honest thing whyle that I drinke.'   40

---

[26] 'By Christ's bones! – unless I have some medicine' (c). *'Corpus bones'* is the Host's own mixture of two oaths: 'by *corpus domini*' (God's body) and 'by Goddes bones'.

[27] *moist and corny*, new and tasting of malt (c).

[28] 'Or unless I immediately hear a pleasant tale.'

[29] 'My heart will break, through pity for this girl.'

[30] *beel amy*, (OF), sweet friend, lover.

[31] 'Tell us something amusing or funny, at once.'

[32] See l. 22.

[33] *at this ale-stake*, at this inn-sign. (Inn-signs at this time commonly consisted of a pole (a 'stake') with a garland hanging on it.)

[34] *eten of a*, eat some.

[35] 'But at once the gentlefolk began to protest' (c).

[36] *ribaudye*, ribaldry, bawdy.

[37] *lere*, learn.

[38] *wit*, wisdom (c).

[39] *I graunte, y-wis*, I agree, certainly.   *moot*, must.

[40] *honest*, worthy, respectable.   *whyle that*, whilst.

Here folweth the Prologe of the Pardoners Tale

The Prologue to the Pardoner's Tale

'Radix malorum est Cupiditas' *Ad Thimotheum, vi*

'Lordings,' quod he, 'in chirches whan I preche,
I peyne me to han an hauteyn speche,
And ringe it out as round as gooth a belle –
For I kan al by rote that I telle.
My theme is alway oon, and ever was: 45
Radix malorum est Cupiditas.
    First I pronounce whennes that I come;
And thanne my bulles shewe I alle and some.
Our lyge lordes seel on my patente –
That shewe I firste, my body to warente,   50
That no man be so bold, ne preest ne clerk,
Me to destourbe of Crystes hooly werk.
And, after that, thanne telle I forth my tales.
Bulles of popes and of cardinales,
Of patriarkes and bisshopes I shewe –   55
And in Latyn I speke a wordes fewe,
To saffron with my predicacioun,
And for to stire hem to devocioun.
Thanne shewe I forth my longe cristal stones,
Y-crammed ful of cloutes and of bones   60

---

41 *Lordings*, ladies and gentlemen.
42 'I take pains to make my words impressive.'
43 'And deliver them as clearly as a bell rings.'
44 'For I know everything that I say by heart.'
45 'My subject always is and was [just] one'.
46 (Lat.) 'Covetousness is the root of [all] evil' (1 Timothy, vi, 10).
47 *pronounce whennes that I come*, proclaim where I come from.
48 'And then I show the whole range of my documents.'
49 'Our liege lord's seal upon my licence' (c).
50 'I show that first, as proof of the authority vested in me.'
51 *ne . . . ne*, neither . . . nor.
52 'To distract me from [doing] Christ's holy work.'
53 *thanne*, then.
54 *bulles*, documents (so called because of the *bulla* (Lat. = 'seal') that was attached to them).
55 *patriarkes*, patriarchs (Church leaders, especially in the Eastern (Byzantine) Church).
56 *a wordes fewe*, a few words.
57 'To season my preaching with.'
58 *stire hem*, encourage them.
59 *shewe I forth*, I exhibit.   *cristal stones*, glass vessels.
60 *y-crammed*, crammed.   *cloutes*, rags.

(Relikes been they, as wenen they echoon).
Thanne have I, in latoun, a sholder-boon,
Which that was of an hooly Jewes sheep.
"Goode men," I saye, "take of my wordes keep!
If that this boon be wasshe in any welle –   65
If cow or calf or sheep or oxe swelle,
That any worm hath ete, or worm y-stonge –
Take water of that welle, and wassh his tonge,
And it is hool anon! – and forthermoore,
Of pokkes and of skabbe, and every soore   70
Shal every sheep be hool that of this welle
Drinketh a draughte! Take keep eke what I telle:
If that the goode-man that the beestes oweth
Wol every wyke, er that the cok him croweth,
Fasting, drinken of this welle a draughte,   75
As thilke hooly Jew our eldres taughte –
His beestes and his stoor shal multiplye!
    And, sires, also it heeleth jalousye.
For, though a man be falle in jalous rage,
Lat maken with this water his potage,   80
And never shal he moore his wyf mistriste,
Though he the soothe of hir defaute wiste –
Al hadde she taken preestes two or three.
    Here is a mitayn, eke, that ye may see.
He that his hand wol putte in this mitayn,   85
He shal have multiplying of his grayn,
Whan he hath sowen, be it whete or otes –

---

61 'They are relics, so they all think.'
62 *in latoun*, in a brass case.
63 *Which that*, which.   The 'holy Jew' would probably be an Old Testament patriarch – perhaps Jacob (see Genesis, xxx, 31–43).
64 *take of my wordes keep*, mark my words.
65 *If that*, if.
67 'That has eaten any worm (this was believed to cause diseases in animals), or that any snake has bitten' (c).
68 *his*, its (the animal's – see *ST*, l. 592).
69 *And it is hool anon*, and it will be cured at once.
70 'From pox and scab (diseases of sheep) and every disease.'
72 *Take keep eke what I telle*, mark also what I [now] say.
73 'If the householder who owns the animals.'
74 'Will every week, before the cock crows.'
76 *thilke*, that.   *eldres*, ancestors.
77 *stoor*, livestock.   *multiplye*, increase.
79 *be falle in jalous rage*, had fallen into a fury of jealousy.
80 'Let his soup be made with this water.'
81 *mistriste*, suspect (of infidelity).
82 'Though he knew the truth about her offence.'
83 'Even if she had taken [as lovers] two or three priests'.
84 *mitayn*, mitten.

So that he offre pens, or elles grotes.
   Goode men and wommen – oo thing warne I yow:
If any wight be in this chirche now   90
That hath doon sinne horryble, that he
Dar nat for shame of it y-shriven be,
Or any womman, be she yong or old,
That hath y-maked hir housbond cokewold –
Swich folk shal have no power, ne no grace   95
To offren to my relikes in this place.
And whoso fyndeth him out of swich blame,
He wol come up and offre in Goddes name,
And I assoille him, by the auctoritee
Which that by bulle y-graunted was to me!"   100
   By this gaude have I wonne, yeer by yeer,
An hundred mark sith I was pardoner!
I stonde lyk a clerk in my pulpet –
And whan the lewed peple is doun y-set,
I preche so as ye han herd bifore,   105
And telle an hundred false japes moore.
Thanne peyne I me to strecche forth the nekke,
And est and west upon the peple I bekke,
As dooth a dowve sitting on a berne.
Myn handes and my tonge goon so yerne,   110
That it is joye to see my bisinesse.
Of avaryce, and of swich cursednesse,
Is al my preching, for to make hem free

---

[88] 'So long as he offers pence, or else groats' (fourpenny-pieces).
[89] *oo thing warne I yow*, I warn you about one thing.
[90] *wight*, person
[91] *That hath doon sinne horryble*, who has committed a horrible sin.
[92] *y-shriven be*, be shriven (i.e. make confession and receive absolution).
[94] 'Who has made her husband a cuckold.'
[95] *swich folk*, such people.   *grace*, favour, privilege.
[96] *offren*, offer money (in return for benefits from the relics).
[97] 'And whoever finds himself free of such guilt.'
[99] *I assoille*, I shall absolve.
[100] 'Which was granted to me by licence.'
[101] *gaude*, pretty little trick.
[102] *mark*, marks (c).   *sith I was*, since I have been.
[103] *clerk*, cleric, or possibly, learned man, in contrast to the 'lewed peple'.
[104] *lewed*, ignorant (see *ST*, l. 264 (c)).   *is doun y-set*, have sat down.
[105] *so as*, just as.   *han*, have.
[106] *false japes*, false tales, tall stories.
[107] *peyne I me to*, I make an effort to.
[108] 'And I jerk my head at the people in all directions (lit.: "east and west").'
[109] *dowve*, dove.   *berne*, barn.
[110] *goon so yerne*, move so eagerly.
[112] *swich cursednesse*, such wickedness.
[113] *for to make hem free*, to make them ready (c).

To yiven hire pens, and namely unto me.
For myn entente is nat but for to winne,   115
And nothing for correccioun of sinne.
I rekke never whan that they been beried,
Though that hire soules goon a-blakeberied!
For certes many a predicacioun
Comth ofte-tyme of yvel entencioun: 120
Som for plesànce of folk, and flaterye,
To been avaunced by ipocrisye –
And som for veyne glorie, and som for hate.
For whan I dar noon other wayes debate,
Thanne wol I stinge him with my tonge smerte   125
In preching, so that he shal nat asterte
To been defamed falsly, if that he
Hath trespassed to my bretheren, or to me.
For, though I telle noght his propre name,
Men shal wel knowe that it is the same,   130
By signes, and by other circumstances.
Thus quyte I folk that doon us displesances –
Thus spitte I out my venim, under hewe
Of hoolynesse, to seeme hooly and trewe!
But shortly myn entente I wol devyse: 135
I preche of nothing, but for coveityse.
Therfore my theme is yet, and ever was:

114 *pens*, pence, money.   *namely*, especially, particularly.
115 'For my aim is solely to make a profit' (c).
116 'And not at all to reprove sin.'
117 'I never care about when they are buried' (i.e. what state their souls are in when they die).
118 'Even if their souls go straying' (lit.: 'go blackberrying'. On the form, *goon a-blakeberied* see *ST*, l. 114 (c)).
119 *predicacioun*, sermon.
120 'Often proceeds from an evil purpose.'
121 *Som for plesànce of folk*, some (sermons) from a desire to please people.
122 'In order to gain advancement by means of hypocrisy.'
123 *for veyne glorie*, from conceit ('vainglory').
124 'For when I dare not fight in any other way.'
125 *him* – i.e. any opponent of the Pardoner's.   *smerte*, sharply.
126 *asterte*, escape.
127 *To been defamed*, being slandered.
128 *trespassed to*, offended against.
129 'For, though I don't actually mention him by name.'
131 'By hints and other details accompanying [what I say].'
132 'Thus I repay those who offend us.'
133-4 'Thus I spit out my poison under colour of holiness/By seeming holy and honest.'
135 'But I will briefly explain my purpose.'
136 *but for coveityse*, except through covetousness.
137 *is yet, and ever was*, is still and always was.

Radix malorum est Cupiditas.
Thus kan I preche agayn that same vyce
Which that I use – and that is avaryce.   140
But, though myself be gilty in that sinne,
Yet kan I maken other folk to twinne
From avaryce, and soore to repente.
But that is nat my principal entente;
I preche nothing but for coveityse.   145
Of this matere it oughte ynough suffyse.
    Thanne telle I hem ensamples many oon,
Of olde stories, longe tyme agoon,
For lewed peple loven tales olde;
Swiche thinges kan they wel reporte and holde.   150
What – trowe ye that, whyles I may preche
And winne gold and silver for I teche –
That I wol live in poverte wilfully?
Nay, nay – I thoghte it never, trewely!
For I wol preche and begge in sondry landes.   155
I wol nat do no labour with myn handes,
Ne make baskettes, and live therby,
By-cause I wol nat beggen ydelly.
I wol noon of the Apostles countrefete;
I wol have moneye, wolle, chese and whete,   160
Al were it yeven of the poverest page,
Or of the poverest widwe in a village –
Al sholde hir children sterve for famyne.
Nay, I wol drinke licour of the vyne,

138 See l. 46 (n).
139 *agayn*, against.
140 *Which that I use*, which I practise.
141 *myself be gilty in*, I myself am guilty of.
142–3 'Yet I can make other people renounce/Avarice, and repent heartily.'
145 See l. 136 and the note on it.
146 'That ought to be enough concerning this matter.'
147 *ensamples many oon*, many exemplary moral stories (Lat. *exempla*), (c).
148 *longe tyme agoon*, (of) a long time ago.
149 *loven tales olde*, love old tales.
150 'They can easily repeat and remember such things.'
151 'What, do you believe that as long as I can preach.'
152 *winne*, earn.   *for I teche*, because I teach (morality).
153 *wilfully*, willingly.
154 *I thoghte it never, trewely*, I honestly never intended to.
155 *sondry*, sundry, various.
156 *nat do no*, not do any.
158 'Since I don't intend to beg in vain.'
159 *countrefete*, imitate (by living in poverty) (c).
160 *wolle*, wool.
161 *of* (here), by.   *page*, lad, or possibly, servant.
163 'Even if her children should die of hunger' (c).
164 *licour of the vyne*, wine (lit.: 'liquor from the vine').

And have a joly wench in every town! 165
  But herkneth, lordings, in conclusioun:
Your lyking is that I shal telle a tale.
Now have I dronke a draughte of corny ale –
By God, I hope I shal yow telle a thing
That shal by resoun been at your lyking! 170
For, though myself be a ful vicious man,
A moral tale, yet, I yow telle kan,
Which I am wont to preche for to winne.
Now holde your pees! My tale I wol biginne.

The Tale

Here biginneth the Pardoners Tale

In Flaundres, whylom, was a compaignye 175
Of younge folk that haunteden folye,
As ryot, hasard, stewes and tavernes,
Where-as with harpes, lutes and giternes
They daunce, and pleyen at dees, bothe day and night –
And ete also, and drinke over hire might, 180
Thurgh which they doon the devel sacrifyse,
Withinne that develes temple in cursed wyse,
By superfluitee abhominable.
Hire othes been so grete, and so dampnable,
That it is grisly for to heere hem swere. 185

---

166 *herkneth*, listen (plural imperative).
167 *lyking*, wish, pleasure.
170 'That will rightly be to your liking.'
171 *myself*, I myself.   *ful*, very.
172 'I can still tell you a moral tale.'
173 'Which I am accustomed to preach for profit.'
174 *pees*, peace.
175 *Flaundres*, Flanders (c).   *whylom*, once.
176 *haunteden folye*, indulged themselves recklessly.
177 'Such as extravagance and gambling, and [frequented] brothels and taverns.'
178 *Where-as*, where.   *giternes*, guitars.
179 *dees*, dice.
180 *over hire might*, beyond their capacity.
181 'By means of which they performed sacrifice to the Devil.'
182 'Within that Devil's temple wickedly' (c).
183 'Through disgusting excess' (see *ST*, l. 342).
184 'Their oaths are so strong and so damnable.'
185 *grisly for to*, horrible to.

Our blissed Lordes body they to-tere –
Hem thoghte that Jewes rente him noght ynough –
And ech of hem at otheres sinne lough.
And, right anon, thanne comen tombesteres,
Fetys and smal, and yonge frutesteres,   190
Singeres with harpes, bawdes, wafereres,
Whiche been the verray develes officeres,
To kindle and blowe the fyr of lecherye,
That is annexed unto glotonye.
The hooly writ take I to my witnesse   195
That luxurie is in wyn and dronkenesse.
    Lo! how that dronken Loth unkyndely
Lay by his doghtres two unwitingly –
So dronke he was, he niste what he wroughte.
Herodes (whoso wel the stories soughte),   200
Whan he of wyn was repleet at his feeste,
Right at his owene table he yaf his heste,
To sleen the Baptist John, ful giltelees.
    Senec saith a good word, doutelees:
He saith he kan no difference fynde   205
Bitwix a man that is out of his mynde,
And a man which that is dronkelewe –
But that woodnesse, y-fallen in a shrewe,
Persevereth lenger than dooth dronkenesse.
O glotonye – ful of cursednesse!   210

186 *blissed*, blessed.   *to-tere*, tear to pieces (c).
187 'It seemed to them that the Jews did not tear him enough.
188 *lough*, laughed (c).
189 'And then at once there came dancing-girls.'
190 'Shapely and slim, and young girls selling fruit.'
191 *bawdes*, procuresses.   *wafereres*, cake-sellers (c).
192 'Who are indeed the Devil's servants.'
193 *blowe the fyr*, fan the flames.
194 *annexed unto glotonye*, linked to gluttony (c).
195 'I take the Holy Scriptures as my witness.'
196 *luxurie*, lechery (c).
197 *how that*, how.   *Loth*, Lot (see Genesis, xix, 29–38).   *unkyndely*, un-
naturally ((c) on *ST*, l. 42).
198 'Unknowingly slept with his two daughters.'
199 *he niste what he wroughte*, he did not know what he was doing.
200 'Herod [as may be seen by] whoever looks through the histories carefully'.
201 *repleet*, replete, full.
202 *yaf his heste*, gave his promise (to his daughter – see Mark, vi, 16–29).
203 'To kill John the Baptist [who was] quite guiltless.'
204 *Senec*, Seneca (c).   *doutelees*, undoubtedly.
206 *Bitwix*, between.
207 *which that is dronkelewe*, who is drunk.
208 'Except that madness occurring in a vicious man.'
209 *Persevereth*, lasts.
210 *cursednesse*, wickedness.

O cause first of our confusioun!
O original of our dampnacioun,
Til Cryst hadde bought us with his blood agayn!
Lo, how deere, shortly for to sayn,
Aboght was thilke cursed vileinye!   215
Corrupt was al this world for glotonye.
   Adam, our fader, and his wyf also,
Fro Paradys, to labour and to wo,
Were driven for that vyce, it is no drede.
For, whyl that Adam fasted, as I rede,   220
He was in Paradys, and whan that he
Eet of the fruit defended on the tree,
Anon he was out cast to wo and peyne.
O glotonye, on thee wel oughte us pleyne!
O, wiste a man how many maladyes   225
Folwen of excesse and of glotonyes,
He wolde been the moore mesurable
Of his diete, sitting at his table!
Allas, the shorte throte, the tendre mouth
Maketh that est, and west, and north, and south,   230
In erthe, in air, in water men to swinke,
To gete a glotoun deyntee mete and drinke!
Of this matere, O Paul, wel canstow trete:
"Mete unto wombe, and wombe eke unto mete –
Shal God destroyen bothe", as Paulus seith.   235
Allas, a foul thing is it, by my feith,
To saye this word, and fouler is the deede –

211 *cause first*, first cause.   *confusioun*, ruin, damnation.
212 *original*, cause, source.
213 *bought*, redeemed.
214–15 'In short, look how dearly/That wicked sin was paid for.'
216 *Corrupt was*, became corrupted.   *for*, because of.
219 *it is no drede*, there is no doubt.
220 *whyl that*, whilst.   *as I rede*, I read.
221 *whan that*, when.
222 *the fruit defended*, the forbidden fruit ((c) on *ST*, l. 170).
223 *out cast*, cast out.
224 *on thee wel oughte us pleyne*, we ought indeed to complain against you.
225 'Oh, if only a man knew how many illnesses.'
226 *Folwen of*, result from.
227 *mesurable*, temperate.
228 *Of his diete*, in his diet.
229 *shorte throte*, 'brief pleasure of swallowing' (Robinson) (lit.: 'short throat') –
an allusion to St Jerome's treatise *Against Jovinian* ((c) on *ST*, l. 265).   *tendre*,
delicate, fastidious.
230–1 'Makes men labour everywhere (lit.: "east and west, etc.")' (c).
232 *mete*, food.
233 'O Paul [St Paul], you can deal with this matter well'.
234–5 ' "Food [is meant] for the stomach, and the stomach for food, [but] God
will do away with both", as St Paul says' (see 1 Corinthians, vi, 13).

Whan man so drinketh of the whyte and rede,
That of his throte he maketh his pryvee,
Thurgh thilke cursed superfluitee!   240
    The apostle, weping, saith ful pitously:
"There walken many, of whiche yow told have I –
I saye it now weping with pitous vois –
That they been enemys of Crystes crois,
Of which the ende is deeth – wombe is hire god!"   245
O wombe! O bely! O stinking cod,
Fulfilled of donge, and of corrupcioun!
At either end of thee foul is the soun!
How grete labour and cost is thee to fynde!
Thise cookes, how they stampe, and streyne, and grynde,   250
And turnen substaunce into accident,
To fulfille al thy likerous talent.
Out of the harde bones knokke they
The mary – for they caste nought away
That may go thurgh the golet softe and swoote.   255
Of spycerye of leef, and bark, and roote
Shal been his sauce, y-maked by delyt,
To make him yet a newer appetyt.
But, certes, he that haunteth swich delyces
Is deed, whyl that he liveth in tho vyces!   260
    A lecherous thing is wyn, and dronkenesse
Is ful of stryving and of wrecchednesse.
O dronke man – disfigured is thy face!
Sour is thy breeth – foul artow to embrace!

238 *whyte and rede*, white and red (wine).
239 'That he makes his throat his privy (lavatory)' – i.e. he vomits.
241 *The apostle* – i.e. St Paul (see Philippians, iii, 18).
242 'There are many now going around, of whom I have told you.'
244 *crois*, cross.
245 *Of which the end*, whose goal.   *wombe*, stomach ((c) on *ST*, l. 224).
246 *cod*, bag, paunch.
247 *Fulfilled of*, brim full of.   *corrupcioun*, rotten matter.
248 *soun*, sound.
249 'What a lot of toil and expense there must be, to provide for you.'
250 *streyne*, strain (liquids).
251 'And turn reality into appearance' (c).
252 'To satisfy your greedy appetite' (c).
254 *mary*, marrow.   *caste nought away*, throw nothing away.
255 *golet*, gullet.   *softe and swoote*, easily and pleasantly.
256–7 'His [the glutton's] sauce has to be made beautifully out of spices from leaves, bark and roots.'
258 *newer*, renewed.
259 'But certainly he who worships such luxuries.'
260 *tho*, those.
262 *stryving*, quarrelsomeness.   *wrecchednesse*, nastiness.
264 *artow* (= 'art thou'), you are.

And, thurgh thy dronke nose semeth the soun,   265
As though thou saydest ay, "Sampsoun! Sampsoun!"
And yet, God woot, Sampsoun drank never no wyn!
Thou fallest as it were a stiked swyn.
Thy tonge is lost, and al thyn honeste cure –
For dronkenesse is verray sepulture   270
Of mannes wit, and his discrecioun.
In whom that drinke hath dominacioun,
He kan no conseil keepe, it is no drede.
Now keepe yow fro the whyte and fro the rede –
And namely fro the whyte wyn of Lepe,   275
That is to selle in Fissh-strete or in Chepe!
This wyn of Spaigne crepeth subtilly
In othere wynes growing faste by –
Of which there ryseth swich fumositee,
That, whan a man hath dronken draughtes three,   280
And weneth that he be at hoom in Chepe,
He is in Spaigne, right at the town of Lepe,
Nat at the Rochele, ne at Burdeux town –
And thanne wol he sayn, "Sampsoun! Sampsoun!"
    But herkneth, lordings, oo word, I yow praye,   285
That alle the sovereyn actes, dar I saye,
Of victories in the Olde Testament,
Thurgh verray God that is omnipotent,
Were doon in abstinence and in prayere.

[265] *semeth the soun*, a sound seems to come.
[266] 'As if you were continually saying "Samson! Samson!" ' (c).
[267] *God woot*, God knows.
[268] *stiked swyn*, stuck pig.
[269] *honeste cure*, concern for decency.
[270] *verray sepulture*, indeed the grave (lit. 'the true grave'; (c) on l. 288).
[271] *wit*, reason ((c) on l. 38). *discrecioun*, judgment.
[272-3] 'Unquestionably, a man who is under the influence of drink cannot keep a secret.'
[274] 'Now keep away from white and red [wine].'
[275] *namely*, especially. *Lepe* – a town in Spain (c).
[276] *to selle*, for sale. *Fissh-streete*, Fish Hill Street (London). *Chepe*, Cheapside (London) (c).
[277] *subtilly*, subtly.
[278] *growing*, maturing (in the wine-merchants' barrels). *faste by*, nearby.
[279] *Of which*, from which mixture (of wines). *fumositee*, vapour affecting the brain (which was thought to be given off by drinks like this in the stomach).
[281] *weneth that he be*, thinks that he is.
[282] *Spaigne*, Spain.
[283] 'Not at La Rochelle or in the town of Bordeaux' (c).
[284] See l. 266 and the note on it.
[285] *oo*, (just) one. *I yow praye*, I beg you.
[286-7] '[Namely] that all the most notable victorious deeds in the Old Testament, I dare say'.
[288] *verray God*, the true God (c).

Looketh the Bible, and there ye may it lere.   290
   Looke Attila, the grete conquerour,
Deyde in his sleep with shame and dishonour,
Bleding ay at his nose in dronkenesse.
A capitayn sholde live in sobrenesse.
And, over al this, avyseth yow right wel   295
What was comaunded unto Lamuel
(Nat Samuel but Lamuel saye I) –
Redeth the Byble, and fynd it expresly
Of wyn-yiving to hem that han justyse.
Namoore of this – for it may wel suffyse!   300
   And, now that I have spoken of glotonye,
Now wol I yow defenden hasardrye.
Hasard is verray moder of lesinges,
And of deceite, and cursed forsweringes,
Blaspheme of Cryst, manslaughtre, and wast also   305
Of catel, and of tyme – and forthermo,
It is repreve and contrarie of honour
For to been holde a commune hasardour.
And ever the hyer he is of estaat,
The moore is he holden desolaat.   310
If that a prince useth hasardrye,
In alle governaunce and policye
He is, as by commune opinioun,
Y-holde the lasse in reputacioun.
   Stilbon, that was a wys embassadour,   315
Was sent to Corinth, in ful grete honour,

290 'Consult the Bible, and there you may learn about it' (c).
291 *Looke Attila*, remember (how) Attila (c).
293 *ay*, continually.
295 'And, in addition to all this, remember carefully.'
296 'What orders were given to Lemuel' – see Proverbs, xxxi, 4ff.
297 'I'm speaking of Lemuel, not Samuel' (c).
298 *it* – i.e. the orders (see l. 296). *expresly*, clearly, specifically.
299 'About giving wine to those who administer justice.'
300 *Namoore*, no more.
302 'I will now warn you against gambling.'
303 *verray moder of lesinges*, the true mother (i.e. cause) of lies.
304 *cursed forsweringes*, wicked perjuries.
305 *Blaspheme*, blasphemy. *wast*, wasting, squandering.
306 *catel*, wealth.
307–8 'It is a reproach to and the contrary of honour/To be considered a common gambler.'
309 'And always, the higher he [the gambler] is in rank.'
310 *holden desolaat*, kept at a distance, ostracised.
311 *useth hasardrye*, makes a habit of gambling.
312 'In all matters of administration and statesmanship.'
313–14 'He is generally thought to be the lower in reputation [because of it].'
315 *that* (here), who.
316 *in ful grete honour*, with very much ceremony.

Fro Lacidomie, to make hire alliaunce.
And, whan he cam, him happede, *par chaunce*,
That alle the grettest that were of that lond,
Playinge atte hasard he hem fond.   320
For which, as soone as it mighte be,
He stal him hoom agayn to his contree,
And sayde, "There wol I nat lese my name,
Ne I wol nat take on me so grete defame,
Yow for to allye unto noon hasardours.   325
Sendeth othere wyse embassadours –
For, by my trouthe, me were levere dye,
Than I yow sholde to hasardours allye!
For ye that been so glorious in honours
Shul nat allyen yow with hasardours,   330
As by my wil, ne as by my tretee."
This wyse philosophre, thus sayde he.
    Looke eke, that to the king Demetrius
The king of Parthes, as the book saith us,
Sente him a paire of dees of gold in scorn.   335
For he hadde used hasard ther-biforn –
For which he held his glorie or his renoun
At no value or reputacioun.
Lordes may fynden other maner play
Honeste ynough to dryve the day away.   340
    Now wol I speke of othes false and grete
A word or two, as olde bookes trete.
Grete swering is a thing abhominable –

---

[317] *Lacidomie*, Lacedaemon, Sparta.   *hire alliaunce*, an alliance with them.
[318] 'And when he arrived, it happened to him, by chance.'
[319-20] 'That he found all the most important people in the country playing gambling games.'
[321] *For which*, because of which.
[322] *He stal him hoom*, he stole away home.
[323] *There wol I nat lese my name*, I do not want to lose my reputation there (in Corinth).
[324-5] 'Nor will I dishonour myself so much/[as] to ally you to gamblers.'
[327] *by my trouthe*, upon my honour (c).   *me were levere*, I had rather.
[329] *been*, are.
[330] *yow*, yourselves.
[331] 'With my consent, or through my negotiations.'
[333] *Looke eke*, remember also.
[334] *Parthes*, Parthians.   *saith*, tells.
[335] *dees*, dice.
[336] *used*, made a habit of.   *ther-biforn*, before that.
[337-8] 'Because of which, he [the king of Parthia] considered his [Demetrius'] glory or renown/To be of no value or standing.'
[339] *other maner play*, other kinds of games.
[340] '[Which are] honest enough to pass the day with.'
[342] *trete*, describe, treat (them, *sc.* the oaths).
[343] *a thing abhominable*, a detestable thing.

And fals swering is yet moore reprevable.
The hye God forbad swering at al   345
(Witnesse on Mathew) – but in special
Of swering saith the hooly Jeremye:
"Thou shalt swere sooth thyne oothes, and nat lye,
And swere in doom, and eke in rightwisnesse."
But ydel swering is a cursednesse;   350
    Bihold and see, that, in the firste table
Of hye Goddes hestes honurable,
How that the seconde hest of him is this:
"Take nat my name in ydel or amis."
Lo, rather he forbedeth swich swering,   355
Than homicyde, or many a cursed thing!
I saye that, as by ordre, thus it standeth –
This knowen, that his hestes understandeth,
How that the seconde heste of God is that.
And, forther-over, I wol thee telle al plat,   360
That vengeance shal nat parten from his hous,
That of his othes is to outrageous:
"By Goddes precious herte, and by his nayles!
And by the blood of Cryst, that is in Hayles!
Seven in my chaunce, and thyn is cink and treye!   365
By Goddes armes! if thou falsly playe,
This dagger shal thurghout thyn herte go!"

[344] *reprevable*, blameworthy, reprehensible.
[346] *Witnesse on Mathew*, as St Matthew's Gospel shows (Matthew, v, 34).
in special, especially.
[347] *Jeremye*, Jeremiah the prophet (see Jeremiah, iv, 2).
[348-9] 'You must swear your oaths truthfully and not lie,/And swear justly and honestly also.'
[350] *ydel*, empty, pointless. *cursednesse*, wickedness.
[351] *the firste table*, the first of the two tablets (of the Ten Commandments).
[352] *hestes honurable*, commandments (which are to be) respected.
[353] *seconde hest of him*, his (God's) second commandment (the third in the Authorised Version).
[354] 'Do not use my name pointlessly or wrongly' (see Exodus, xx, 7).
[355] *rather he forbedeth*, he sooner forbids.
[356] *homicyde*, homicide, murder.
[357] 'I say that the commandments stand in this order.'
[358] 'They who understand his [God's] commandments know this.'
[360] 'And, furthermore, I will tell you straight out.'
[361] 'That vengeance shall never miss that man (lit.: "leave his house")' (c).
See Ecclesiasticus, xxiii, 11.
[362] 'Who is too violent in his oaths.'
[363] *his nayles*, the nails of the Cross, or perhaps, the nails of Christ's body. (The Pardoner is imitating a swearing gambler.)
[364] *Hayles*, the abbey of Hailes in Gloucestershire, where there was a bottle which was believed to contain some of Christ's blood.
[365] 'My lot is the seven, and yours is five and three.'
[367] 'This dagger shall go straight through your heart.'

This fruit cometh of the bicched bones two:
Forswering, yre, falsnesse, homicyde.
Now for the love of Cryst, that for us dyde,   370
Lete your othes, bothe grete and smale!
But sires, now wol I telle forth my tale.

  Thise ryotoures three, of whiche I telle,
Longe erst er pryme rong of any belle,
Were set hem in a taverne to drinke.   375
And, as they sat, they herde a belle clinke,
Biforn a cors was caried to his grave.
That oon of hem gan callen to his knave:
"Go bet," quod he, "and axe redily,
What cors is this that passeth here forby –   380
And looke that thou report his name wel!"
  "Sire," quod this boy, "it nedeth never a del.
It was me told, er ye cam here, two houres.
He was, pardee, an old felawe of youres,
And sodeynly he was y-slayn tonight,   385
Fordronke, as he sat on his bench upright.
There cam a pryvee theef men clepeth Deeth,
That in this contree al the peple sleeth –
And with his spere he smoot his herte atwo,
And went his way withouten wordes mo.   390
He hath a thousand slayn this pestilence.

368 'This fruit [these consequences] comes from the two cursed bones [dice].'
369 'Perjury, anger, treachery and murder.'
370 *dyde*, died.
371 *Lete*, give up.
372 *telle forth*, go on with.
373 *ryotoures*, gamblers, drunks, hooligans (c).
374 'Long before any bell rang for Prime (the service sung at 6 a.m.)' (c).
375 *Were set hem*, had settled down.
377 *Biforn a cors was caried*, in front of a corpse which was being carried (in procession).
378 'One of them called to his servant'. (On the meanings of 'knave' see (c) on *ST*, l. 115.)
379 ' "Off with you," he said, "and ask at once".'
380 *here forby*, by here.
381 *looke that*, see that.
382 *boy*, servant (probably) – see (c) on l. 58 of the *FT*.   *it nedeth never a del*, there's no need at all (for that).
383 'It was told me two hours before you came here.'
384 *pardee*, by God.   *felawe*, fellow, mate.
385 *sodeynly*, suddenly.   *y-slayn*, killed.
386 *Fordronke as he sat*, as he sat dead-drunk.
387 *pryvee*, sly (c).
388 'Who kills all the people in this country.'
389 *Smoot his herte atwo*, struck his heart in two.
390 'And went his way without another word.'
391 *this pestilence*, (during) this period of plague (c).

And, maister, er ye come in his presence,
Me thinketh that it were necessarie
For to be war of swich an adversarie.
Beth redy for to meete him evermoore –   395
Thus taughte me my dame; I say namoore."
    "By Seinte Marie!" sayde this taverner,
"The child saith sooth – for he hath slayn this yeer,
Henne over a myle, withinne a grete village,
Bothe man and womman, child, and hyne, and page!   400
I trowe his habitacioun be there.
To been avysed, grete wisdom it were,
Er that he dide a man a dishonour."
    "Ye, Goddes armes!" quod this ryotour,
"Is it swich peril with him for to meete?   405
I shal him seeke by way and eke by streete –
I make avow to Goddes digne bones!
Herkneth, felawes – we three been al ones;
Lat ech of us holde up his hand til other,
And ech of us becomen otheres brother,   410
And we wol sleen this false traytour Deeth;
He shal be slayn, he that so manye sleeth,
By Goddes dignitee, er it be night!"
    Togidres han thise three hire trouthes plight,
To live and dyen, ech of hem for other,   415
As though he were his owene y-bore brother.
And up they stirte, al dronken in this rage,

392 *in*, into.
393 'It seems to me that it would be necessary.'
394 *For to be war*, for (you) to be on your guard against.
395 *Beth*, be (plural imperative).   *for to*, to.   *evermoore*, always.
396 *Thus taughte me my dame*, so my mother taught me.
397 *taverner*, inn-keeper.
398 *saith sooth*, is speaking the truth.   *he* – i.e. Death.
399 *Henne over a myle*, over a mile from here.
400 *hyne and page*, servant and lad.
401 'I think his home is there.'
402–3 'It would be very wise to be cautious,/In case he caused you trouble.'
404 *Ye, Goddes armes*, What (lit.: 'yes'), by God's arms.
405 'Is it such a danger to meet him?'
406 'I shall seek him high and low (lit.: "through paths and streets").'
407 'I vow by God's holy (lit.: "worshipful") bones.'
408 *been al at ones*, are all together (in this business).
409 *holde up his hand til other*, raise his hand towards the other (as when an oath is taken in court today).
410 *otheres*, the other's.
411 *sleen*, kill ('slay').
413 *dignitee*, honour, worthiness.   *er it be night*, before night comes.
414 'These three have pledged their word to one another.'
416 *y-bore brother*, blood-brother (lit.: 'brother born').
417 *up they stirte*, up they leapt.

And forth they goon towardes that village,
Of which the taverner hadde spoke biforn.
And many a grisly ooth thanne han they sworn,   420
And Crystes blessed body they to-rente;
Deeth shal be deed, if that they may him hente!
    Whan they han goon nat fully half a myle,
Right as they wolde han troden over a style,
An old man and a povre with hem mette.   425
This olde man ful meekely hem grette,
And sayde thus, "Now, lordes, God yow see!"
    The proudest of thise ryotoures three
Answerde agayn, "What, carl, with sory grace!
Why artow al for-wrapped, save thy face?   430
Why livestow so longe in so grete age?"
    This olde man gan looke in his visage,
And sayde thus, "For I ne kan nat fynde
A man, though that I walked into Ynde,
Neither in citee, ne in no village,   435
That wolde chaunge his youthe for myn age.
And therfore moot I han myn age stille,
As long tyme as it is Goddes wille.
    "Ne Deeth, allas, ne wol nat han my lyf!
Thus walke I, lyk a restelees caityf,   440
And on the ground, which is my modres gate,
I knokke with my staf, bothe erly and late,
And saye, 'Leeve moder, leet me in!

420 *grisly ooth*, terrible oath.
421 *to-rente*, tore apart (see ll. 184–7 and the notes on them).
422 *if that they may him hente*, if they can catch him.
424 *wolde han troden*, were about to step.
425 *An old man and a povre*, an old man, and a poor one.
426 *hem grette*, greeted them.
427 *God yow see*, God protect you.
428 *thise*, these.
429 'Answered back, "Hey, you ruffian – bad luck to you!" '
430 *for-wrapped*, muffled up.   *save*, except for.
431 *livestow* (= 'livest thou'), do you live.
432 *in his visage*, into his (the young man's) face.
433 *For I kan nat*, because I cannot.
434 *though that*, even if.   *Ynde*, India (a larger part of the Middle and Far East in medieval usage).
436 *chaunge*, exchange.
437 *moot I han*, I must keep.
438 'For as long a time as God wishes.'
439 *Ne Deeth . . . ne wol*, nor will Death.   *han*, have, take.
440 *caityf*, wretch, outcast.
441 *modres*, mother's (c).
442 *bothe erly and late*, all day (lit.: 'both early and late').
443 *Leeve*, dear.

Lo how I vanissh – flessh, and blood and skin!
Allas! whan shal my bones been at reste?   445
Moder, with yow wolde I chaunge my cheste,
That in my chambre longe tyme hath be –
Ye, for an haire-cloute to wrappe me!'
But yet to me she wol nat do that grace,
For which ful pale and welked is my face.   450
    "But, sires, to yow it is no curteisye
To speken to an old man vileinye –
But he trespasse in word or elles in deede.
In hooly writ ye may yourself wel rede:
'Agayns an old man, hoor upon his heed,   455
Ye sholde aryse – ' wherfore I yive yow reed:
Ne dooth unto an old man noon harm now,
Namoore than that ye wolde men dide to yow
In age – if that ye so longe abyde.
And God be with yow wher ye go or ryde;   460
I moot go thider as I have to go."
    "Nay, olde cherl, by God, thou shalt nat so!"
Sayde this other ryotour anon,
"Thou partest nat so lightly, by Seint John!
Thou spak right now of thilke traitour Deeth,   465
That in this countree alle our freendes sleeth.
Have here my trouthe, as thou art his espye!
Telle where he is, or thou shalt it abye –
By God, and by the hooly sacrament!

444 *vanissh*, wither away.
446 *chaunge my cheste*, exchange my clothes chest (c).
447 *longe tyme hath be*, has been a long time.
448 'Yes, [just] for a hair-cloth (i.e. a shroud) to wrap myself in'.
449 *grace*, favour.
450 *welked*, withered, wrinkled.
451 'But, sirs, it is not courteous of you.'
452 *speken to . . . vileinye*, say insulting things to.
453 *But he trespasse*, unless he offends.
454 *hooly writ*, the Scriptures, the Bible.
455-6 ' "You should stand up (as a sign of respect) in front of an old man with white hair", (Leviticus, xix, 32) so I give you [this piece of] advice' (c).
457-9 'Do not do to an old man any more harm now than you would wish men to do to you in old age – if you should live so long' – see Ecclesiasticus, viii, 6.
460 *wher ye go or ryde*, whether you walk or ride.
461 *thider as*, where.
462 *shalt nat so*, shan't do that.
464 *partest nat so lightly*, won't get away so easily.
465 *right now*, just now.
466 See l. 388.
467 'You can take my word for it, you're his spy.'
468 *shalt it abye*, will suffer for it.

For soothly thou art oon of his assent,   470
To sleen us yonge folk, thou false theef!"
  "Now, sires," quod he, "if that yow be so leef
To fynde Deeth, turn up this croked way.
For in that grove I laft him, by my fay,
Under a tree, and there he wol abyde;   475
Nat for your boost he wol him nothing hyde.
See ye that ook? right there ye shal him fynde.
God save yow, that boughte agayn mankynde,
And yow amende!" thus sayde this olde man.
And everich of thise ryotoures ran,   480
Til they came to that tree, and there they founde,
Of florins fyne of gold, y-coined rounde,
Wel ny an eighte busshels, as hem thoughte.
No lenger thanne after Deeth they soughte –
But eche of hem so glad was of the sighte,   485
For that the florins been so faire and brighte,
That doun they sette hem by this precious hoord.
The worst of hem, he spak the firste word:
  "Bretheren," quod he, "take keep what I saye;
My wit is grete, though that I bourde and playe.   490
This tresor hath Fortune unto us yiven,
In mirthe and jolitee our lyf to liven.
And lightly as it cometh, so wol we spende.
Ey, Goddes precious dignitee! Who wende
To-day that we sholde han so fair a grace?   495
But mighte this gold be caried fro this place,
Hoom to myn hous, or elles unto youres,
(For wel ye woot that al this gold is oures) –

470 'For indeed, you're one of his accomplices.'
472 *if that yow be so leef*, if you're so eager.
473 *croked*, crooked, winding.   *way*, path.
474 *laft*, left.   *by my fay*, upon my word.
475 *abyde*, wait.
476 'He will not by any means hide on account of your boasting.'
478 *bought agayn*, redeemed.
479 *yow amende*, make you better.
480 *everich*, each one.
482–3 'Very nearly eight bushels of fine gold florins (c), in good round coins.'
485 *of the sighte*, at this sight.
486 *For*, because.
489 *take keep*, pay attention to.
490 'My intelligence ((c) on l. 38) is great, although I joke and play about.'
491–2 'Fortune has given us this treasure,/For us to live our lives in pleasure and enjoyment.'
493 'And we will spend it as easily as it has come.'
494 *Who wende*, who would have thought.
495 'That we should have such good luck today.'
496 *mighte this gold*, if this gold could.
498 *wel ye woot*, you know well.

Thanne were we in hye felicitee.
But trewely, by day it may nat be;   500
Men wolde sayn that we were theves stronge,
And for our owene tresor doon us honge!
This tresor moste y-caried be by nighte,
As wysely and as slyly as it mighte.
Wherefore I rede that cut among us alle   505
Be drawe, and lat see where the cut wol falle.
And he that hath the cut, with herte blythe,
Shal renne to the town, and that ful swythe,
And bringe us breed and wyn ful prively.
And two of us shul keepen subtilly   510
This tresor wel, and, if he wol nat tarie,
Whan it is night we wol this tresor carie,
By oon assent, where-as us thinketh best."
That oon of hem the cut broughte in his fest,
And bad hem drawe, and looke where it wol falle;   515
And it fil on the yongest of hem alle,
And forth toward the town he wente anon.
And, al-so soone as that he was gon,
That oon of hem spak thus unto that other:
"Thou knowest wel thou art my sworen brother;   520
Thy profit wol I telle thee anon.
Thou woost wel that our felawe is agon,
And here is gold, and that ful grete plentee,
That shal departed been among us three.
But, nathelees, if I kan shape it so   525

499 'Then we would be at the height of happiness.'
500 *may nat be*, cannot be (done).
501 *theves stronge*, flagrant thieves.
502 'And have us hanged for [stealing] our own treasure.'
503 *y-caried be*, be moved.
504 'As carefully and as quietly as can be.'
505-6 'So I propose that lots be drawn among us all, and let us see where the lot falls' (c).
507 'And he whom the lot falls upon, with a merry heart.'
508 *renne*, run.   *ful swythe*, very quickly.
509 *prively*, secretly.
510 *keepen*, guard.   *subtilly*, carefully.
511 *wol nat tarie*, does not linger.
513 'With one accord, to wherever seems best to us.'
514 *That oon of hem*, one of them.   *cut* (c).   *fest*, fist.
515 *bad hem drawe*, asked them to draw lots.   *it* – i.e. the lot.
518 *al-so soone as that*, just as soon as.
519 *That oon . . . that other*, one . . . the other.
521 'I'll tell you at once what's in your interest.'
522 *woost*, know (2nd person singular).   *is agoon*, has gone away.
523 *that ful grete plentee*, a great deal, at that.
524 *shal departed been*, is to be shared.
525 'But nevertheless, if I could arrange things so.'

That it departed were among us two –
Hadde I nat doon a freendes torn to thee?"
   That other answerde, "I noot how that may be;
He woot how that the gold is with us tweye.
What shal we doon? what shal we to him saye?"   530
   "Shal it be conseil?" sayde the firste shrewe,
"And I shal tellen, in a wordes fewe,
What we shal doon, and bringe it wel aboute."
   "I graunte," quod that other, "out of doute,
That, by my trouthe, I wol thee nat biwreye."   535
   "Now," quod the firste, "thou woost wel we be tweye,
And two of us shul strenger be than oon.
Looke whan that he is set, that right anon,
Arys, as though thou woldest with him playe –
And I shal ryve him thurgh the sydes tweye,   540
Whyl that thou strogelest with him as in game –
And with thy dagger looke thou do the same.
And thanne shal al this gold departed be,
My deere freend, bitwixe me and thee.
Thanne may we bothe our lustes al fulfille,   545
And playe at dees, right at our owene wille!"
And thus acorded been thise shrewes tweye
To sleen the thridde, as ye han herd me saye.
   This yongest, which that wente to the town,
Ful ofte in herte he rolleth up and doun   550
The beautee of thise florins newe and brighte.
"O Lord!" quod he, "if so were that I mighte
Have al this tresor to my self allone,

527 'Wouldn't I have done a good turn for you?'
528 *noot*, don't know.
529 'He knows that the gold is with us two.'
531 ' "Shall it be secret?" said the first villain.' (On the meanings of 'shrewe' see (c) on *ST*, l. 380.)
533 *bringe it wel aboute*, manage it well.
534 ' "I promise" said the other "certainly".'
535 'That I won't betray you, upon my word.'
537 *shul strenger be*, shall be stronger.
538-9 'Make sure that, once he has sat down, you get up straight away as if you wanted to wrestle (lit.: "play") with him.'
540 'And I shall stab him in both sides.'
541 *strogelest*, are wrestling.   *as*, as if.
542 *looke thou do the same*, make sure you do the same.
543 *departed be*, be shared.
545 *our lustes al fulfille*, fulfil all our desires (c).
546 *right at our owene wille*, just as much as we want to.
547 'And so these two villains have agreed.'
549 *which that wente*, who was going.
550 'Turns over very frequently in his mind.'
552 *if so were that I mighte*, if only it might happen that I could.

There is no man that liveth under the trone
Of God that sholde live so mery as I!"   555
And atte laste the Feend, our enemy,
Putte in his thought that he sholde poyson beye,
With which he mighte sleen his felawes tweye –
For-why the Feend fond him in swich livinge
That he hadde leve him to sorwe bringe.   560
For this was outrely his ful entente,
To sleen hem bothe, and never to repente.
And forth he gooth, no lenger wolde he tarie,
Into the town, unto a pothecarie,
And prayed him that he him wolde selle   565
Som poyson, that he mighte his rattes quelle.
And eke there was a polcat in his hawe,
That, as he sayde, hadde his capouns y-slawe,
And fayn he wolde wreke him, if he mighte,
On vermin that destroyed him by nighte.   570
    The pothecarie answerde, "And thou shalt have
A thing that, al-so God my soule save,
In al this world there is no creature,
That ete or dronke hath of this confiture
Nat but the montaunce of a corn of whete,   575
That he ne shal his lyf anon forlete.
Ye, sterve he shal, and that in lasse whyle
Than thou wolt goon a paas, nat but a myle,
The poysoun is so stronge and violent."
    This cursed man hath in his hand y-hent   580
This poysoun in a box, and sith he ran

---

554 *under the trone*, beneath the throne (i.e. subject to the power).
556 *the Feend*, the Devil ('fiend') (c).
557 'Put it into his mind that he should buy poison.'
559–60 'Because the Devil found him following such a way of life that he (the Devil) was given permission to bring him to grief.'
561 'For he was firmly and fully resolved' (*outrely* = 'utterly').
564 *a pothecarie*, an apothecary, a seller of drugs and medicines.
566 *that he mighte his rattes quelle*, so that he might kill his rats.
567 *hawe*, yard.
568 *hadde his capouns y-slawe*, had killed his capons.
569 'And he would gladly take revenge if he could.'
570 'On pests that harassed him by night.'
572 *al-so God my soule save*, as God may save my soul.
574 'Who has eaten or drunk just an amount equivalent to a grain of wheat from this concoction.'
576 'That will not at once lose his life.'
577–8 'Yes, he will die, and that in less time/Than you would take to go just a mile at walking pace' (c).
580 *y-hent*, grabbed.
581 *sith*, then.

Into the nexte streete, unto a man,
And borwed of him large botels three,
And in the two his poysoun poured he.
The thridde he kepte clene for his drinke –   585
For al the night he shoop him for to swinke,
In carying the gold out of that place.
And whan this ryotour, with sory grace,
Hadde filled with wyn his grete botels three,
To his felawes agayn repaireth he.   590
    What nedeth it to sermone of it moore?
For right as they hadde cast his deeth bifore,
Right so they han him slayn, and that anon.
And, whan that this was doon, thus spak that oon:
"Now lat us sitte, and drinke, and make us merye,   595
And afterward we wol his body berye."
And, with that word, it happed him *par cas*
To take the botel there the poysoun was,
And drank, and yaf his felawe drinke also –
For which anon they storven, bothe two.   600
    But, certes, I suppose that Avicen
Wroot never in no canon, ne in no fen,
Mo wonder signes of empoisoning
Than hadde thise wrecches two, er hire ending.
Thus ended been thise homicydes two,   605
And eke the false empoisoner also.
    O cursed sinne of alle cursednesse!
O traytours homicyde – O wikkednesse!
O glotonye, luxurie, and hasardrye!
Thou blasphemour of Cryst with vileinye   610

583 *of*, from.   *large botels three*, three large bottles.
585 *thridde*, third.   *clene*, clean, not poisoned.
586 *he shoop him for to swinke*, he meant to toil.
588 *with sory grace*, bad luck to him.
590 *repaireth he*, he returns.
591 'What need is there to preach about it any more?' (c).
592 'For just as they had previously plotted his death.'
594 *whan that*, when.
597-8 'And as he said that, he happened by chance/To take the bottle in which the poison was.'
600 'As the result of which they died at once, both of them.'
601 *certes*, certainly.   *Avicen*, Avicenna (c).
602 *canon*, textbook (i.e. the *Canon of Medicine*).   *fen* – a word for the chapters into which Avicenna's *Canon of Medicine* was divided.
603 '[About] stranger symptoms of poisoning.'
604 *er hire ending*, before their death.
605 *thise homicydes two*, these two murderers.
607 'O sin cursed above all sins.'
608 *traytours homicyde*, treacherous murder.
610-11 'You who blaspheme Christ with coarseness/And great oaths, through habit and pride.'

121

And othes grete, of usage and of pryde!
Allas, mankynde! – how may it bityde,
That to thy creatour, which that thee wroughte,
And with his precious herte-blood thee boughte,
Thou art so fals and so unkynde, allas?   615
   Now goode men, God foryive yow your trespas,
And ware yow fro the sinne of avaryce!
Myn hooly pardoun may yow alle waryce,
So that ye offre nobles or sterlinges,
Or elles silver brooches, spoones, ringes.   620
Boweth your heed under this hooly bulle!
Cometh up ye wyves! offreth of your wolle.
Your name I entre here in my rolle anon –
Into the blisse of hevene shul ye goon!
I yow assoille, by myn hye power   625
(Yow that wol offre), as clene and eke as cleer
As ye were born!
                – And lo, sires, thus I preche.
And Jesu Cryst, that is our soules leche,
So graunte yow his pardoun to receyve –
For that is best, I wol yow nat deceyve.   630
   But, sires – oo word forgat I in my tale.
I have relikes and pardoun in my male,
As faire as any man in Engelond,
Whiche were me yiven by the popes hond.
If any of yow wol, of devocioun,   635
Offren, and han myn absolucioun –
Com forth anon, and kneleth here adoun,

612 *how may it bityde*, how can it happen.
613 *which that thee wroughte*, who made you.
614 *thee boughte*, redeemed you.
615 *so fals and so unkynde*, so treacherous and unnatural.
617 *ware yow fro*, be on your guard against.
618 *may yow alle waryce*, can cure you all (of sin).
619 'Provided that you offer nobles (gold coins, worth one-third of a pound at the time) or silver pence.'
621 *Boweth* (plural imperative) *your heed*, bow your heads (in reverence).
622 *offreth of*, offer some of.
623 *rolle*, list ('roll') of names.
625-7 'I will absolve you through my sacred authority (you who will make a contribution), so that you will be as clean and also as pure as you were at birth! – And look, sirs, this is how I preach' (c).
628 *that is our soules leche*, who is the physician for our souls.
629 'May he allow you to receive *his* pardon.'
631 *oo word*, (just) one word.
632 *male*, bag. (Present day 'mail' is derived from this.)
634 *me yiven*, given to me.
635 *of devocioun*, out of devotion.
636 *han*, take.
637 *kneleth here adoun*, kneel down here.

And mekely receyveth my pardoun!
Or elles taketh pardoun as ye wende,
Al newe and fressh at every myles ende –   640
So that ye offren, alway newe and newe,
Nobles or pens, which that been goode and trewe.
It is an honour to everich that is here
That ye mowe have a suffisant pardoner,
T'assoille yow in contree as ye ryde,   645
For aventures whiche that may bityde.
Peraventure, there may falle oon or two
Down of his hors, and breke his nekke atwo.
Looke which a seuretee is it to yow alle
That I am in your felaweship y-falle,   650
That may assoille yow, bothe moore and lasse,
Whan that the soule shal fro the body passe!
I rede that our Hoost here shal biginne,
For he is moost envoluped in sinne!
Com forth, sire Hoost! and offre first anon,   655
And thou shalt kisse the relikes everichoon,
Ye, for a grote – unbokele anon thy purs!'
    'Nay, nay!' quod he, 'thanne have I Crystes curs!
Lat be!' quod he, 'it shal nat be, so theech!
Thou woldest make me kisse thyn olde breech,   660
And swere it were the relik of a seint –
Though it were with thy fundement depeint!
But, by the crois which that Seint Eleyne fond,

639 *as ye wende*, as you travel.
640 *at every myles ende*, at the end of every mile.
641 'Provided that you always offer, again and again.'
642 *which that been*, which are.   *trewe*, genuine.
643 *everich*, everyone.
644 'That you should have a competent pardoner.'
645 *in contree as ye ryde*, as you ride through the country.
646 'In case of accidents that may happen' (c).
647 *Peraventure*, perhaps.
648 *of* (here), from.   *atwo*, in two.
649 'Look what security it gives all of you.'
650 *in your felaweship y-falle*, fallen into your company.
651 *moore and lasse*, greater and lesser (in rank).
652 *Whan that*, when.
653 *I rede*, I propose.
654 'For he is the one most steeped in sin' (c).
656 *the relikes everichoon*, every one of the relics.
657 *unbokele*, unbuckle, undo.
658 *thanne have I Crystes curs*, Christ curse me if I do.
659 ' "Enough of that!" he said. "That won't happen, so help me!" '   (*theech*
is the contracted form of '*thee ich*', lit.: 'may I thrive').
660 *breech*, pair of breeches, trousers.
662 'Although it was stained by your anus.'
663 *Seint Eleyne*, St Helen (c).

I wolde I hadde thy coilons in myn hond,
In stede of relikes, or of seintuarie!   665
Lat kutte hem of! – I wol thee helpe hem carie.
They shul be shryned in an hogges toord!'
    This Pardoner answerde nat a word;
So wrooth he was, no word ne wolde he saye.
    'Now,' quod our Hoost, 'I wol no lenger playe   670
With thee, ne with noon other angry man.'
But right anon, the worthy Knight bigan,
Whan that he saugh that al the peple lough:
'Namoore of this, for it is right ynough!
Sire Pardoner, be glad and mery of cheere.   675
And ye, sire Hoost, that been to me so deere,
I pray yow that ye kisse the Pardoner.
And, Pardoner, I pray thee, drawe thee neer –
And, as we diden, lat us laughe and playe!'
Anon they kiste, and riden forth hire waye.   680

Here is ended the Pardoners Tale

664 'I wish I had your balls in my possession (lit.: "in my hand")' – i.e. as if they were relics.
665 *seintuarie*, holy things.
666–7 'Have them cut off! I'll help you to carry them – they shall be enshrined in a pig's turd!'
669 *wrooth*, angry.
670 *playe*, joke.
672 *bigan*, broke in, began to speak (c).
673 *lough*, were laughing.
674 *right ynough*, quite enough.
675 *mery of cheere*, cheerful.
676 *that been*, who are.
678 *drawe thee neer*, come closer (to the other pilgrims, from whom the Pardoner seems to have drawn away in a huff).
679 *as we diden*, as we did before.
680 *riden forth hire waye*, rode along on their way.

Commentary

Abbreviations and references

Lists of the books referred to more than once and the abbreviations used for them can be found on pp. vi and 45.

Line-references to *Tales* and *General Prologue* portraits, *other* than those printed in this volume, are preceded by the letters (A–I) which are given to each of the Fragments of the *Canterbury Tales* in the standard editions of Chaucer.

OED = *The Oxford English Dictionary* (13 vols. and Supplement) (Oxford, 1933).

GP   the *General Prologue* to the *Canterbury Tales*
FT   the *Friar's Tale*
ST   the *Summoner's Tale*
PT   the *Pardoner's Tale*

The Friar's Tale

1. *limitour*. Begging was the standard means by which the friars raised funds to maintain themselves and their convents, and this was one of the reasons for their unpopularity in some circles (see the Introduction, p. 4). The soft-soaping techniques used by this Friar are described in his portrait in the *General Prologue* to the *Canterbury Tales* (printed in this volume, pp. 49–51). The procedures of begging-friars are also satirically presented by the Friar's enemy, the Summoner, in his *Tale* (especially ll. 45–96).

4. *vileyns*. 'Villain' originally meant simply 'peasant' ('villein' in the feudal sense), and this meaning was still current in Chaucer's time. An insulting sense of 'oaf, churl' was also current, however, and the meaning of the word has since become progressively worse – the present day sense of 'evil-doer' being established by the early sixteenth century.

7–13. The Friar is probably referring here in particular to the discourse on nobility, etc., at the end of the Wife of Bath's *Tale* (D 1109–1216). The 'authorities' cited there include Dante, Seneca and Juvenal. Academic argument and preaching at this time laid heavy stress on the quoting of 'authorities' (usually Classical Latin writers, pagan and Christian philosophers, and theologians) – as the Friar points out in l. 13.

16–21. The summoner was the official who summoned people to appear before ecclesiastical courts. Fornication was one of the offences dealt with by such courts – for the others, see ll. 38–56. Such officials were – like bailiffs and debt-collectors – naturally unpopular, and attacks on them, of the kind mentioned by the Friar, seem to have been quite common.

22–5. The Host is clearly having a hard time keeping order between the Friar and Summoner – as is also the case in ll. 34–6 and 70–3, below, and at the end of the Wife of Bath's *Prologue* (ll. 22–5 of the extract in this volume).

38–52. The archdeacon was the assistant to the bishop in the administration of a diocese. In Chaucer's time he also presided over one of the ecclesiastical courts. The way in which he 'dide execucioun' upon offenders (l. 39) was through the imposition of penances. Penances were of various kinds – including, at one period, whipping for breach of promise ('contractes', l. 44) – but they tended in the course of time to become less severe and to take the form of money-payments (the 'pecunial peyne' referred to in l. 50).

Those hardened cases who resisted the archdeacon's authority and refused either to do penance or pay the fine, were liable to be forbidden to enter church, or, in the last resort, excommunicated. Excommunication was a threat to be taken seriously; it did not mean simply exclusion from the church and the sacraments. Excommunicated persons who remained disobedient for forty days or more could, at the request of the Church, be arrested and imprisoned indefinitely by the secular authorities. Chaucer ironically warns guilty men about this in ll. 38–40 of the pilgrim-Summoner's portrait (in this volume).

53–4. The bishop also presided over an ecclesiastical court, and there may be a suggestion here that some unlucky people were tried here as well as in the archdeacon's court, for the same offence. 'Hook' here ironically alludes to the bishop's crook, which symbolized his disciplinary powers.

57–62. This description of the summoner's underhand methods is similar to that in the *GP* portrait of the pilgrim-Summoner (especially ll. 41–2).

58. *Boy* originally meant simply 'serf' or 'servant', a meaning still current in Chaucer's time. An insulting sense of 'rascal', 'ruffian' had also developed, however (cf. 'vileyns' above, l. 4) – and this is the one that is present here. The word could also be used jokingly or affectionately in this sense – for example when the carter, later on in this tale (l. 299), calls his horse 'myn owene lyard boy' ('my old grey rascal'). The modern meaning of the word is not clearly current before the early fifteenth century. The nearest Chaucer comes to it is in l. 382 of *PT* (in this volume). The 'ryotoures'' 'boy', though, is both their servant *and* a child (l. 398) – so Chaucer may be using the word in both senses there.

63. 'Furious as a hare' seems a strange comparison. The word 'wood' here can, however, mean 'mad' in general, as well as

'furious'' – and it may be that the Friar is using it to express a contemptuous view of the Summoner's anger, which breaks out again in l. 68. The hare was, however, thought to be 'mad' when mating furiously in early spring (this is the origin of the modern phrase 'mad as a March hare'). So the Friar may also be using the comparison to hint at a similar kind of sexual madness in the Summoner, who has already been described as 'lecherous as a sparwe' (l. 4 of his *GP* portrait. It might, therefore, be possible to take the phrase as meaning: 'Although the Summoner were to be as angry as he is lecherous'. This comparison is the first of several drawn from the animal world and hunting in this tale (see the Introduction, p. 12).

64. *harlotrye*. 'Harlot' originally meant 'vagabond' or 'rogue' (of either sex). This sense remained in the language until the seventeenth century (according to the *OED*) – as in the description of the pilgrim-Summoner as a 'harlot' (l. 25 of his *GP* portrait). Other senses of the word also current in Chaucer's time were those of: 'professional entertainer' (male or female), 'lecher' (male or female), 'prostitute' (now most familiar from the Authorized Version of the Bible), and 'male servant' (in a rather contemptuous sense – as in l. 90 of *ST*).

The word 'harlotrye' in Chaucer has two main senses (*a*) (as here) 'evil conduct' generally, or 'sexual immorality' in particular; (*b*) 'buffoonery' or 'obscenity' (as in, e.g., the *Miller's Prologue*, A 3145).

68–73. The pattern of activity in these lines (interruption by the 'victim' of the tale and restoration of order by the Host) is repeated at a similar point in *ST* (ll. 97–9). This sort of outbreak doesn't occur elsewhere in the *Canterbury Tales*; the angry exchanges between Miller and Reeve, Pardoner and Host, for example, are confined to the prologues or endings of the tales concerned. The effect of the Summoner's and Friar's interruptions is therefore to reinforce the dramatic framework of their two tales.

The 'wommen of the styves' (l. 68) were the prostitutes, who were licensed to practise, without being prosecuted by the Church, within a certain area of a town – the 'styves' or 'stews'. This licence was withdrawn about the middle of the sixteenth century. The word 'stew' earlier meant 'stove' or 'heated room'; it then came to refer to such a room when used for a hot bath; then, because of the use of public baths by prostitutes for meetings with their customers, it came to mean 'brothel'. Finally 'the stews' came to be used as a general term for the 'red light district' of a town.

74–80. The Friar now takes up the tale again with obvious relish. He has already said (in ll. 61–2) that his summoner spares a few lechers in order to get his hands on a much larger number. He here goes on to show him actually involved in the prostitution business – through his use of procuresses as informers and as members of his 'espiaille' (the body of spies that has been referred to in l. 59). A few lines further on (ll. 90–4) he adds that the summoner is himself a procurer, and that he gets his information directly from the prostitutes he employs.

75–6. The 'lure' is a bunch of feathers on a thong in which a hawk's meat is placed when it is being trained. The falconer is thus later able to recall the hawk when in flight by showing it the lure.

85. The acceptance by this summoner of bribes in the form of entertainment at the alehouse recalls – as it is probably meant to do – the habitual drunkenness of the pilgrim-Summoner, as described in his portrait (ll. 13–16). The pilgrim-Summoner is also said in *GP* to be willing to allow a 'companion' to keep a mistress for a year without interference, in return for a quart of wine (ll. 27–9 of the portrait).

86–7. According to John, xii, 6, Judas kept the purse for Christ and the Apostles. Several medieval legends relate this to his betrayal of Christ – for example, the dramatic and impressive thirteenth-century ballad of Judas (No. 18 in R. T. Davies's anthology, *Medieval English Lyrics*).

88. It seems from this that the summoner embezzled the funds, or exacted double the fines – perhaps both.

92. 'Sir' was a title for priests as well as knights in medieval England.

The indirect accusation of lechery here may have been slipped in by the Friar as a gibe against the parish priests, who were his professional rivals for the attention (and the money) of the ordinary people. Priests, like friars and monks, were frequently attacked on these grounds by the satirists and reformers of the time.

96–102. Besides searching out offenders and delivering the summons to them, the summoner was also obliged to bring them to court. At the court itself he acted as a kind of usher, maintaining order while it was in session, and taking charge of the witnesses. There seem to have been opportunities for summoners to take bribes even when doing this part of their job, since a Council of the Church at London in 1342 had to decree that they should not receive gifts in any form from people in court.

In the kind of case that the Friar mentions, it would probably have been very necessary for the summoner to extract a bribe at this stage. For, if the proceedings went any further, he would run the risk of losing the 'customer', or even of having his forgery (of the 'summons') discovered.

The summoner's offer to the man to strike the girl's name out of 'our black books' is ironic in these circumstances. Since the summons is forged, her name cannot have been entered on the court records anyway – unless, of course, the summoner has falsified these as well.

113. The word 'ribybe' (a kind of stringed instrument) is here used jokingly to mean 'old woman'. Later on in this tale (l. 309) the summoner speaks contemptuously of the old woman in question as a 'rebekke' – another word meaning 'fiddle'. It has been suggested that the words came to be used of old women because of the squeaky sound made by such fiddles. Skeat also suggests that the joke involves 'a pun upon "rebekke", a fiddle, and "Rebekke", a married woman, from the mention of Rebecca in the marriage service' (as in the *Merchant's Tale*, E 1703–5). Both ideas may be present here.

116. A 'yeoman' was originally an attendant or retainer to a knight or lord (the term being a compound of the words 'yeong' ('young') and 'man'). This is the meaning here and in *GP* (A 101–17). In Chaucer's time the word was also coming to be applied to members of this class who had become small landowners. This 'middle-class' meaning survived into the twentieth century in such military and archaic usages as: 'yeomanry' and 'yeoman stock'.

116–19. The appearance of the devil as a huntsman follows appropriately on the number of metaphors from hunting and animal-life that have been used in connexion with the summoner (see Introduction, p. 12). His green clothing has been thought to be symbolic of his devilry in some respects – but it could just imply that he is as well equipped with camouflage as he is with weapons (l. 117). This description could be compared with that of the Yeoman attending the Knight in *GP* (A 101–17). Both characters are shown to be well equipped for their different types of 'hunting'. In the case of the yeoman-devil there may be a sinister touch in the reference to the 'black borders' on his hat.

121. The word 'felawe' could be used in both a friendly and a contemptuous way in Chaucer's time – as it can be now. The phrase 'good felawe' describes both the summoner in this tale and the pilgrim-Summoner in the *GP* (l. 26 of his portrait). In both cases the friendly meaning of the word ('companion', 'mate') seems to be used ironically as a thin covering for the contemptuous one.

122. The yeoman-devil addresses the summoner from the start in the familiar second person *singular* ('thou') form. He twice slips into the second person *plural* form (in ll. 135 and 303), but this doesn't seem to have any special significance. The 'thou' form (as well as being the one used between close friends or members of a family) was commonly used to a junior or inferior – by a father to his child, for example, or by a master to a servant. The devil may, therefore, be 'speaking down to' the summoner in this way. As a yeoman (even if a bogus one) he would be socially a bit above the summoner, and in his own right he is without doubt intellectually superior to his companion, as he implies in ll. 216–17.

The summoner, on the other hand, begins by using the respectful second person plural form (in ll. 146, 147, 153, etc.). He proceeds to the familiar 'thou' form, when asking his 'leeve brother' for his name, in l. 180 – but then (perhaps as a sympton of his shock at hearing that his companion is a devil) returns to the 'ye' form from l. 192. Then (perhaps to show that his confidence is returning) he starts to use the 'thou' form again in l. 262, where he declares to his companion that he will keep his pledge, 'though thou were the devel Sathanas.' He continues to use this form from here to the end.

143–4. This simile in its simplest terms means just that the summoner was as full of chatter as shrikes are of 'venomousness'. The behaviour of the red-backed shrike is described as follows in the *Oxford Book of Birds*: 'As well as large insects, the shrike takes lizards, young birds and small mammals, sometimes sticking them on thorns in the shrike's "larder", from which habit he has been called the butcher-bird.' According to the late twelfth-century writer, Giraldus Cambrensis, such thorns were afterwards thought to be poisonous.

So 'venim' here seems to refer to both the aggression and the supposed poisonousness of the shrike. Through using such a comparison the Friar probably also means to suggest that the summoner is like a shrike in other ways too – especially, perhaps, in the viciousness with which he preys on his fellow-creatures.

149. The devil says that he comes from 'far in the north', perhaps because he thinks that this part of the country will be unfamiliar to the summoner. But he may also be referring indirectly and ironically to his true home – since there was a belief, found both in pagan Germanic myth and in Biblical tradition (e.g., Isaiah, xiv, 13–14) that Hell was situated in the north. Both Shakespeare and Milton – drawing on the Biblical tradition – refer to Satan as ruling in the north (*I Henry VI*, V, iii, 6 and *Paradise Lost*, V, 755–60).

162–9. Here again (see l. 149) the devil may be telling something of the truth in an indirect and ironic way – as well as leading the summoner on to reveal something of his own attitude to his work (as he does in ll. 170–9). In fact it was believed that some of the devils sent, like this one, to work in the world were given a hard time by Satan. A fifteenth-century writer tells the following story about the activities of one of them – a well-known devil, by the name of Tutivillus:

We read of a holy Abbot of the order of Citeaux that while he stood in the choir at matins he saw a fiend that had a long and great poke [pouch] hanging about his neck and went about the choir from one to another and waited busily after all letters and syllables and words and failings that any made; and them he gathered diligently and put them in his poke. . . .

When the Abbot questions him about his job, Tutivillus replies:

'I must each day bring my master a thousand pokes full of failings and negligences and syllables and words that are done in your order in reading and singing, and else I must be sore beaten'.

(quoted by Eileen Power, in *Medieval People*, p. 70)

163. The word 'danger' (ult. fr. Lat. *dominationem*, through OF) in Chaucer's time had three main meanings: those of 'power', 'liability', and (in love-poetry, etc.) 'standoffishness' in the woman (her power over the lover). The modern meanings of 'risk' or 'peril' did not become current until the late fifteenth century (out of the sense of 'liability'). 'Dangerous' in Chaucer's time generally meant 'hard to please', as here. The modern senses of the adjective developed at about the same time as those of the noun (see above).

195–209. The summoner's questions and the devil's replies here (together with the lecture that is given in ll. 218–48) reflect the workings of the popular imagination on the subject of devils. Owst (p. 112) quotes a number of opinions about their appearance and activities, from writers roughly contemporary with Chaucer:

They ... 'flye above in the eyer [air] as thyke as motis [specks of dust] in the sonne', dropping 'unclene maters' from the sky, leaving storm and ruin in their path, transforming themselves into a dozen shapes in as many different situations, now a swine, now a dog, now an ape, now a black horse, now a spider, now a fair damsel, now some innocent-looking parish clerk, manorial servant, or even well-known neighbour: now perched on a lettuce-leaf, now riding on a rich lady's train or a 'nightmare', now haunting the chambers of the dying, now 'sittyng in the stockis' [the stocks], now presiding at the altar – *'in habitu pontificali'* [in priest's robes], or escaping in confusion from the church door.

203. 'Jogelour' probably means 'magician' – particularly one who entertained people with illusions and conjuring-tricks. The word (like the French *jongleur*) originally meant simply 'entertainer', 'minstrel' or 'jester'. It then came to be applied (as here) especially to those who performed with the aid of magic or witchcraft. The modern word 'juggler' has further altered in meaning, and refers of course to sleight of hand, rather than reliance on magic. The kinds of trick performed by the magician-'jogelour' (sometimes called a *tregetour* by Chaucer) are further described in the *Franklin's Tale* (F 1139–51).

210–17. By addressing his companion as 'leeve sire somnour', the devil shows that he has seen through his disguise. The summoner, however, doesn't seem to notice this immediately, since in l. 260 he is still insisting on being thought of as 'a yeman, knowen is ful wide'.

218–36. The devil's words here contain some ominous pointers to the summoner's own situation – though the summoner typically remains unaware of them (see the Introduction, p. 13).

237–9. Several saints are said to have had tame devils to do jobs for them. This was seen as an extension of God's power over devils, which has already been referred to in ll. 219–24, and which is said to have been exercised by Christ's disciples (Luke, x, 17). As l. 238 suggests, St Dunstan (A.D. 924–88), the Anglo-Saxon archbishop, also had a reputation for putting devils to work for him; the 'Lay of St Dunstan', in R. H. Barham's *Ingoldsby Legends*, seems to be based on this tradition. The 'Apostles' whom the devil says he has served might have included St Paul (see Acts, xix, 11–17), and St James and St Bartholomew, about whom there are similar medieval legends.

243–8. According to Skeat, ' "Phitonissa" . . . is another spelling of "pythonissa", which is the word used, in the Vulgate (Latin) version of 1 Chronicles, x, 13, with reference to the Witch of Endor'. The word is related to the Greek-derived 'python', which was originally the name of the huge mythical serpent killed by Apollo (hence the commonest modern meaning). 'Python', however, *also* came to mean 'familiar spirit', or, later, someone possessed by a spirit – and 'Phitonissa' (or 'pythoness') is the feminine form of this word which was frequently used, in Chaucer's time and after, to describe the Witch of Endor.

The episode referred to here is the calling up of the dead Samuel to speak to Saul before his final battle with the Philistines (1 Samuel, xxviii). As Robinson points out, there was at this time 'a common theory [that] the spirit of Samuel was not raised, but [that] he was personated by the Devil' – which the devil seems to dismiss in ll. 247–8.

249–54. Here the devil gives the summoner an even stronger warning than that in ll. 218–36, though he expresses it humorously in terms drawn from the academic language of the time. He tells his companion that he will shortly be qualified by first-hand knowledge to lecture about Hell as an authority on the subject.

A lecture at a medieval university usually took the form of a reading (Latin, *lectura*) of the text being studied – followed by a commentary upon it. It was necessary for the text to be read aloud first, since books were expensive, and students would often have taken the opportunity of copying down as much as they could during the lecture. To 'read' (l. 254) eventually came to mean delivering both parts of a lecture (the basic reading aloud and the commentary) – and this is the meaning here.

The chair (l. 254) from which the medieval lecturer addressed his students came to be regarded as a symbol of his authority. Hence, in modern English, a professor's post is usually spoken of as a 'chair'.

The original meaning of the word 'sentence' (l. 254) was that of 'opinion' of any kind. The academic meaning of the word in

Chaucer's time was that of 'learned opinion'. The devil seems to be using it here to refer humorously to his own version of Christian doctrine concerning devils and Hell (ll. 197–248) – and to reinforce his genially sinister promise to provide the summoner with the experience necessary to become qualified in this.

255–6. Both Vergil and Dante were commonly believed at this time to have actually been down to Hell, and seen for themselves what they subsequently described in their poetry. This, it was thought, could be the only explanation for the precise knowledge of the layout of Hell that is shown in Vergil's *Aeneid*, Book VI, and in Dante's *Inferno*.

289. Robinson points out that 'such appearances of the Devil to seize what has been assigned to him are not uncommon' in folk stories and ballads (see Introduction, p. 17).

300. St Eligius ('Sëint Loy') was the patron saint of carters, so it seems right for the carter to call upon him to bless the horses here. He was also well-known for his beauty and courtesy, and this is probably why Chaucer's Prioress is said to use his name for her 'greatest oath' (*GP*, A 120). This may also be in the carter's mind when he asks him to bless the horses, and may help to emphasize his change of mood towards them since l. 283, where he has angrily given them over to the Devil.

306. The devil here is making a rather heavy joke which depends on the audience knowing something about the day-to-day workings of the feudal system. 'Carriage' was the term for a lord's right to use his tenants' horses and carts. (It also came to mean the sum of money that the tenants often preferred to pay instead of providing this service.) The devil is thus saying that he won't gain anything by making this kind of claim, since – as he has explained in ll. 292 and 304 – he has no rights in the matter. It is not a very funny joke, but it is appropriate, at least, to a devil who has earlier on in the story disguised himself as a bailiff.

309. For the meaning of 'rebekke' see the note on l. 113.

312. Twelve pence in Chaucer's time was quite a large sum of money. It would have been thought a good wage for a skilled workman to earn for three days' labour. Hence the old woman's shocked reaction to the summoner's demand when it's actually made (ll. 340–3).

313. The summoner here at last gives up the pretence of being a yeoman and a bailiff which he was still trying to preserve in l. 260. The devil, of course, has shown as early as l. 210 that he has seen through the disguise – but it seems that this has taken a long time to sink in, or that the summoner has actually forgotten about his disguise altogether. Either way, the devil's low opinion of the summoner's intelligence (see ll. 216–17) would be further justified here.

319. This sort of accusation fits in with what we have been told about the summoner's spying methods earlier on (e.g. in ll. 91–110). The inclusion of friars in it is ironic if we remember who is telling the tale. It also recalls Chaucer's other ironic remarks about the friars' methods of working and their reputation for lechery (for example, in the *GP* portrait of the Friar, at the opening of the *Wife of Bath's Tale* and throughout *ST*).

351–3. Adultery was one of the offences dealt with by the Archdeacon's court (see l. 42), and the summoner is here accusing the old woman not only of being guilty of this, but also of having got him to pay the fine for her.

374. Here the devil takes up again the humorously academic tone that he has adopted in ll. 251–4. He now promises the summoner actual 'qualifications' in the knowledge of Hell – in addition to the first-hand 'experience' that he has pointed forward to in l. 253.

383. The 'words of Christ' about Hell are most likely those which describe 'outer darkness', or 'a furnace of fire', and 'weeping and gnashing of teeth' (e.g. in Matthew, viii, 12; xiii, 42; and xxii, 13). The 'text of Paul' is probably the apocryphal *Vision of St Paul*, which describes how the saint was granted a view of the torments of Hell. The 'text of John' is probably Revelation – especially xix and xx.

393–4. The text that the Friar uses to drive home his moral is Psalm x, verse 9. The psalm does not identify the lion with the Devil, but Chaucer may also have in mind here a text which does – i.e. the description of the Devil as 'a roaring lion', who 'walketh about, seeking whom he may devour' in I Peter, v, 8.

398. Christ is frequently represented as a knight in medieval literature – especially in poems on the Crucifixion. See especially the opening of Passus XVIII of *Piers Plowman* (pp. 255–6 of the Penguin translation).

399–400. Compare with this the Friar's prayer for summoners in general, at the end of his actual narrative (ll. 379–80). Here, on the other hand, his prayer for the pilgrim-Summoner in particular ends the whole *Tale* on an appropriate note of personal vindictiveness, which is all the sharper for being so piously expressed. This helps to prepare dramatically for the outbreak of the Summoner's rage, which follows immediately in the *Prologue* to the next *Tale*.

The Summoner's Tale

8. The Summoner is referring here to the Friar's few pious words about Hell at the end of his *Tale* (ll. 381–8, in this volume).

10. This insult is typical of the propaganda against friars (see p. 5 of the Introduction). One of their chief opponents in the mid-thirteenth century – a teacher at the University of Paris, called Guillaume de St Amour – attacked them in a similar way. He claimed that they were the false apostles who, according to St Paul, would be sent by Antichrist to deceive men shortly before the Day of Judgment (2 Timothy, iii, 1–9).

11–13. In spite of the Summoner's claim that this is a well-known story, no parallel form of it has yet been unearthed. Visions of Hell and its torments, though, were common in medieval legend and imaginative literature – Dante's *Inferno* being the best example. Such visions were supposed to have been granted to saints and (as a grim warning) to sinners – see, for example, the stories of St Fursey and various other people in Bede's *History* (Penguin translation, pp. 167–71 and 284–93). It was also believed that during such visions the soul was actually absent from the body, as ll. 12–13 here suggest.

22. Satan is often described as being fixed in the lowest part of Hell (see, for example, Dante's *Inferno*, XXXIV, 28 ff.).

28. If Chaucer's own estimate of walking speed as 3 m.p.h. is taken as a strict standard (*Treatise on the Astrolabe*, part I, par. 16) – then 'half a furlong way of space' would be equivalent to $1\frac{1}{4}$ minutes. But we're probably not expected to work out the 'muzzle velocity' of 20,000 friars in such precise detail; this kind of arithmetical problem isn't considered until the end of the Tale.

37. This meaning of the word 'sorry' (= 'wretched') is not found very often today, except in some slightly archaic expressions like 'a sorry sight'.

42. In the expression 'of verray kynde', the word 'kynde' has the sense of 'nature' or 'natural character' which is often found in Chaucer and has been obsolete since about Shakespeare's time. The modern noun 'kind' (meaning 'group' or 'sort') is broadly related to it through the sense of 'kind' as 'natural group' or 'species' – as in the 1611 version of the Bible, Genesis, vi, 20: 'Of fowls after their kind', etc. On the relationship between the words 'Nature' and 'Kind' and the development of their meanings, see ch. 2 of *Studies in Words* by C. S. Lewis.

43. Compare with this the Friar's pious hopes that the summoners may become good men (*FT*, l. 380) and that this particular Summoner may repent before the Devil takes him. (*FT*, ll. 399–400).

45–6. It is not clear why Chaucer chose this part of the country

135

(the south-eastern corner of Yorkshire) as a setting for the story. It has been suggested that he knew several of the important families there, and that this influenced his choice – but such theories have little to do with the work as we have it. In any case, there does not seem to be anything especially Northern in the rest of the story, and such unexplained detail often seems to be used by Chaucer in order to give an impression of actuality as also in l. 118 of this Tale.

48. The friars had a great reputation as preachers and critics of society at this time (see Introduction, p. 3), though this particular friar's preaching seems to have degenerated into mere sales-promotion.

53. On 'trentals' see the note on ll. 60–7.

54. Money for buildings is again the object of the friar's appeals to Thomas later in this tale (ll. 313–16 and 435–42). The eagerness of the friars to build impressive churches is also satirized by Langland in *Piers Plowman* (Penguin translation, pp. 84–5), when he shows a friar offering salvation in return for a contribution to the building-fund.

56–9. The friar evidently sees the monks (the 'possessioners') as competitors for funds and endowments, just as in ll. 62–4 he sees the parish-priests as competitors for 'trentals'. He attacks the 'possessioners' more viciously and at greater length later on in the Tale (see ll. 260–70 and note).

60–7. A 'trental' was a sequence of thirty masses (Medieval Lat. *trentale* – from Lat. *triginta*, thirty). They were paid for in order to speed up the progress of a friend or relative through Purgatory to Paradise. Although the commercialization of this activity by clerics like Friar John attracted the attention of satirists and reformers, it was still strongly believed that prayer of any kind could help a soul towards Heaven. Some of the souls that Dante meets in Purgatory are particularly anxious about this (see *Purgatorio*, VI, ll. 1–48).

The trentals were usually delivered at the rate of one mass a day for thirty days. The friar however claims that they should be 'hastily y-songe' in order to be effective. According to Skeat, 'the friars used occasionally to sing all the thirty masses in one day, and so save a soul from twenty-nine days of purgatory'.

Through the remarks he makes about the productivity of priests in ll. 62–4 the friar seems to be trying to outbid possible competition for trentals-business. This is the first of several scornful asides with which he tries to undermine the relationship between the parsons and their parishioners. The others are in ll. 152–4 and 344–5. (On the enmity between friars and parish-priests see Introduction).

Friar John's description of flesh-hooks and burning makes the penances of Purgatory sound more like the torments of Hell. But some medieval accounts of Purgatory do include one or both of these details (e.g. Dante's *Purgatorio*, XXV, 109f. and XXVII, 49f.), and it is in the friar's interests to make the penances sound as gruesome as possible, in order to ensure a quicker sale of the trentals.

73–4. It's ironic that Christ's instructions to his apostles (Matthew, x, 5–42 and Luke, ix, 3–5 and x, 1–12), which formed the basis of the friars' ideals and written rules, forbade them to take either a bag or a staff with them on their journey. In Luke, x, 7, Christ also adds: 'Go not from house to house'.

75–89. The Rule of St Francis (see the Pelican *Documentary History of England* vol. 1, pp. 114–29) encourages friars to 'go forth confidently to seek alms, nor be ashamed to do so, since Our Lord made himself poor for us in this world'. Also, in return for any work done, they could receive 'bodily necessities for themselves and their brothers'. But St Francis would definitely not have approved of the kind of bargain (prayers in return for provender and cash) that Friar John is trying to drive here. In any case, the taking of 'A Goddes halfpenny or a masse-peny' was strictly forbidden by section 4 of the Rule – though this article must often have been ignored in between St Francis's time and Chaucer's.

90. Friars were meant to go begging in pairs – possibly to prevent either of them from falsifying the returns. But they were not supposed to take a third person with them – especially not for the purpose mentioned here.

On the meanings of 'harlot' see the note on l. 64 of *FT*.

97–9. See the note on ll. 68–73 of *FT*.

106–10. The Rule of St Francis (section 3 – see the note on ll. 75–89) says of travelling friars that 'Whenever they enter a house, their first words shall be: "Peace upon this house", and, as it is written in the Holy Gospel (Luke, x, 5–8), they may then eat of any dish that is set before them.' Friar John's behaviour on entering Thomas's house is a characteristic distortion of this. His blessing and good wishes are followed up by a heavy hint that another 'mery meel' would not come amiss.

114. *was go walked*. The past participle (rather than the present) is often used with the verb 'to go' in Middle English. Another example is 'goon a-blakeberied', in l. 118 of the *PT*.

115. 'Knave', like 'boy' and 'harlot' (see the Commentary on ll. 58 and 64 of the *FT*) is a word that has lost several meanings since Chaucer's time. At first it meant simply 'boy' – until about the end of the fifteenth century (according to the *OED*). The further meaning of 'servant' – which is the one here – didn't become obsolete until the seventeenth century. The main modern meaning, of 'rogue', has been current since the thirteenth century.

118. The reason or reasons for Chaucer's choice of March as the time for the story don't seem to be much clearer than those for

his choice of Holderness as the place (see the Commentary on ll. 45–6). It could be that he wanted to suggest a time when 'madness' (in the sense of practical jokes, etc.) might be expected – or that he was used to making spring a time for action in his tales (as in *Troilus and Criseyde*, the *Knight's Tale* and the Canterbury pilgrimage itself – see ll. A 1–18 of *GP*). But there is no further mention of March or suggestion of spring in the rest of the Tale.

125. *simple wit*. Both of these words have changed a great deal in meaning since Chaucer's time. In *Studies in Words* C. S. Lewis traces the development of each in full (chs. 4 and 7). 'Simple' is (paradoxically) a very complex word in this context – since it seems to cover the meanings of 'unlearned', 'sincere', and 'humble', all of which are referred to by Lewis. 'Wit' here has the general meaning of 'intelligence' – a meaning which survives today only in compound-words like 'quick-witted', and in phrases like 'to have the wit (to do something)'.

126–30. The technique of preaching that the friar describes here seems to be far from 'simple'. The 'glosing' that he refers to in l. 129 could be a very complicated as well as 'glorious' business. Theologians had realized early on that the Bible (especially the Old Testament) could not always be taken literally, and often had to be interpreted metaphorically – that is, according to the 'spirit' rather than the 'letter'. In doing so they took as their motto a quotation from the Bible itself: 'the letter killeth, but the spirit giveth life' (2 Corinthians, iii, 6) – which the friar refers to in l. 130. However, this approach to the Bible, which began as a genuine attempt to make sense of obscure or contradictory passages, had by Chaucer's time developed into something of a critical industry, which could provide charlatans like Friar John with glib excuses for their own sins of omission or commission. Awareness of this perversion of learning caused the reformers of Chaucer's time (especially the Lollards) to lay stress on the literal truth of the Bible, though they in turn tended to go to extremes in this direction. The greatest of them, John Wyclif, attacked the 'glosers' with the following arguments (translated from Owst, p. 62): 'Bastard theologians say . . . that these words of Christ are false, and so no words of Christ are binding except through the understanding [the original has 'witt'] of them that the "glosers" give. But here we say to these renegades that they blabber thus through lack of understanding.'

138–45. Although kissing at this time was quite a usual form of greeting between friends (see the description of the reconciliation between Host and Pardoner in ll. 675–80 of the *Pardoner's Tale*), this kind of behaviour by a cleric would still have been thought rather suspicious. The description of the friar chirping 'like a sparrow' as he kisses Thomas's wife (ll. 140–1) is even more suggestive. Birds, especially the dove and sparrow, were often associated with Venus, the goddess of love, and it is worth remembering here that Chaucer also uses the expression 'lecherous as a sparrow' to describe the Summoner (l. 4 of his *GP* portrait).

153. *grope.* This religious meaning of the word has been obsolete since the late seventeenth century (according to the *OED*). The modern (physical) meaning was also current in Chaucer's time – and it may be part of the joke against the friar that the word is used in *this* sense to describe his activities later on (in ll. 477 and 484). The use of this vivid verb to express *both* the professed spiritual methods and the real material aims of the friar thus helps to highlight his hypocrisy.

156–7. These lines illustrate how the friar, using the technique described in ll. 126–30, twists Biblical texts in order to justify his activities in general and fit in with his immediate commercial purposes. The metaphor in l. 156 is clearly based on Matthew, iv, 19 ('I will make you fishers of men'), whilst the one in l. 157 could be a distorted echo of Matthew, xxii, 21 ('Render . . . unto Caesar the things which are Caesar's; and unto God the things that are God's').

168, 174. The friar's use of French phrases when speaking to Thomas and his wife shows that he has social pretensions as well as commercial aims, and that he likes to appear 'genteel' in front of the churls. The kind of French that had been brought over by the Norman conquerors as the standard language of the upper and educated classes was in Chaucer's time being replaced by English, even at Court. Nevertheless for a long time afterwards the use of French in some form or another was regarded as a mark of social or educational superiority. Characters who, like Friar John, lard their conversation with French words or phrases for this purpose are common enough in literature and life up to the present day.

The pilgrim-Friar also seems to be concerned to make a good impression through his manner of speaking. In the *GP* it is said that he cultivates his lisp, in order to 'make his English sweete upon his tonge' (l. 58 of his portrait) – and thus presumably to make a better impression on his 'clients', especially the female ones.

170. *defend.* This meaning of the word (= 'forbid') has been obsolete since the late seventeenth century (according to the *OED*). The modern meaning of 'protect' was, however, also current in Chaucer's time, and is frequently evident in his poetry (e.g. in l. 933 of the *Man of Law's Tale*). The related verb in French (*défendre*) still has both meanings.

196–8. According to Skeat, friars 'having served fifty years in the convent . . . obtained certain privileges, one of which was to go about alone'. Friars normally went begging in pairs (see the note on l. 90). To 'walk alone' seems to be a very attractive prospect for the friar; he refers to it in a pious awestruck tone, similar to that in which he describes the child being 'born to blisse'. The advantage from his point of view is probably that it would allow him greater scope for salesmanship of the kind he practises here.

205–20. According to W. Curry – in ch. 8 of *Chaucer and the Medieval Sciences* (pp. 215–17) – it was thought at this time that abstinence and plain living were necessary before a man could receive celestial visions – so the friar's general argument here is all right. But, as Professor Curry says, 'in this particular case one cannot forget the pig's head and the capon's liver'.

213–37. Catalogues of brief illustrative examples or *exempla* (Lat.) like this (usually drawn from the Bible or the classics) formed the stock-in-trade of medieval moralists. Preachers (including bogus ones like Friar John and the Pardoner) were expected to have them at their fingertips.

224. *womb*. This meaning of the word (= 'stomach') has been obsolete since about the middle of the eighteenth century. It is also used (again in the process of an attack on gluttony) in ll. 234, 245 and 246 of the *PT*. The modern meaning, of 'uterus', is not clearly distinguished in Middle English usage from that of 'woman's belly' in general.

238–9. This is another of the friar's satirical stabs at the parish-priests or the monks (see the notes on ll. 60–7 and 260–70).

242. 'Sely' in Chaucer's time had the following main meanings (according to the *OED*): 1. 'happy', 2. 'blessed', 3. 'pious, holy, good', 4. 'innocent, harmless', 5. 'pitiable', and 6. 'insignificant, feeble'. Friar John characteristically seems to want his audience to apply all of the first four meanings to 'sely freres' here – but when describing Thomas's wife later as 'this sely innocent' (l. 319) he probably intends only the meanings of 'harmless' or perhaps 'good'.

The word is related to the modern adjective 'silly', which began to be used (though not with its modern meaning) in the fifteenth century. By the early sixteenth century 'silly' had come to mean 'pitiable'. During the course of the sixteenth century it also gained the present-day meaning of 'foolish'.

251–3. Although Gluttony is presented here as the original sin committed by Adam, it was not thought to be the worst. Pride (the sin of Lucifer) was generally held to be the most serious of the Seven Deadly Sins – and the others (Envy, Anger, Sloth, Covetousness, Gluttony and Lechery) were said to derive from it. Nevertheless, preachers like Friar John and the Pardoner (ll. 210–23 of his Tale) emphasized the seriousness of Gluttony by pointing out that it was the sin that 'our forefather Adam' committed by eating the forbidden apple, and was thus the immediate cause of Man's being driven out of Paradise. Here – as also in ll. 210–23 of *PT*, and in the *Parson's Tale*, I 818 – Chaucer's source for the idea is a quotation from the works of St Jerome (fourth century A.D.): 'As long as Adam fasted he was in Paradise; he ate, and was thrown out.'

In ll. 252–3 there may be a pun on the words 'chaced' and 'chaste'. It doesn't seem though to have much significance as a way of developing the friar's argument, and l. 253 seems to be there solely for the sake of the pun itself. On the other hand, this kind of irrelevant playing with words could well illustrate the perversity of Friar John's 'glosing' method. Puns generally are not very common in Chaucer, though there are one or two bawdy ones in this tale (see the notes on ll. 303–5 and 554–76).

254–9. Friar John's approach to the Biblical text here and his use of it to justify the friars are typical of the methods and aims of the 'glosers' (see the note on ll. 126–30).

260–70. On the motives for this attack on the 'possessioners' see the note on ll. 56–9. Preachers of Chaucer's time (including friars like John Bromyard) frequently denounced the monks for faults like those mentioned here. Chaucer's own portrait of the Monk in *GP* (A 165–207) could be compared with this as a description of a sleek and pompous possessioner.

264. The word 'lewednesse' is used here in a sense (= 'ignorance') which has been obsolete since about the end of the sixteenth century (according to the *OED*). The modern meaning has been current since that time.

The adjective 'lewd' is used in a similar way, to mean 'ignorant' in l. 344 of this tale (also in l. 82 of *FT* and ll. 104 and 149 of *PT*) – a meaning which has been obsolete since the early eighteenth century. In l. 502 of the *GP* Chaucer uses a still older meaning of the word (= 'not clerical' or 'lay') which has been obsolete since about the middle of the sixteenth century. He also uses the modern meaning of the word in the Prologue to the *Miller's Tale* (A 3145), where the Reeve accuses the Miller of being about to tell a 'lewed' tale.

Also in this line, the word 'diffye' is used with a meaning (= 'despise') that has been obsolete since about the middle of the eighteenth century (according to the *OED*). Chaucer also uses the word in or near this sense in the *Nun's Priest's Tale*, where Chauntecleer the cock decides to 'diffye' the bad dream that he has had (B 4361).

265. Jovinian was a heretical monk who lived in the fourth century A.D. According to Skeat, 'Gibbon in his *Decline and Fall of the Roman Empire*, ch. 30, refers in a footnote to "Jovinian, *the enemy of fasts and celibacy*, who was persecuted and insulted by the furious Jerome" '. St Jerome wrote a treatise called *Against Jovinian* which is often quoted or referred to by Chaucer (see ll. 251–3 and note). Skeat also compares the description in l. 266 with Jerome's description of Jovinian as 'that fine monk – fat, sleek, whitewashed and always walking like a bridegroom'.

Friar John goes further than this in his satirical portrayal of such monks, and in ll. 268–70 shows them suffering from the effects of overeating even when saying prayers. 'Buf!' in l. 270 is an imitation of a smothered belch. The 'psalm of Davit' which follows it (No. 44 in the Vulgate, 45 in the Authorized Version) is not really appropriate as a psalm 'for soules' of the dead – as it is mainly about the marriage of a king. Its opening line reads in full: '*Cor meum eructavit verbum bonum*' – 'My heart has brought forth a good utterance'. But *eructavit* can also mean 'has belched' – so the quotation *is* appropriate as a punning comment on what the monk has just done.

273. *werkers*. This very broad meaning of the word (= 'doers') has been archaic since about the early seventeenth century.

'Auditours' (in the same line) has the sense of 'hearers', or 'members of an audience', which is rare now. The modern meaning of 'examiner of accounts' was also current in Chaucer's time, and is used by him when describing the Reeve in the *GP* (A 594).

279. St Yves was an honest lawyer who became a diocesan judge and then a parish priest in Brittany in the late thirteenth century. He died in 1303 and was canonized in 1347. According to the *Penguin Dictionary of Saints*: 'he was distinguished for his equity, incorruptibility, and concern for the interests of the poor and ignorant . . .' and when he became a priest 'his legal knowledge was always at the disposal of his parishioners, as were his time and his goods; he gave an example of frugal and unassuming living, and found his forensic experience valuable in the pulpit'. He thus seems to be a fairly appropriate saint for a subtle and legalistic persuader like Friar John to swear by, when claiming to be concerned about an ordinary 'churl'.

283. *weelden*. This broader sense of the word (applied to limbs) has been obsolete since about the middle of the eighteenth century. The more specialized modern meaning of 'wield' (applied to instruments, weapons, etc.) was also current in Chaucer's time – though the metaphorical meaning (applied to power, authority or influence) has been current only since the early seventeenth century.

303–5. Friar John's arguments about concentrating and dividing the gifts he wants may have some connexion with a problem that arises later in the *Tale*. This is the problem of the equal distribution of the fart – the gift he actually gets. There might even be a hint of a pun here on 'ferthing' and 'farting' – though only people who knew the story already could be expected to get the joke. The argument of these lines as a whole, however, could be what gives Thomas the idea of laying down the condition that his gift should be shared equally between Friar John and his twelve colleagues (see ll. 465–72).

315–16. St Thomas the Apostle (Doubting Thomas) was supposed to have been the first missionary to India. Marco Polo, the traveller, claims that St Thomas also converted the peoples of Nubia and Abyssinia, and that he is buried in India in the small town of San Thomé Maïlapur), a few miles south of Madras (see *The Travels of Marco Polo*, Everyman edition, pp. 364–5 and 399). According to Skeat, 'the mention of the "building up of churches" refers to a well-known legend of St Thomas, who built churches with the money given to him by King Gondoforus for the purpose of building a palace'. Friar John seems here to be cunningly trying to arouse Thomas the churl's interest by referring to the legend of a saint who is his namesake. He obviously hopes that Thomas will be inspired to follow the example given, and contribute to the building of the friars' church.

319. *sely*. See the note on l. 242.

321–40. It's a bit difficult to see why Friar John is so concerned to warn Thomas against the possible wrath of his wife as well as his own anger. The gist of the argument seems to be: 'Don't get angry, especially not with your wife, because the Bible forbids it (ll. 324–7), and also because by doing so you'll get her angry – **and** although, as you know, she's usually meek and mild, the anger of women, when roused, is a very dangerous thing.' The friar's aim in warning Thomas against his own anger is probably to get him to feel guilty about it, so that he will be prepared to make a formal confession (see ll. 425–9) – which would be profitable from the commercial point of view. There may be a more subtle purpose behind the warning about women's anger – namely to make Thomas less willing to oppose his wife when she sides with the friar, as she seems to have done in ll. 159–67.

341, 346. Anger is said here to be 'one of the greatest of the Seven (Deadly Sins)' because, like Pride, Envy and Avarice, it was one of the sins of the spirit, which were thought to be more serious than those of the flesh (Sloth, Gluttony and Lechery). Anger is also described in l. 346 as 'the henchman of Pride', because Pride was thought to be the worst sin, and it was sometimes said that all the others were dependent on it. Chaucer says in the *Parson's Tale* that 'Of the roote of thise sevene sinnes, thanne is Pryde, the general roote of alle harmes' (I 387).

353–78. We have already seen how Friar John uses catalogues of brief Biblical or Classical illustrations to give weight to his arguments (see the note on ll. 213–37). Here and in ll. 379–409 he tells a couple of longer stories for the same purpose. The Pardoner in his Tale (ll. 315–32) uses an illustration of similar length and type, to attack gambling.

The 'Senec' referred to in l. 354 is Seneca the younger, the Roman philosopher and playwright, who was tutor and adviser to the Emperor Nero, and died in A.D. 65. He wrote a treatise *On Anger* in which he tells the story that Friar John retails here. The

143

'yrous potestat' in Seneca's story was Piso, governor of Syria in the reign of Tiberius.

In l. 360 the special legal meaning of the word 'deeme' (= 'sentence') is used – a meaning which has been obsolete since about the early seventeenth century (according to the *OED*). In l. 572 of this tale the word is used in a slightly broader sense (= 'decide' or 'judge' in a scientific way) – when the puzzled lord of the manor says that there is no man who can 'deeme' whether a fart and its effects have been distributed evenly. The still broader modern meaning of 'consider', 'maintain' or 'think' was also current in Chaucer's time, and is evident, for example, in l. 1881 of the *Knight's Tale*). The verb 'deem' is related to the noun 'doom' (see l. 349 of *PT*).

'Hool' (cf. modern 'whole') in l. 369 has the general sense of 'in good condition, sound, uninjured' – which is now applied to things rather than people. The personal meaning, however, survived for a long time after Chaucer, and is found frequently in the 1611 (Authorized) Version of the Bible, for example in Matthew, ix, 12: 'They that be whole need not a physician'.

379–409. This story of Cambyses is also from Seneca's treatise *On Anger* (see the note on l. 354). Cambyses, king of Persia, was the son of Cyrus the Great (see ll. 415–20), and reigned from 529 to 522 B.C. Herodotus also speaks about him and his crimes in the *Histories* (Penguin translation pp. 188–9).

380. The meaning of 'shrewe' (= 'vicious or malicious person' of either sex) has been obsolete since about the middle of the seventeenth century. It can be found also several times in the *PT* (ll. 208, 531 and 547). 'Shrew' is still used sometimes to describe a nagging wife, and this meaning is found several times in Chaucer – for example, in the *Prologue* to the *Merchant's Tale* (E 1222).

The adjective 'shrewd' is related to this. Up to the middle of the seventeenth century it could be used to mean 'malicious' or 'villainous' (cf. the earlier meaning of 'shrew'). The modern sense of 'shrewd' (= 'clever' or 'acute') did not become current until about the early sixteenth century – but Chaucer seems to be approaching this meaning in l. 574 of the Tale, where the lord of the manor says he is amazed at how 'shrewedly' Thomas the churl has spoken to Friar John. The meaning here though, seems to be slightly closer to the original sense of 'malicious' than the modern one is – so 'cunningly' would be a better equivalent for it than 'cleverly'.

There are also two obsolete verbs related to the noun 'shrew'. These are the verbs 'beshrew' and 'shrew'. Of the two 'beshrew' shows more clearly the connexion with the noun and adjective, since, up to the middle of the sixteenth century it could mean 'make wicked', and up to the late seventeenth century could also mean 'curse'. The verb 'shrew' was, as far as we know, used only to mean 'curse', up to the late seventeenth century. Chaucer uses 'shrewe' with this meaning in l. 563 of this tale.

The *OED* suggests that all these meanings might be traced back to the *animal* shrew, which is well known to be aggressive.

410–14. This does not seem to be a very suitable moral for a preacher to draw from the story (see the Introduction, p. 21).

In l. 411 'Singeth *Placebo*' refers to the ninth verse of Psalm 116 (114 in the Vulgate): '*Placebo Domino in regione vivorum*' – 'I shall please the Lord in the land of the living' – which was often sung as an anthem for the dead. As Skeat says, 'this anthem was familiar to everyone, and "to sing Placebo" came to mean "to be complaisant"; as in Bacon, Essay 20'. In the *Merchant's Tale* 'Placebo' is the name of a man who flatters his friend by agreeing with everything that he says.

415–20. Yet another story from Seneca's treatise *On Anger* (see the note to ll. 353–78). The Cyrus referred to here was Cyrus the elder (*d.* 529 B.C.), who defeated Croesus, and was the father of Cambyses (see the note on ll. 379–409). The story of how he destroyed the river 'Gysen' (Gyndes) is also told in Herodotus' *Histories* (Penguin translation, pp. 89–90). According to Herodotus, Cyrus destroyed the river by splitting it up into 360 separate channels.

427. Anger is often shown in medieval and Renaissance paintings holding a knife. By claiming that Thomas is pointing the 'knife' at his *own* heart Friar John is reminding him of the suicidal nature of anger which he has already mentioned in l. 343.

431–4. The way in which Thomas refuses Friar John's offer here provides yet another reminder of the quarrelling between friars and parish-priests over the right to hear confessions (see also the note on ll. 60–7).

436–8. Mussels and oysters do not seem to have been thought such delicacies in Chaucer's time as they are now. Friar John is citing them here as examples of very cheap and simple food, such as would be fitting for poor and abstemious friars. (Compare with this, though, the actual meal that he orders in ll. 174–86 of the Tale.)

442. Forty pounds was a very large sum of money at this time. It was, for example, four times the annual salary that Chaucer himself earned (between 1374 and 1386) as controller of customs in the Port of London. (See also the note on l. 312 of the *FT*.)

443. It was believed that, between the Crucifixion and the Resurrection, Christ broke into Hell and robbed ('harrowed') it of the souls of the Old Testament patriarchs and prophets which had previously had to go there because of the sin of Adam. The source for the story was an apocryphal Gospel – the Gospel of Nicodemus – and, in medieval painting and drama especially, the Harrowing of Hell became a very vivid way of expressing the idea

of redemption (e.g. in the York Cycle of Miracle Plays, No. 37 – as also in *Piers Plowman*, pp. 258–68 of the Penguin translation).

447–9. This is one view of the way in which friars operated in the world. Another, less complimentary one is expressed by the Wife of Bath at the opening of her *Tale* (D 868), where she describes the friars swarming everywhere 'as thikke as motes in the sonne-beem' – 'as thick as specks of dust in the sunlight'.

451–4. According to Skeat, 'there was great strife among the four orders of friars (Franciscans, Dominicans, Augustinians and Carmelites) as to the priority of their order'. The Carmelites, in their more extravagant moments claimed to have been founded by Elijah on Mount Carmel (see 1 Kings, xviii, 19–20). Friar John's echoing of this claim here suggests that he himself may be a Carmelite.

462–4. The idea of brotherhood and the sealed letter mentioned here refer, according to Skeat, to 'the *letters of fraternity*, which friars were accustomed to grant under the conventual seal, to such laymen as had given them benefactions or were likely to leave them money in their wills. The benefactors received in return a brotherly participation in such spiritual benefits as the friars could confer.' Friar John has already reminded Thomas that he is privileged to be one of the friars' 'brothers'. But the friar is by now such a suspect character that we might even doubt whether the letter he refers to exists – let alone whether he means to fulfil the promises that he says it contains.

'Took' in l. 464 has the meaning of 'hand over, deliver, give', which has been obsolete since about the middle of the sixteenth century. This sense is related to one of the main modern meanings – that of 'carry' – which was also current in Chaucer's time.

498. A large house, a manor house or even a castle could be called a 'court' up to about the end of the sixteenth century. This was probably because they consisted of buildings grouped around an open space – a 'court' in one of the modern senses. The word is still used in the names of some buildings of this kind – notably Hampton Court.

520–4. Skeat points out that although Friar John hypocritically refuses to be called 'master' here, he has twice allowed Thomas's wife to give him the title (in ll. 136 and 172). Here in ll. 522–4 he characteristically quotes from the Gospels (Matthew, xxiii, 7–8) to support his 'modest' attitude. The degree of Master (probably of Divinity) which he claims to hold (l. 522) was of higher standing at universities and in society in the Middle Ages than it is now, and it gave the holder great prestige. Thus the pilgrim-Friar in *GP* is said to be so prosperous and impressive in appearance that he looks 'lyk a maister or a pope' (l. 54 of his portrait).

531. *Distempre.* This verb was originally used in a medical sense,

to mean 'make ill through upsetting the balance ("temper") of the "humours" (the four basic fluids) in the body'. The 'four humours' were: blood, phlegm, yellow bile, and black bile – and the four temperaments in which each was believed to predominate were, respectively, the 'sanguine', 'phlegmatic', 'choleric', and 'melancholic'. For further information on this subject, see either pp. 105–7 of *Chaucer's World*, by M. Hussey, or pp. 169–74 of *The Discarded Image*, by C. S. Lewis. By Chaucer's time it had also come to mean 'upset' in the emotional sense, and this is the meaning here. It has been archaic since about the end of the seventeenth century. The noun 'distemper' has been used to describe the disease that dogs get since about the middle of the eighteenth century.

532. This phrase is used by Christ to describe his disciples in Matthew, v, 13. Chaucer is using it here to mock the friars, who claimed to be following the life of the Apostles. Friar John has made this claim for himself several times in the *Tale*, in ll. 156 and 523, for example.

542. *cherl*. The word in Anglo-Saxon times ('ceorl') meant simply 'free man'. With the decline of this class after the Norman Conquest it came to mean 'serf' (a sense which became obsolete in the early seventeenth century). This is probably the meaning here but there is also a suggestion of the more offensive sense – that of 'boor' which had also become current by Chaucer's time. Compare the development of the word 'villain' (see the note on l. 4 of the *FT*).

545. 'Frenzy' in the sense of actual madness or delirium is rarely used today. The figurative meaning (e.g. 'a frenzy of rage') is now more common.

547. *Wreke*. This meaning of the word has been obsolete since about the end of the sixteenth century. It is also found in *PT* (l. 569). Another main meaning of the word, which is also used by Chaucer, is that of 'to give vent or expression to'. This can still be found in phrases like: 'wreak vengeance', 'wreak havoc', or 'wreak one's wrath'.

554–76. As might be expected in the lord of the manor's learned discussion of the problems raised by Thomas's fart a number of academic terms, like 'demonstracioun' (560) and 'demoniak' (576) are used. Of these probably the most interesting is 'Ars-Metryke' (l. 558). Arithmetic (literally: 'the art of measurement') was one of the Seven Liberal Arts studied at medieval universities (the others being Grammar, Rhetoric, Logic, Geometry, Music and Astronomy) – and so is a highly respectable subject for the lord to appeal to when faced with such a problem. But the strong possibility of a pun on 'Ars' (= 'art' or 'arse') helps to keep the basic joke in front of us.

'Nyce' in ll. 563 and 568 is a complimentary word for the

academically-minded lord to use of his churl – but it is not, however, complimentary in its modern weakened sense of 'generally pleasant' or 'agreeable' (which did not become current until the late eighteenth century). Here it is used in the sense of 'academically precise', as a term of high praise for the way in which Thomas has posed the problem. This meaning has been archaic since about the middle of the sixteenth century, but it is related to a later sense which is still found in phrases like: 'nice distinctions', or 'a nice sense of timing'. The word originally meant 'foolish' – a sense that has been obsolete since the late sixteenth century.

On the meanings of 'shrewe' (l. 563) and 'shrewedly' (l. 574) see the note on l. 380 – and on that of 'deeme' (l. 572) see the note on l. 360.

579–80. One of the duties of a squire, even at the King's court, was that of carving for and waiting on his lord at the table. In *GP* (A 100) this is said to be one of the services performed by the pilgrim-Squire for his father, the Knight.

583. Skeat quotes the nineteenth-century scholar Thomas Wright on the subject of the 'gowne-clooth': 'In the middle ages, the most common rewards, and even those given by the feudal landholders to their dependants and retainers, were articles of apparel, especially the gown. . . . Money was comparatively very scarce in the middle ages; and as the household retainers were lodged and fed, clothing was almost the only article they wanted.'

589–622. The Squire does not say exactly how his fantastic apparatus is to be set up. I suppose that the cartwheel and Thomas would have to be supported on some sort of frame – *low* enough to allow the twelve friars to set their noses to the spokes while in a kneeling position – yet *high* enough to allow Friar John to crawl underneath and hold his nose upright under the hub.

In l. 595, the Squire points out that the usual number of friars in a convent is 13. Skeat quotes Thomas Wright again on the reason for this: 'The regular number of monks or friars in a convent had been fixed at twelve, with [i.e. besides] their superior; in imitation, it is said, of the number of twelve apostles and their divine master.' So here we have another reminder of the friars' claims to be living the life of the Apostles (see the note on l. 532). A 'coven' of witches also numbers 13.

'Sadly' in l. 600 has the meaning of 'closely' or 'firmly', which has been obsolete since the end of the fifteenth century. C. S. Lewis traces the full development of the meaning of 'sad' in *Studies in Words*, ch. 3.

624. 'Jankin' (Jack) is often the name of a clever lad or cunning lover in popular literature of this time. Both the apprentice that the Wife of Bath goes out with and her fifth husband are given this name (see the *Wife of Bath's Prologue*, D 303–7 and 627–31). In a

fifteenth century lyric there is a clerical seducer called Jankin (see R. T. Davies, *Medieval English Lyrics*, No. 73).

627. *wit*. See the note on l. 125.

630. The town that the pilgrims have nearly reached may be Sittingbourne in Kent – about 40 miles from London and 19 miles from Canterbury. The Summoner threatened at the end of the *Wife of Bath's Prologue* to tell 'two or three' stories about friars 'er I come to Sidingbourne' (l. 19 of the extract in this volume). If this is really the place that the company has now arrived at, it seems that the Summoner has, as usual, been exaggerating.

The Pardoner's Tale

1–12. The Host is here talking about the *Physician's Tale*, which has just finished. In it the 'fals justyse' (l. 3) is the judge Appius, who wants to get the 'sely mayde' Virginia (l. 6) into his power, and so bribes the 'fals cherl' Claudius (l. 3) to claim in court that she is a slave of his. Appius thus hopes to get hold of the girl by having her made a ward of the court, but her father Virginius prevents him by killing her. The Host reacts in a characteristically straightforward and emotional way to this 'pitous tale' – showing both sincere indignation about this particular case (up to l. 5), and a rueful concern about the broader problems that it implies (up to l. 12).

9. The 'gifts of Fortune and Nature' are, respectively, those which a person receives or gains during life on earth (e.g. wealth), and those with which he is born (e.g. beauty).

16. *gentil*. This complimentary meaning of the word is now obsolete, except in self-consciously archaic forms of address like 'Gentle Reader'. The root meaning of 'noble' is also now obsolete, except in a usage like 'the gentle art of boxing' – where the modern meaning is also ironically present. In Chaucer, though, 'gentil' usually means 'noble' in one way or another – as 'gentle' frequently does in Shakespeare. By Shakespeare's time, though, the modern meanings of 'mild' and 'not violent or rough' had become current (since about the middle of the sixteenth century).

21–3. The Host seems to have his tongue fairly firmly in his cheek as he admires the Physician's imposing professional appearance here. So does Chaucer when describing the Physician in *GP* (especially in A 422–44). On the other hand, the Physician isn't seen by either of them as an impostor or quack. He holds the degree of Doctor of Medicine (see *GP*, A 411), which required not less than eight years of study, and would have given him genuine status among the pilgrims. This impression is strengthened by his maintenance of what is probably meant to be a dignified silence in the face of the joking about 'urinals', etc. (ll. 17–19). So the Host's apology for the crudeness of his language here (l. 23) may be half-serious.

'St Ronyan' (in l. 22) is a non-existent saint whom the Pardoner also swears by in l. 32. Robinson suggests that the name is a corrupt form of 'St Ninian' (a genuine fourth/fifth-century Irish saint). If this were true it would be typical of the way in which the Host distorts words and phrases – such as 'cardinacle' (see l. 25 and the notes on it) and 'By Corpus bones' (l. 26).

24–9. Although the Host has said (l. 23) that he is unable to speak in learned terms, he seems to know something about the common medical expressions (see also ll. 16–20). When describing his condition as a result of hearing the Physician's tale, he says that his main symptom is something near to a 'cardinacle' (l. 25) – which is a malapropism for 'cardiacle', the word for 'heart-attack'.

'Triacle', on the other hand (l. 26), was the proper word at this time for 'medicine' or 'remedy'. It is related to the modern word 'treacle', and originally meant 'antidote against snake-bite or poison generally' – a meaning which survived until the early nineteenth century. The meaning here (= 'medicine') was current until the early eighteenth century. 'Treacle' came to mean 'unrefined syrup' in the late seventeenth century – perhaps because medicine was often mixed with something sweet.

In l. 27 ale is described as 'corny' because at this time it was brewed only with malt (which is made from barley or other kinds of grain). Hops were not used by English brewers until they were introduced from the Continent in the early sixteenth century.

35. *gentils*. 'Gentle' as a noun, meaning 'a person of high social class', has been obsolete since about the middle of the seventeenth century. It is related to the adjective 'gentle' in its meaning of 'noble' (see the note on 'gentil' in l. 16). The 'gentils' on the pilgrimage would thus certainly have included the Knight, Squire, Prioress and Monk, and perhaps also the Man of Law, the Doctor of Physic and the Franklin.

38. *wit*. This meaning of the word (= 'wisdom') is now obsolete, except in expressions like 'to have the wit to . . .'. For other meanings see the Commentary on l. 125 of the *ST*.

47–58. The Pardoner is here describing the kinds of credentials that he uses to impress his audience. Chaucer's contemporary Langland also shows a pardoner softening up his victims in this sort of way, in the Prologue to *Piers Plowman* (p. 65 of the Penguin translation). This Pardoner first announces where he comes from. According to the description of him in the *GP* (l. 2 of the portrait in this volume), he probably came from the hospital of St Mary of

Roncesvalles, which was near Charing Cross in London. According to Robinson, there were a number of pardoners about in Chaucer's time who claimed to be collecting on behalf of this hospital. On the other hand, the Pardoner may be referring here to a claim he makes of having come from the Pope's Court at Rome – which is where he seems to have been just before coming on the Canterbury pilgrimage (see l. 3 of his portrait in this volume). This, in any case, is the place where he says he has got some of the documents authorizing him to sell pardons.

'Our lyge lordes seel' on one of these documents (l. 49) is probably the Pope's seal – or possibly the local bishop's. The basic meaning of 'patente' in the same line is 'licence'. In Chaucer's time the word had the special meaning of 'licence or indulgence granted by the Pope'. The modern meaning of 'exclusive licence to make or market a certain article' has been current since the late sixteenth century.

62–3. The shoulder-bone of a sheep, according to Skeat, was often used by magicians to foretell the future. Chaucer's Parson denounces this superstitious practice in his *Tale* (I 602). So in making such astounding claims about the properties of his relics, the Pardoner seems to be building up a foundation of popular belief.

67. The meaning of 'worm' (= 'snake') in the second half of this line has been obsolete, except in archaic poetry, etc., since the seventeenth century. The asp in Shakespeare's *Antony and Cleopatra* is described as a 'worm' (Act V, sc. ii).

78–83. On the Pardoner's tactics at this stage of his campaign see the Introduction, pp. 28–9.

101–2. An English mark at this time was worth two-thirds of a pound – so the Pardoner seems to have been earning more than £66 a year, in the money of the time. This would have been a very large income indeed. It was more than three times the amount of Chaucer's own basic pension (£20) in the last years of his life, and more than six times what he had earned as controller of customs (£10). The Pardoner seems to be either a great salesman or a great liar – perhaps a bit of both.

105. The Pardoner here is talking about the account of preaching technique that he has given in ll. 41–58 – and especially about his use of avarice as the main theme for his sermon. The reason for this choice of subject is made blatantly clear in ll. 112–14.

113. *free*. This meaning of the word (= 'ready' or 'generous') survives today only in expressions like 'free with money (or compliments)'. Another important meaning of 'free' which is frequently found in Chaucer is that of 'noble' (used, for example, to describe Chauntecleer strutting around the yard and crowing, in the *Nun's Priest's Tale*, B 4459). This meaning has been obsolete since about

the early seventeenth century. C. S. Lewis examines the meanings of 'free' and words related to it in *Studies in Words*, ch. 5.

115. *winne*. This use of the verb without an object, to mean simply 'make a profit', has been obsolete since about the late seventeenth century. This meaning is also apparent in l. 173 of this Tale. A related meaning of 'gain (something) as a profit' is also common in Chaucer, and is found, for example, in l. 189 of the *FT*. It has been obsolete since the early seventeenth century, except in dialect and in the modern noun 'breadwinner'.

124–31. The friar in the *ST* also threatens to take this kind of revenge on the churl Thomas who has insulted him (see ll. 546–51 of the *ST*).

147–50. The Pardoner uses these 'olde stories', as he has used his documents and seals (ll. 47–58), to impress his audience, and to give his preaching and his merchandise more authenticity. 'Ensamples' from Biblical, classical or popular legend were the stock-in-trade of preachers in the Middle Ages, and anthologies of them were compiled for use in sermons. In a sermon a number of them might be run through briefly to support a particular argument, as in ll. 197–223 of this tale – or else one or two of them might be related at greater length for the same purpose, as in ll. 315–40. Their general purpose was twofold: to hold the attention of the 'lewed peple', and to give the weight of tradition and authority to the preacher's words.

On Chaucer's use of such 'ensamples' elsewhere, see the Commentary on ll. 213–37 and 353–78 of the *ST*.

156–9. In this frank confession the Pardoner contrasts his way of earning a living with that of the Apostles – the original exponents of the Christian religious way of life whom the Pardoner, as a cleric, should ideally be imitating. In the Middle Ages the Cistercian monks and the Franciscan friars, especially, stressed the value of manual labour as a foundation for the religious life. In earlier Christian times St Paul the Hermit (fourth century) is said to have made baskets for a living, and this is probably the legend that the Pardoner is referring to in l. 157. The more well-known St Paul (the apostle) is said to have made tents for a living (Acts, xviii, 3) – this is probably being referred to in l. 159.

159. 'countrefete' did not necessarily have the discreditable meaning of 'counterfeit' in Middle English. The word may, however, be balanced on the edge of this sense in Chaucer's description of the Prioress and her desire to 'countrefete cheere/Of court (courtly behaviour)' (*GP*, A 139–40).

163. *sterve*. 'Starve' (the modern form of the word) now means only 'to die of hunger'. (It has had this special meaning since the late sixteenth century.) But in Chaucer's time the word meant 'to die' regardless of the cause – hence Chaucer has to add 'for famyne'

('of hunger') here, to make the meaning clear. This older meaning can also be found in l. 600 of this tale. It had become obsolete, except in the archaic language of some poets, by the early sixteenth century.

168. This refers to the drink that the Pardoner has had before beginning his Prologue (see ll. 33–40) and the note on l. 27.

175. There seem to be some clearer reasons for the *Pardoner's Tale* being set in Flanders than there are for the *Summoner's Tale* being set in Holderness (see the Commentary on ll. 45–6 of the *ST*). One reason is that the Flemish seem to have had a reputation in England for hard drinking and money-grabbing (the latter perhaps because of their prominence in trade and industry). Another reason may be that, as Skeat suggests, an earlier form of the story may have come from Flanders. Themes and subjects like those of the *Pardoner's Tale* were common in the art of the Low Countries (the early sixteenth-century play of *Everyman*, in which the character of Death plays such an important part, is thought to have been translated from a Dutch original).

182. The tavern was often denounced by medieval preachers as a kind of anti-church, where the Devil was worshipped in various ways. One of these preachers, quoted by Owst (pp. 438–9), says that 'when good men are at their service on a holy day, gluttons sit fast at the Devil's service, with many ribald words and lecherous songs, blaspheming God with many great oaths ... and each of them is trying hard to deceive the other with cunning tricks'. In Langland's *Piers Plowman* (Passus V) the figure of Glutton is presented as a peasant, setting out to go to church, but ending up at the tavern instead (Penguin translation, pp. 108–9).

184–7. 'Tearing Christ's body in pieces' here means swearing oaths like 'God's bones', 'God's blood', 'God's wounds', etc. This metaphor was a vivid traditional way of making people feel guilty about swearing. Like the idea of the tavern as the Devil's church (see l. 182 and the note on it) it featured frequently in the sermons of the time. Chaucer's Parson (who has already rebuked the Host for swearing in the Epilogue to the *Man of Law's Tale*) also uses the metaphor in his sermon to the pilgrims at the end of the *Canterbury Tales* (I 590).

There is also a painting on this subject which probably dates from very shortly after Chaucer's time. It is on the north wall of the nave at Broughton church (North Buckinghamshire), and shows Christ (having just been taken down from the Cross) in the arms of the Virgin Mary, surrounded by people in medieval costume carrying (i.e. swearing by) bits of him (foot, bones, etc.). What makes this painting especially interesting in relation to the *PT* is that at the bottom it shows a couple of figures sitting round what seems to be a gaming-table, holding crosses (i.e. swearing by the

Cross) and hitting each other over the head with swords. This illustrates the connexion between gambling, swearing and murder which the Pardoner also points out later in the Tale (ll. 303–5 and 363–9).

188. Even such a small detail of behaviour as the laughter of people at hearing others swearing had been noticed and denounced by the preachers of Chaucer's time. One of them, the friar John Bromyard, comments on this by saying that such people 'laugh to hear such things, who, nevertheless, if insulting remarks were made in front of them about their father or their earthly lord, would either defend the outraged by fighting, or at least be offended and withdraw' (quoted by Owst, pp. 418–19).

191. The 'wafereres', according to Skeat, seem to have been employed as go-betweens by lovers, and by prostitutes and their clients.

193–4. The idea of lechery being a consequence of gluttony (and especially of drunkenness) is common and obvious enough. A Latin proverb, found in Terence's play *The Eunuch*, points out the connexion metaphorically: '*Sine Cerere et Libero friget Venus*' ('Without Ceres and Bacchus (i.e. food and wine) Venus (i.e. sexual desire) is cold'). In medieval times gluttony and lechery were also associated by being sins of the flesh.

196. 'Luxury' (derived from Lat. *luxuria*) continued to be used as a synonym for 'lechery' until about the beginning of the nineteenth century. By that time its main modern meanings had developed; the meaning of 'high living' had been current since the early seventeenth century, and that of 'a non-essential thing' since the late eighteenth century.

204–9. Chaucer often refers to Seneca on moral questions (see the Commentary on ll. 353–78 of the *ST*). This quotation is from his *Letters* (No. 83).

210–23. On the view of gluttony reflected here see the Commentary on ll. 251–3 of the *ST*.

229–32. The labour and expense that are caused by gluttony is yet another theme drawn by the Pardoner from the tradition of medieval preaching. Owst (p. 442) quotes an anonymous preacher of about this time who says that 'At the beginning of the world Man's food was only bread and water – and now gluttony is not satisfied with all the harvest of trees, of all roots, of all herbs, of all beasts, of all birds, of all fishes in the sea'. The Pardoner uses such well-tried sermon-topics, as he uses his documents and old stories, to impress the 'lewed peple'.

246–8. Chaucer's contemporary Langland is even more violent in his expression of disgust at the results of gluttony, when he is describing the behaviour of Glutton in the tavern (Passus V of *Piers Plowman* – pp. 109–10 of the Penguin translation). This moral indignation at the relationship between delicate foods and 'corrup-cioun' of various kinds is also suggested in a different way by Chaucer's description in *GP* (A 379–87) of a Cook who is expert at making subtle dishes and sauces, but 'unfortunately' has a scabby ulcer on his shin.

249–58. This description of cooks' activities fills out the view of gluttony as a waster of work and money that has been presented to us in ll. 229–32. Owst's anonymous preacher (quoted in the note on ll. 229–32) develops his argument in a similar but less vivid way: 'The meats', he says, 'have to be cooked with great activity and with the skill of cooks, more for the pleasure of a man's body than for the benefit of a man's constitution, for the constitution of a man is little improved by this'.

In l. 251 the Pardoner uses the language of medieval philosophy to describe what goes on in the kitchen. 'Substaunce' was the term used by the philosophers to describe the basic material of which an object was composed (here the raw food used by the cooks) – and 'accident' referred to the form or shape that it took (here the finished dish, in which the original ingredients are unrecognizable). Medieval cooks devoted much of their skill to disguising the in-gredients of a dish – as was often necessary because the meat might well be going 'off'. With this in mind they specialized in dishes and sauces that would probably seem to us to be a kind of anonymous mush, flavoured with almost every seasoning or spice that was available. The Cook who is described in the *GP* is an expert at producing these kinds of creation – which are what the wealthier classes (such as the gourmet Franklin in *GP*, A 351–2) had come to expect.

'Likerous' in l. 252 is an obsolete form of the adjective 'lecherous'. Chaucer also uses it to mean 'lecherous' (in his description of Alison in the *Miller's Tale*) – a meaning that became obsolete by about the middle of the seventeenth century.

Also in l. 252 the meaning of 'talent' is related to the Biblical one (see Matthew, xxv, 14–30), but it is borrowed or imitated from Old French, where the word had already developed the sense of 'appetite' or 'desire'. This meaning has been obsolete since about the beginning of the sixteenth century – whilst the modern meaning of 'natural ability' had begun to develop in the early fifteenth century.

259—60. This is an indirect warning about the punishment that was thought to await gluttons in the next world. 'Dead' in l. 260 means 'spiritually dead' and therefore likely to be damned. There is a manuscript illustration of this sin and its consequences, on p. 91 of *Chaucer's World* by M. Hussey. In Canto VI of the *Inferno*, Dante shows gluttons in the third circle of Hell, grovelling in mud and being rained on.

266–7. 'Sampsoun! Sampsoun!' of course imitates the sound of the drunkard's heavy breathing. But, as the Pardoner points out in the next line, it also provides an ironic reminder that Samson himself (see Judges, xiii, 7) is said to have gained his strength partly by abstaining from wine – as opposed to the drunkard, who is shown losing control of himself *because* of wine, and collapsing like a stuck pig (the pig itself being, in medieval art and literature, symbolic of gluttony and sensuality).

275–84. The cheap and powerful 'whyte wyn of Lepe' seems to have been the 'hard liquor' of the time. (Distilled liquors like gin didn't become widely available in England until the eighteenth century.) The better and safer wines were imported from France, especially Bordeaux. In ll. 277–8 the Pardoner is warning his congregation about wine-merchants who mixed these more expensive wines with the cheaper stuff – whilst, presumably, still charging the higher price. (Medieval preachers often acted as consumer-advisers in this way – as Owst shows in pp. 352–61 of his book.)

B. H. Bronson, in *In Search of Chaucer* (p. 82), thinks that the Pardoner is also suggesting that the Host adulterates his wine like this. He argues that 'Fish Street and Cheapside, as all the pilgrims of course knew, lie just at the other end of London Bridge from where the Tabard Inn (the Host's inn) stood; and in view of this fact the reference to "othere wynes growing faste by" is surely sufficiently pointed'. He also suggests that this is a further reason for the quarrel that breaks out between the Pardoner and the Host at the end of the *Tale*.

288. 'Very' as an adjective is now obsolete except in phrases like 'the very thing'. This usage is often found in Shakespeare and the 1611 (Authorized) Version of the Bible.

290. By advising his audience here to do their own reading on this subject the Pardoner avoids having to deliver a long string of examples of abstinence such as Friar John bores his victim with in ll. 213–37 of the *ST*.

291–3. This story is told of Attila the Hun – the 'Scourge of God' – who reigned from A.D. 434 to 453. He is said to have died of a burst blood-vessel on his wedding-night.

296–7. One reason why Chaucer emphasized so heavily that the Pardoner is talking about Lemuel was to ensure that the scribes who copied the *Tales* for publication didn't confuse him with Samuel, who was and is the better-known of the two Biblical figures. (Chaucer also shows anxiety about unreliable scribes at the end of *Troilus* (Book V, ll. 1793–5), and in a short ironic poem *Unto Adam, His Owne Scriveyn* [scribe].) The poet's warning in these lines seems to have got through to most of the copiers of the eighty or so existing manuscripts of the *Tales* – but even so one or two of them still managed to get the names mixed up.

301–2. Changes of subject have to be clearly pointed out to the audience, both in sermons and in poetry that is written to be read aloud. The *Pardoner's Tale* is both of these – a sermon to be delivered by the Pardoner, and poetry mainly to be read aloud by Chaucer or someone else – so it is doubly important that divisions like the one here and those in ll. 341–2 and 372 should be clearly marked.

303–5. Here and in ll. 363–9 gambling is said to result in lying, swearing and violence. 'Lesinges' and 'deceite' in ll. 303–4 refer to the various kinds of cheating and swindling that are associated with gambling – whilst 'forsweringes' and 'blaspheme' in ll. 304–5 describe the violent language that accompanies almost any game that causes uncertainty and excitement. 'Manslaughtre' in l. 305 could be seen as the end-result of all these activities – as is suggested by the gambler's threat in ll. 366–7.

315–40. The two stories from ancient history that the Pardoner tells here are taken from the *Policraticus*, a work on political theory by a twelfth-century scholar, John of Salisbury.

The word 'trouthe' in l. 327 is an earlier form of the now archaic word 'troth', which has the meanings of 'fidelity' or 'pledged word' (the expression of fidelity). 'Troth' survives now mainly in the marriage service (in the *Book of Common Prayer*) and as part of the verb 'betroth'. 'Trouthe' elsewhere in Chaucer is also found as an earlier form of the word 'truth', in the sense of 'true statement or account'.

341–2. Here the Pardoner combines another clearly-marked change of subject (see the note on ll. 301–2) with a further reference to the authority of 'olde bookes' which was supposed to give weight to his preaching (see the note on ll. 147–50).

360–7. The sin of swearing or blasphemy is one that was often shown in a dramatic way being followed by a sudden and violent punishment – probably because it can be seen as a direct defiance of God. In the *Inferno* (XXV, 1–16) Dante shows a damned soul who makes an obscene gesture in the direction of Heaven, and immediately receives extra punishment as a result. Owst quotes several lurid stories about Divine vengeance on swearers – including one which, like the Pardoner's sermon, associates swearing with gambling. In it a 'blaspheming dice-player' is 'struck dead at the game before his companion's eyes, while a voice from heaven declares – "I will no longer endure the shame that you cause me through your horrible oaths and your vindictive and malicious cursing!"' (see Owst, p. 418). Swearing is also seen by the Pardoner in the conclusion to his sermon as one of the sins for which the three 'ryotoures' are punished (see ll. 610–11).

368–9. Here, in preparation for the story of the 'ryotoures', the connexions between gambling, swearing and murder are emphasized again (see the note on ll. 303–5).

372. As with his other changes of subject (see the note on ll. 301–2), the Pardoner here shows clearly that he has finished the detailed denunciation of particular sins that began in l. 195, and that he is now going on to something else. The 'sermon' which he is preaching to an imaginary congregation still continues, though – with the story of the 'ryotoures' as its main illustration and example. But, with the Pardoner addressing his fellow-pilgrims (as 'sires') here, we are reminded that it is also the 'tale' that they have asked him to tell.

373. This is the first time the Pardoner tells us that he is talking about three 'ryotoures' in particular. At the beginning of the *Tale* he has spoken generally about 'a compaignye/Of yonge folk that haunteden folye' (ll. 175–6).

It's very difficult to find a good modern equivalent for the word 'ryotour'. It seems in Chaucer's time (and probably up to the early seventeenth century, according to the *OED* to have been used of people who were both disorderly and dissipated in their way of life. It would be misleading to call the Pardoner's characters 'rioters', since the word now has exclusively the political sense which, according to the *OED*, has been current since the later fifteenth century. Other possible alternatives, such as 'hooligan', 'playboy' and 'reveller' also have drawbacks. 'Hooligan' is a word associated just with disorderly or destructive behaviour – 'playboy' has largely upper-class connotations (which would not suit the broadly representative character of the Pardoner's figures) – and 'revellers' doesn't sound disapproving enough. Because of this difficulty, of finding a present day word that expresses adequately the blend of aggression and dissipation that characterizes the three figures, I have (in most cases in the Introduction and Commentary) fallen back on Chaucer's own word.

374–5. Mention of the *time* here shows that the 'ryotoures' started their drinking very early in the day. But its association with the ringing of a bell for a church-service suggests also that, from the narrator's point of view, the 'ryotoures' would do better to answer such a summons. There may thus be a further reminder here of the description of the tavern as the Devil's 'temple' (l. 182), where his followers worship instead of going to church.

387. This description of Death as a 'privee theef' may perhaps owe something to Christ's warning in Revelation, xvi, 15: 'Behold I come as a thief. Blessed is he that watcheth . . .' In both cases the visitation is also a judgment, and people are warned to be ready for it. Elsewhere in medieval art, literature and legend Death often appears as a dancer or a chess-player.

391. The boy's reference to '*this* pestilence' reminds us that death by plague was something that the Pardoner's audience always had to reckon with. The Black Death (1348–9) was itself

one of a number of plagues that struck England during Chaucer's lifetime (though it isn't certain how many of these were actually outbreaks of bubonic plague, as opposed to epidemics of more 'normal' diseases).

392–6, 402–3. Both these warnings about death and being ready for it are simple enough in origin (l. 396), morality and expression. But, as they later show in their reaction to the Old Man, the 'ryotoures' are incapable of seeing Death as anything more than a literal enemy.

404–21. The defiance of Death that the 'ryotoures' express here is peppered with the sort of swearing that the Pardoner has just been preaching against (especially in ll. 184–7 and 341–71). The first long speech made by any of them contains three such oaths in ten lines (404–13) – and it is made clear that the rest follow his example (420–1), by 'dismembering Christ's body' in the way that has already been described (see the note on ll. 184–7).

441–50. The Old Man's description of the Earth as his 'mother', from whom he came and to whom he must return, is (like the description of Death as a 'privee theef' in l. 387) a simple metaphor which probably has a Biblical origin. In Genesis, iii, 19 God tells Adam: 'In the sweat of thy face shalt thou eat bread, till thou return unto the ground; for out of it wast thou taken: for dust thou art, and unto dust shalt thou return'. In ll. 446–8 the Old Man speaks about the actual process of dying in the same simple, everyday way, when he offers to exchange his chest of clothes (regarded as a form of wealth in the Middle Ages – see the Commentary on l. 583 of the *ST*) for a shroud.

451–9, 471. The Old Man's advice to the 'ryotoures', and their reply, remind us of the difference in age as well as attitude that there is between them. The Pardoner has already pointed out at the beginning of the Tale (l. 176) that the 'ryotoures' are 'younge folk'.

469. The 'ryotour' characteristically suses an oath to reinforce his threat (see the note on ll. 404–21). One of the figures in the Broughton painting (see the note on ll. 184–7) is carrying some-. thing that looks rather like a hot-cross-bun, but is in fact a communion-wafer. In other words, he is also swearing 'by the hooly sacrament'.

482. 'Florins', according to Skeat, 'were so named because originally coined at Florence, the first coinage being in 1252.' The value of the coin was half an English mark (see l. 102) or one-third of a pound.

505–15. The 'cut' here probably consists, as it often does today, of pieces of grass or straw held in the fist – the lot usually falling on whoever draws the shortest piece. The same method is used by the Host at the beginning of the Canterbury pilgrimage, to decide who is to tell the first tale (A 835–58).

545. 'Lustes' here has the general meaning of 'desire' or 'pleasure', which in Chaucer's time could include the modern meaning of 'passionate (usually sexual) desire'. As often happens, the sexual meaning of the word has squeezed out the others – and in the case of 'lust' this had taken place by about the end of the seventeenth century. The older meanings of the word survive only in the adjectives 'lusty' and 'listless'.

556–60. The Devil is also shown giving ideas to the corrupt judge in the *Physician's Tale* (C 130–2) – the tale which immediately precedes this one. In the *FT* (ll. 218–36) the devil explains to the summoner the circumstances in which he and his colleagues are allowed by God to tempt human beings – an aspect of Divine justice which the Pardoner is probably referring to here in ll. 559–60. In this context there seems to be some irony in the 'ryotour's' referring to himself as living 'beneath the throne of God', in ll. 554–5.

578. If 3 m.p.h. is taken as walking-speed (see the Commentary on *ST*, l. 28), the time taken to walk a mile would be 20 minutes. But obviously 'a fairly short time' is all that is meant here.

591. 'To sermone' is used here in the ironic sense of 'to go on at length about something' – but it also reminds us that on one level of the narrative a sermon *is* actually going on.

601–4. Avicenna (A.D. 980–1037) was an Arab writer on philosophy, science and medicine. He was one of the greatest medieval thinkers, and his work was well-known in the West by Chaucer's time. His *Canon of Medicine*, which is referred to in l. 602, was a standard textbook for students of the subject, and the Physician in *GP* (A 432) is said to know it well.

618–27. The Pardoner here has a similar style of 'patter' to that used by Friar John as he goes begging from door to door in *ST* (ll. 49–89). Compare, for example, the 'buttonholing' effect of the Pardoner's 'Your name I entre here in my rolle anon' (l. 623) – with Friar John's equally vivid 'lo! here I write your name' (*ST*, l. 88). Both of them are prepared to take offerings either in kind or in cash, but Friar John is less ambitious in this respect. He asks only for 'a Goddes halfpenny or a masse-peny' (*ST*, l. 85) – whilst the Pardoner here (l. 619) is hoping for 'nobles or sterlinges'. In other ways also Friar John doesn't quite match the Pardoner's sheer effrontery. He doesn't hawk his wares quite so brazenly while in church, and doesn't start on his begging-rounds until the service is over.

627. At this point the Pardoner switches his address from his imaginary congregation back to his audience of pilgrims. The 'sermon' is over.

631 ff. Here – for whatever reason – the Pardoner begins to treat the pilgrims in the same way as he has treated his 'congregation',

and tries to offer them just the kind of wares that he has shown to be bogus in his Prologue. (On this problem see Introduction, p. 37.)

646. *aventures*. This meaning of the word has been obsolete since about the mid-eighteenth century (except in legal language). The modern meaning of 'adventure' has been current since the late fifteenth century.

653–7. Why does the Pardoner pick on the Host as the 'moost envoluped in sinne' of the pilgrims? Because he swears such a lot? Because he's a taverner? Because he's avaricious? The Pardoner may be hinting at all of these possibilities – but he is also making a tactical choice here. If the Host falls for this kind of approach, most of the other pilgrims will probably follow.

663. St Helen (*c.* A.D. 255 – *c.* 330) was the mother of Constantine the Great, and is supposed to have discovered the True Cross. This was probably the most famous of all relics. It seems to have been divided up into more fragments than it can possibly have been composed of, and distributed lavishly around Christendom. Through swearing by 'the cross that St Helen found' the Host is thus challenging the Pardoner in two of his roles – as dealer in bogus relics, and as preacher against swearing.

664–6. As well as being another crude joke about the Pardoner's ability to turn anything into a 'relic' (see also ll. 660–2), the Host's remark here could also be an ironic reference to suspicions that the Pardoner is a eunuch. For further evidence about this see ll. 20–3 of his *GP* portrait, and ch. 3 of *Chaucer and the Medieval Sciences* by W. Curry. But, if the Pardoner really is sterile and/or impotent (a 'eunuch from birth', as Professor Curry suggests), what are we to make of his own references to dealings with women, and even possible marriage, in l. 165 here and in the *Wife of Bath's Prologue* (D 163–8)? Is this yet another example of his 'selling false relics'?

672. Since the Host himself is involved in the quarrel, it is left to the Knight, as the most high-ranking of the pilgrims, to intervene and set things right.

677. Kissing, even between people of the same sex, was very common as a form of greeting or sign of reconciliation at this time. (See also the note on ll. 138–45 of *ST*.)

Textual Notes

The text of this edition is based on the Ellesmere MS as printed by the Chaucer Society – with reference being made to the other MSS printed in their '6-text' volume and to the readings and variants in J. M. Manly and E. Rickert *The Text of the Canterbury Tales*, as well as those in the major modern editions (Skeat and Robinson). As in the other Chaucer editions in this series, the spelling of the MS has been normalized and simplified somewhat. The punctuation is editorial.

The Friar's Tale

399–400. In the reading of this final couplet there are two alternatives. We could take it that the Friar is referring still (as in ll. 377 and 380) to summoners *in general*, and read (as both Skeat and Robinson do):

> And prayeth that *thise* somnour*s* *hem* repente
> Of *hir* misdedes, er that the feend *hem* hente.

Or we can take it that the Friar is referring to the pilgrim-Summoner in particular, and so read: 'And prayeth that *this* Somnour', etc. (following Manly and Rickert). Since the manuscript evidence seems to be evenly divided between these two alternatives, I have chosen the reading which suits the context best. It would make a rather lame ending to the *Tale* if the Friar were here to make the *same* kind of remark about summoners in general as he has already made in ll. 377 and 381. It seems more appropriate that the Friar – having begun the *Tale* as part of a personal quarrel, and having now (since l. 381) turned to address the pilgrims directly – should finish off on a personal note, with an ironically pious stab at his immediate enemy – the Summoner himself.

The Summoner's Tale

625. *Ptholomee*. Most of the manuscripts (according to Manly and Rickert) give this name in a corrupt form, as 'Protholomee'. In the best of them, the Ellesmere manuscript, the line as a whole is:

> As wel as Euclide or Protholomee.

I would like to think that the Summoner, rather than Chaucer's scribes, is responsible for this corruption – particularly as it would strengthen his 'presence' here at the end of his *Tale* (compare his twisting of the word 'preamble' at the end of the *Wife of Bath's Prologue* – ll. 9–10 of the extract in this volume). But, as Skeat points out in his note on this line, most of the scribes make exactly the same mistake about the name in the *Wife of Bath's Prologue* (D 182 and 324). Skeat argues in favour of the line having originally been:

> As wel as Euclide or *as* Ptholomee.

He suggests that 'the occurrence of an unpronounceable *P* at the beginning of "Ptholomee' made the scribes think that something must be *omitted*. Hence several of them introduced a stroke through the *p*, which stood as an abbreviation for "ro", and this turned it into "Protholomee", which looked right, but made the second *as* superfluous.' I have followed Skeat's reading, although the second 'as' is not found in any of the manuscripts (according to Manly and Rickert). Robinson's reading of the line is: 'As wel as Euclide dide or Ptholomee'. 'Dide' here is supported by a few of the manuscripts, but these are not among the most important ones – and anyway it gives a rather clumsy sound to the line.

The Pardoner's Tale

10. After this line most editors print the following couplet:

> Hire beautee was hire deth, I dar wel sayn.
> Allas, so pitously as she was slayn!
>> (ll. 297–8 of Robinson's edition)

This couplet is thought by the textual critics (e.g. Manly and Rickert, and A. Brusendorff (pp. 100–3 of *The Chaucer Tradition*)) to belong to Chaucer's earlier version of the link between the *Physician's* and *Pardoner's Tales*. I have here followed what is considered (according to the evidence of the various manuscript groups) to be Chaucer's later version of the passage, as printed by Manly and Rickert. A further reason against including this couplet is, I think, that it confuses the line of the Host's argument without being particularly typical of his style of speech – though it could be argued that such confusion might be a symptom of the Host's emotional state at this particular moment.   N. R. H.

How to Read Chaucer's Verse

To read Chaucer's verse properly we need to combine a basic knowledge of the original sound-values of his words with the ordinary sensitivity we would bring to the reading of any poetry. A great deal can never be recovered, of course – for instance the *tone* of the poetry as read out aloud or recited – but on the whole the meaning is a reliable guide to the latter.

The Sounds

No manuscript of Chaucer's work survives in his own hand, and since spelling was not yet fixed in the fourteenth century, Chaucer's poetry shows inconsistencies of spelling. But the Ellesmere MS of the *Canterbury Tales* (on which this text is based) has a fairly regular spelling which indicates the pronunciation quite clearly. This has been further regularized and simplified (e.g. long ī is spelt *y* in this edition).

Consonants

These are always pronounced – including the *w* in *wryte*, *k* in *knowe*, etc. The letter *r* is rolled or trilled in any position – e.g. *flour*, as well as *croppes*. *ng* is pronounced like *ng* in present day 'finger'; *gh* is like *ch* in German *ach*, except after *i* and *e*, when it is more like *ch* in German *ich* (thus *night* has one sound, *droghte* another).

Vowels

		EXAMPLE
Short ă	as in German *Mann*	*whan, that*
Long ā	as in father	*bathed, name*
Long open (slack) ę̆	as in there	*heeth, were*
Long close (tense) ę̄	as in French *é*, or, less closely, fame	*swete, meeke*
Short ĕ	as in set	*engendred*
Unaccented or neutral e (ə)	as in *a*do, mill*er*	*falle*
Long ī (y)	as in mach*ine*	*ryde, wys*
Short ĭ	as in switch	*swich, blisful*
Long close (tense) ǭ	roughly as in tone, but closer to French *rôle*	*sote*
Long open (slack) ǭ	as in broad	*goon*
Short ŏ	as in long	*croppes*

164

Long ū	as in true	*devout, shoures*
Short ŭ	as in put	*ful, ronne*
'French' u (ü)	as in Fr. *tu*, Ger. Dürer	*vertú, natúre*

Diphthongs

These are sounds composed of two vowels spoken more or less rapidly together. Some are still heard in English:

au	as in brown	*bawdrik, y-taught*
oi	as in joy	*coy, Loy*

About the others scholars still disagree, but the following simplified guide is not too far from the truth.

The sound represented variously by the spellings *ai, ay, ei, ey* (e.g. *day, veyne*) may be pronounced as either a combination of the short *ă* in our *man* with the short *ĭ* of our *thin*, lengthened somewhat (as in *mayde, lay*), or else as a sound like *ai* in our *aisle*. But there are other possibilities.

In diphthongs containing *w* it is simplest to sound the first vowel separately and then articulate the *w* gently: *tre – we, kno – we*.

Au in the group *aun* (mainly in words from the French, like *straunge, daungere*) may be pronounced either as in our *haunt*, or as in *brown*.

Note that the spelling *o* sometimes indicates other than 'o' – sounds: *ronne* (*o* = short *u*), *droghte* (*o* = long *u*). Contrast: *also* (long open *ǫ*), *doon* (long close *ọ*), *oft* (short *ŏ*).

A rough guide to the difference between open and close vowel-sounds is the modern spelling of the Middle English word (where it still exists). Thus present day *ea* usually indicates an original open *ę̆* sound (e.g. head: *heed*), *ee* or *ie* an original close *ẹ̄* sound (e.g. green: *grene*, or lief (er): *levere*); *oa* indicates an original open *ǭ* sound (e.g. broad: *brood*), *oo* an original close *ọ̄* sound (e.g. root: *ro(o)te*).

A useful guide to reading Chaucer aloud is the record of the *General Prologue*, read by Nevill Coghill, Norman Davis and John Burrow (Argo Records). A. V. C. S.